sweet
REGRET

K. BROMBERG

PRAISE FOR K. BROMBERG

"K. Bromberg always delivers intelligently written, emotionally intense, sensual romance . . ."

—*USA Today*

"K. Bromberg makes you believe in the power of true love."

—#1 *New York Times* bestselling author Audrey Carlan

"Always an absolute must-read."

—*New York Times* bestselling author Helena Hunting

"An irresistibly hot romance that stays with you long after you finish the book."

—#1 *New York Times* bestselling author Jennifer L. Armentrout

"Bromberg is a master at turning up the heat!"

—*New York Times* bestselling author Katy Evans

"Supercharged heat and full of heart. Bromberg aces it from the first page to the last."

—*New York Times* bestselling author Kylie Scott

ALSO WRITTEN BY K. BROMBERG

Driven Series
Driven
Fueled
Crashed
Raced
Aced

Driven Novels
Slow Burn
Sweet Ache
Hard Beat
Down Shift

The Player Duet
The Player
The Catch

Everyday Heroes
Cuffed
Combust
Cockpit
Control (Novella)

Wicked Ways
Resist
Reveal

prologue

Bristol

Eleven Years Ago

MY HEART JUMPS OUT OF MY CHEST AS I SCAN THE SHADOWS OF MY room for whatever just yanked me from sleep.

Knock. Knock. Knock.

I bite back a yelp as my eyes register the dark silhouette standing outside my bedroom window.

About the same time as my brain computes the notion that an axe murderer wouldn't be knocking—they'd just break in—my phone vibrates on the nightstand beside me. The illuminated screen shows text after text from Vince.

I scramble out of bed, bleary-eyed and anxious. With a glance toward my bedroom door to make sure it's shut, I pull the curtain aside and open the window as quietly as possible.

"What are you doing?" I whisper-yell before emitting a nervous chuckle and looking over my shoulder again. He's removed the screen.

There's no way he can come in here. What if my parents hear? What if they walk in? What if— "Are you out of your mind? Do you know how grounded I'll be if my parents find you here? How much trouble we'll be in?"

But at the same time, I'm so glad he is. Our fight earlier was a rarity, and I hated the sick feeling I had in my stomach when I went to bed without hearing from him.

"Trouble?" He chuckles, but it doesn't sound like the Vincent I know. He sounds off. Dejected. Maybe even drunk. "Like I care about getting in trouble." He cups the back of my neck and brings his mouth to mine.

For the briefest of seconds, the fight from earlier disappears, and I lose myself in everything Vincent Jennings has become to me. The dark spark in my mundane life. The best friend I can tell anything. The rebel that pushes my boundaries when I'd rather paint inside the lines—or exactly, perfectly on the lines. The person who looks at me and makes me feel beautiful.

My first love.

But there's something more to this kiss and the faint taste of beer on his tongue, and it takes me a few seconds to recognize it.

There's desperation here—*hunger*—an urgency that I can't comprehend.

"Vince?" I ask as the kiss ends and he rests his forehead on mine, his hand still at the base of my neck holding me to him. "What's wrong?"

He gives the slightest shake of his head but doesn't move.

He's been like this before when whatever happens at his house . . . *happens*. He's come to me not wanting to talk but needing my company. He's come to me with a swollen cheek or busted lip but has refused to explain other than to play it off with a "you should've seen the other guy" type of comment.

But he's never knocked on my window at two in the morning. He's never kissed me so it makes me feel like this might be our last kiss. His presence has never caused the panic fluttering in my throat like it is right now.

I don't know what to do so I kiss him again. Soft and slow and unknowingly try to give him everything he needs but won't say that he does.

"Bristol," he murmurs against my lips before forcibly taking a step back.

"What? What is it?" I glance toward my door again. "Tell me." *Please tell me this time.* "Climb in."

He's in my room in a second. When his feet land on the floor, it sounds like a herd of elephants in my head, and I'm more than certain my parents will be rushing in here at any second.

But they don't come.

My door doesn't barge open.

It's just Vince and me facing each other in the darkness of my room, both hands holding on to each other's. But when he shifts and the moonlight hits his face, I can see the bruise on his cheek. I notice his red-rimmed eyes, and for the first time ever, I hope it's from the alcohol and not from crying.

While his kiss tasted like beer, I know it's not from that.

The solemnity in his demeanor tells me what I don't want to know and what he has never talked about in the three years we've been together.

His house.

His dad.

The things that happen there.

I scramble for what to say as he looks at me with a resigned determination I don't understand . . . and don't think I want to.

"Is this about earlier?" I ask, grasping for something to erase the expression on his face.

He gives a smile that is as subtle as the shake of his head for his answer.

"I've thought about it and realized that I caused a fight because I was nervous. What will people think of me if they find out we went all the way? Then I was worried it might be different between us after we did it and . . . I just don't want it to ruin this. Us. And . . ." My nervous chuckle stops my endless ramble that we know can go on forever. I slide my hand around the back of his neck and bring his lips to mine. "I'm ready, Vince. I want to—"

"No, Shug." The tensing of my body has him swearing. "God, yes, I want you. How could you think otherwise? You're all I think about. Sometimes I want you so bad it physically hurts. But not like this. Not now."

"But . . ." His rejection stings and is more confusing than what he's doing here right now.

"Don't you see? You deserve so much better than me. So much more than what I can give you. Than—"

"Don't be ridiculous." I grab his head in both of my hands and stare into those green eyes that are so light they're almost translucent. "You're all I need. You're *everything* to me."

"For now, maybe. But you have a huge future ahead of you. You'll be valedictorian when you graduate. Then off to college. Then law school after that. I mean—"

"We already talked about this. Planned this. You're going to go with me. Play in the local clubs wherever I go and try to be seen there. No one thought we'd last a month, yet here we are. It'll be hard but we'll make it work. We always have."

He nods but refuses to meet my eyes.

"What is it, Vince? What are you not telling me?" That panic resurfaces, clawing its way up my throat.

"I'm leaving, Shug."

"What do you mean you're leaving? Like for the weekend?" My mind races. "I thought we were going to go to . . . never mind. I get it. You have plans. But you'll be back on Sunday, right?"

"No. I'm going. Now. Tonight." He lifts his gaze to meet mine, and all the air is sucked from the room as his expression pulls tight. "For good."

"I—I don't understand." Emotion balls in my throat and chills chase over my skin. "You can't go. We have plans." I shake my head as if the action will help this make sense. It doesn't. "But you—"

"I can't take this anymore." His voice breaks right along with my heart at the sound of it.

"Take what?" I ask but know before he answers. *His dad.* The reason why in the three years we've been dating, I've only met the man once, and why I'm only allowed over to his house when his dad's not home.

Fairfield knows Vince's father, Deegan Jennings, as the man who mostly keeps to himself. The one who sits in his vintage Bronco on the street outside the football stadium to watch the high school games from afar wishing his son were on the field instead of playing with his second-hand guitar. The man who wants a homecoming king for a son instead of an outcast who doesn't care if he fits in. The one who frequents the liquor store a little too regularly but always has a subtle nod or quiet smile to anyone who says hi.

But I know him as the man Vince hates. I know him as the man with sharp criticism and demeaning quips in the background during our phone conversations. I know him as the man responsible for the marks on Vince's face even though he's never confirmed it.

"I just can't, okay?" He swallows, his voice thick from the tears brimming in his eyes that he blinks away. "I should have done it the day I graduated, got the hell out of here . . . but . . ."

"But you stayed because of me."

He put up with whatever hell he won't talk about because of me. My heart breaks a little more.

He nods. "You're the only good thing I have here, Bristol."

"But it isn't enough." My voice is barely audible.

"No. That's not it." He holds my chin up and stares into my eyes as his first tear slips down his cheek. This boy . . . this man that I love, seems so broken, and I don't know how to fix him. How to help him. "You're more than enough. *You're everything*, but if I stay, I don't think I'll ever take the chance at becoming what he thinks I can't be, and I know I can be."

"Yes, you will. I know you will. You're—"

"Shh." He presses a finger to my lips and shakes his head. "And if I stay, you won't take those chances you need to take. You'll hold yourself back because of me. You'll pick a college where you think there's a music scene for me instead of one that's best for you."

"I won't. I promise."

"I know you better than that. You're selfless like that, and I can't do that to you. I can't hold you back from being the person we both know you can be."

"You're just saying this to make it easier to leave. You're just—"

"You're right. I am." He swallows roughly. "I have to believe it." His hands are on my cheeks. His forehead is resting against mine again. "It's the only way I can do this. It's for the best."

Salt is on my lips. My own tears falling hard and fast while my brain tries to process Vince's decision.

That he really is leaving.

That he's walking away without a fight.

We had plans. Tomorrows and forevers. A future.

I love him.

I can see those same thoughts reflected in his eyes. The same pain. The same hurt. The same regret.

I can't make him suffer more because of his loyalty to me. I can't force him to endure whatever hell happens in his house simply because I need him.

He needs so much more. He deserves so much better.

I press the most tender of kisses to his lips. *Goodbye, Vince.* Somewhere deep down, I find the strength to give him what he needs while it slowly kills me.

"I understand," I whisper and choke on the next words. "It's for the best."

His eyes hold mine before he nods and moves back toward the window.

Another kiss.

A squeeze of our linked fingers.

A shuddered breath of acceptance even though I don't want to accept anything.

He climbs out the window.

Fight the tears.

He turns to face me.

Don't let your voice break.

"I'll call you," he says, but I know he won't.

If there's one thing I know about my boyfriend, it's that he's all or nothing. And his *all* is ahead of him, and I'm the *nothing* that must remain behind. I'm the nothing that might pull him back when he can't even chance looking back.

"Don't call," I say.

His eyes flash to mine. Hurt flares in them followed shortly by acceptance.

This is it.

A clean break.

The chance to walk away while I'm holding the broken pieces of myself together . . . so he doesn't have to see them fall apart.

He stares at me long and hard for a moment. The darkness masking so much, and I'm not sure if I'm grateful that it does or if I'd prefer to see it.

"Goodbye, Shug."

"Goodbye, Vince."

"Maybe I'll see you around sometime."

"Maybe."

I struggle for composure. My hands fisting. My teeth digging into my bottom lip. My jaw is clenched tightly.

I watch his shadow disappear into the night . . . "Vince, wait!" But he keeps walking right out of my life.

"I miss you already," I whisper.

I don't even make it to my bed before I fall apart. The tears come fast, hard, and uncontrollably.

He's gone.

My strength dissolves into despair. My resolve shatters into heartbreak.

I'd wait for him. He knows it. I know it. But I also can't spend my life waiting for him either.

Hope is enough to sustain someone and break them simultaneously.

I'd hold it tight if I thought it would help.

But for some reason I think it's already lost.

He deserves so much more than being his father's punching bag.

"Make all your dreams come true, Vince. I know someday your star will shine."

CHAPTER
one

Bristol

I SHOULD HAVE STAYED IN BED.

If the smoke alarm chirping at three in the morning (because isn't that always when the batteries die), the coffee pot breaking, and Jagger throwing up all over my clothes minutes before I headed out the door weren't a warning sign I should have heeded, then I don't know what was.

And now as Simone looks at me with raised eyebrows, expectant eyes, and yet another imposing request, I know being nestled in my warm, soft bed would have been so much better than what I'm about to agree to do.

"Don't give me that look," she says. "I'd do the same for you, if you asked."

"The difference is that I don't ask. Ever."

Her sigh and the shift of her feet are all the proof I need. She knows I'm right. That this is most definitely a one-way relationship—unless you consider the laughter she pulls from me on the daily. If we compared that, then she's the reason I stay sane most days.

And the same reason I glare at her but nod my head. "He better be a damn good lay if you're making me cover for you."

"Really?" Simone clasps her hands and dances a jig, her spiral curls bouncing and her smile reaching megawatt levels. All for covering her shift tonight so she can be with her current flavor of the month—and they do change monthly—who happens to be in town for the night. But who am I to deny someone in love with the notion of being in love and the addictive giddiness that comes with it?

"Really," I say drolly, already hating that I can't say no to her.

"Oh my God. You're the best. Maybe this will put you front and center with Xavier so he sees what a godsend you are and finally treats you what you're worth."

Xavier McMann. Schmoozer to the stars. Hard-ass galore. Our boss. How he led McMann Media Management to be one of the top media and public relations firms in Los Angeles is beyond me. With his grueling schedule, his unyielding demands, and his snap-of-the-fingers-you-better-jump communication skills, he only seems to notice you if you screw up.

And yet we both work here because he's the best of the best. His stamp of approval is the golden ticket to a successful career in the industry. The connections you make working for him guarantee it. If dealing with him and his demands is what I need to do to learn the ropes and get my foot in the door I feel like I've been pushing on for what feels like forever, then so be it.

One day I plan to be him.

My own publicity or talent management firm. My own employees. My own reputation.

I just got a little later start on everything than planned . . .

The roll of my eyes in response says it all.

"Nothing will ever make Xavier see me." *No matter how hard I work, he'll never notice me.* "We're never in the same place either." In the rare instances that we are, my most important job is relegated to grabbing coffee. Apparently, my immediate boss wants the more important tasks to try and make a lasting impression with the top one.

"He's going to be there today."

"No, he's not. He's—"

"Here. In Los Angeles. He came back from Napa early because this thing came up, and he wanted to be here for it. So you know it's a big deal if he cut his trip short."

"And this thing is . . ."

"No clue." Her shrug is as indifferent as her tone is in having this conversation right now. I'm certain her thoughts are already on her date tonight. "It's all being kept under lock and key."

"And you're going to miss it?"

"I know. I'll probably shoot myself in the foot for it when you're promoted to vice president or some shit like that after you kick ass today."

"Yeah. Right." I swing my arm in the aw-shucks motion and snap. "My gofer game is so strong that Xavier will promote me on the spot."

Knowing he's going to be there does at least provide me a positive reason for working the overtime. As much as he's a pain in the ass, there is always opportunity when he's in the room.

"Whatever."

"Now, are you going to tell me what my job duties are tonight?"

"I don't know."

And this is why getting a late start to my career is frustrating. I'm often teamed with younger employees who aren't often aware of the fine points.

Then again, even at Simone's age, I would have known the intimate details.

"Come again?"

"I don't know." She shrugs again, her smile so sugary sweet I feel cavities forming.

"Well, then can you at least tell me who the client is?"

"Nope. Like I said, everything is being kept all hush-hush."

"Great. You don't know what and you don't know who. I'm beginning to not like this idea." I groan. "Last time we had *hush-hush* all hell broke loose."

Simone snorts as we both recall the disaster of taking on a shock jock as a client and trying to redeem him in the public eye. Needless to say, the redemption part was short-lived and futile in the end.

"I don't think it's that kind of hush-hush. I think it's more along the lines of Xavier stealing a big name away from another firm, and we have to keep it under wraps type of thing. He wants a big staff presence to show the talent that we're there to support him in any way possible."

"Ah, the song and dance routine."

"Exactly."

"So it's a *him*, then?"

"Yes. A male. I mean, at least we know it's not some diva with ridiculous demands."

I give her the side-eye because we both know men can rival women in the diva factor at times.

"Look, I owe you like a million . . . something." She waves her hand and laughs. "I can't say dollars because we both know I sure as shit don't have that."

"Same, girl." I sigh, still resigning myself to the fact that I agreed to do this. "Tell me where I need to go and what time I need to be there."

CHAPTER
two

Bristol

"**W**HERE'S SIMONE?" KEVIN ASKS THE MINUTE I ENTER THE STUDIO as he whisks past me like his ass is on fire. Or rather, how us junior associates are required to act regardless of whether there's a fire or not.

But he's not a junior associate, so that tells me the pep in his step is because Xavier is already here.

"You're getting me tonight."

His step falters for half a beat as he cranes his neck over his shoulder and flashes a quick smile. "I'm not going to complain about that. You know we all fight over you. Life is way easier when you're assigned to our events."

"I'm touched." I place my hand over my heart and wink as he holds up a finger telling me he'll be right back.

"Excuse us," comes from my right. I step out of the way from a few grips who are hurriedly pushing the black, wheeled cases that exist on every sound stage I've ever been on. After they pass, I scan the oversized space to try and get a hint of who this hush-hush client is.

The room doesn't give me much more to go on other than I'm clearly at a sound stage (they're a dime a dozen in the Los Angeles area), and there is a hell of a lot of people here. Sound engineers with their headphones hanging on their necks and pieces of random tape stuck to their all-black clothing from where they've taped mics to someone. The hair and makeup team stand whispering furtively in one corner with their belts loaded with brushes or hair accessories either clipped around their waists or worn like a cross-body purse. The lighting crew is on ladders as they adjust moving heads and spotlights toward the middle of the stage area. Toward the far side of the room is a huddle of people where Xavier stands very much in the center, clearly in control given the rapt attention of everyone around him.

There are a few closed doors behind the huddle, but it's too far for me to read the printed pieces of paper in the acrylic holders that typically identify whose door the talent belongs to.

And there are a dozen or more other people milling about who look important—or from my experience, are trying to look important for their own egos' sakes.

I quickly try to call my mom and check on Jagger, but as per usual, her cell goes unanswered. What I'd give for the woman to take it out of her purse and off do not disturb so she can actually hear when I call her.

"Bristol."

I shove my phone in my pocket and look up when my name is called from across the room. Kevin is standing beside Xavier, and they are both intently looking at me. Kevin waves for me to come over.

With a huge gulp of *here we go*, I make my way across the large space, ever aware that they are blatantly scrutinizing me as I go.

I'm too old to worry about Xavier and what he thinks of me. Most of the junior associates with McMann are five to seven years younger than I am and have a lot less backbone.

Both serve as a blessing and a curse for me.

Being twenty-eight means I need to be amiable and not piss off any of the senior associates or managers. It also means I'm old enough to have a good sense of self, a pocketful of experience to pull from, and have dealt with enough bullshit that I'd prefer not to tolerate any more of it.

Like I said, a blessing and a curse. Especially when my mouth opens to stand up for myself without thinking, when my younger counterparts would most likely nod with a smile and suck up whatever shitty task has been set before them.

There's a definite yin and yang, and I'm sure as shit still finding the correct balance to it. One that won't get my ass fired.

It's a weird thing to be a mother, in control of all things when I'm at home, and then to come to work and take orders from everyone else.

"Do you think she's too old?" Xavier asks as I'm within earshot.

A purse of Kevin's lips. A tilt of his head. A bristle of my shoulders in silent rebuke.

This is the only industry where scrutinizing a person's looks is perfectly normal and accepted.

I listen but look over my shoulder to see who they're talking about.

"Nah. Her hair can be fixed to look right. Her skin is flawless. Great coloring with no wrinkles," Kevin says.

"The issue isn't her skin." Xavier's smile pulls tight, his eyes averting from me. "The body type is off."

Kevin shifts on his feet as I stop before them. "True, but body inclusivity is a big thing right now. It might make a statement that looks good for him. The 'all body types are beautiful' type of thing."

"You have a point." Clearly Xavier isn't a fan of this idea by the strained smile and muscle ticking in his jaw.

"I mean, by no means is it what we had planned, but we're in a pinch, and no doubt she can do what needs to be done."

"Who can do what?" I ask, looking from one to the other and then back.

"Our lead actress is sick and casting isn't getting a response from our sourcing firm."

"Meaning?"

"Meaning we might have you stand in until we can get someone here," Kevin says while I process the subtle critiques they were just giving about my body—because that's exactly what every woman wants to hear . . . *said no woman ever.*

"Wait. *What?*" I ask.

"I believe they're saying that they want you to fill in as my love interest."

The deep tenor at my back has my heart beating fiercely because I'd know that gravel dipped in velvet-sounding voice anywhere. And as much as I hope that I'm wrong, when I turn around to face its owner, every part of me stands at attention when I'm proven right.

Vincent Jennings.

Dark hair. Light eyes. A sleeve of tattoos that peeks up and past the neck of his trademark black T-shirt. That fuck-you curl to his lips that's always been there—taunting and seducing simultaneously.

I'm relieved to see shock flashing across that gorgeous face of his. At least I'm not the only one being thrown for a loop right now.

"Hey, Shug." *Shug,* short for sugar—a nickname I originally despised but that he somehow made mine over our time together. It's a name I haven't heard in years that has my heart clenching and rejecting it *and* him all at the same time.

Or trying to, because in that one look, a million feelings come rushing back. The bittersweet feeling of first love and the soul-crushing despair of first heartbreak. The utter humiliation of rejection and the constant reminder that I will always somehow be indebted to him. *Not that he will ever know.*

I stand frozen in surprise with my head and heart racing, but my first words aren't to the man who has owned my life in ways he doesn't even know. Rather they are directed at Xavier and his curious gaze. "I-I d-don't understand. We don't take on rock stars. McMann doesn't do that. We manage movie stars. And Food Network chefs. And social media influencers . . . but not him."

Kevin sucks in a quick breath as Xavier crosses his arms over his chest and narrows his eyes at me. "We represent whoever it is that I say we do," he says in that authoritative, soft tone of his. The one that says don't question or fuck with him. "Or have you forgotten it's my name on your paycheck?"

"Yes. I know. I mean . . ." *Stop, Bristol. Just stop.* My tongue feels like it weighs a pound while my entire body vibrates with the adrenaline coursing through it. "But not *him.*"

Kevin's quick clearing of his throat is a warning. So are his eyes flitting between the four of us as if he's taking stock of who I've offended more. "What I think you meant to say was how exciting it is that McMann Media Management has decided to venture into representing musicians now. And how lucky we are that the super talented, rock god Vincent Jennings is going to be our first client in that realm."

"Our client?" I mouth as realization breaks through the heavy fog seeing him again has weighed me down with.

"Yes. Our client." The muscle ticks in Xavier's jaw as he stares at me. "One who may not feel welcome given your delightful reception."

"It's good to see you again," Vincent says to my back, completely disregarding Xavier and his sarcasm, as if he and I are the only ones in the room.

His voice has always owned me, and this time it's no exception regardless of the ocean of history the two of us are treading water in right now.

Expectant eyes stare at me as I force myself to turn and face Vince. Eyes that ask a million questions in that one simple exchange.

How are you?

What are you doing here?

How come it's been so long?

This is so not a good thing—you being here.

I've seen him on television, in the tabloids, at award shows more times than I care to count, and yet standing here, face-to-face with him, I'm on that razor-thin edge of bittersweet nostalgia and indifferent disbelief.

Indifferent.

Isn't that what I promised myself I'd be if we were ever face-to-face again?

Then why is my heart racing? Why is my mouth dry? Why am I telling myself he can't be here—that this can't happen—all while being unable to tear my eyes away from him?

Why is it so hard to be indifferent when I'm standing before him?

"Vincent." I nod as my head swims with memories. First kisses. Linked fingers and shoulders for support. Midnight farewells and endless tears. Desperate sex to make up for lost time. Final words I'll never forgive or forget. I shake my head, trying to focus on the here and now. On doing my job and not letting him screw up my plans.

"Bristol."

"I don't understand," I say when my rational mind catches up. "What are you doing here?"

Vince's lips curl up on one side, a dimple I know all too well denting in one cheek. "Pretty self-explanatory. We're shooting a music video."

My smile is halfhearted as I look over his shoulder because it hurts too much to look at his eyes. They're too familiar. Too overwhelming.

Time and life experiences may have dulled the hurt, but it doesn't erase it or my own participation.

"We have big plans with Vincent, here," Xavier says, stepping forward, his chest puffed, his smile in full-on big-dick mode as he pats Vince's shoulder.

"Tonight, we're shooting a video for his up-and-coming single *Heart of Mine.* The rest of this week will be various brainstorming sessions with your PR team. Then we'll start working on some behind the scenes for the documentary. We've got a lot to do with him while he's in town."

"Documentary?" I snort. Vince isn't exactly the documentary type. And it's way easier to focus on that than hear that he's going to be in town for an extended period.

"Yes. About Vince. As you know when you control the narrative, it makes it easier to do damage control," Xavier says. "It's better if we have the paparazzi on our side instead of with their blood on our fists."

"He had it coming to him." Vince rolls his eyes.

"And that's why we'll do the talking for you," Xavier admonishes but with a smile.

Vince's chuckle is a warning I'm certain Xavier believes he can pacify and that I know from experience he can't. "No one talks for me."

Xavier nods, clearly placating Vince. "The documentary will and we'll make sure it says exactly what we want it to say." His smile is quick and unwitting when he looks at me. "When we're done with his campaign, everybody who doesn't already know his face will recognize him."

"And hopefully that translates into a monster release week for his first full solo album," Kevin interjects, trying to wiggle his way back into this conversation.

Vince is the bass guitarist for one of the biggest bands in the rock scene, Bent.

Was.

He *was* the bass guitarist for one of the biggest bands on the rock scene.

A year ago, Bent took a break to pursue individual projects after years together. Passion projects, I believe they'd called it.

Vince has released an extended-play album since then—a few songs on a mini album. They did well, but not anywhere near as successful as Bent's music. But he's summitted all the peaks before with them—he's won Grammys, topped the Billboard charts, sold out stadium tours, had albums go platinum . . . so why this new push? Why is he so desperate to prove himself when he already has? "Sorry to repeat myself, but why does Vince need—"

"Because no press is bad press?" Vince answers. It may have been years since we've last seen each other—almost seven to be exact—but I know the man standing before me well enough to see the shadow in his eyes hiding behind his flippant answer. *There's more to his reasoning.*

And I'll be damned if I want to know what it is. Or even care what it is.

"Exactly," Xavier says. "Reinvention is the key to this business. Vince here did incredible with Bent. We're here to ensure that he kicks ass as a front man. I mean, who knew the guy could belt out a tune like he does, right?" Xavier pats Vince on the shoulder. "And now McMann is going to help take him to the next level. Let the world see the man outside of the spotlight. Keep the aura of everything that is Vincent Jennings while making people feel that they know the real person beneath."

I nod, used to Xavier's ego-stroking bullshit, but *what am I missing?* Why did Vince switch agencies? Why is he here? Why is McMann diversifying to musicians now? Why after why after why?

"Sounds perfect," Vince says but he doesn't move, his eyes still locked on mine.

I wondered if this day would ever come. I've rehearsed and imagined what I'd do and say. How I'd feel. If that visceral punch to the gut that seeing Vince has always made me feel would still be there.

The answer is yes.

It's always been yes.

"Can you give us a minute?" Vince asks.

"Sure." Gladly. I'm about to move out of the way so Vince and Xavier can talk when Vince reaches out and grabs my arm.

"Not you," he says to me before looking at Xavier and Kevin with raised eyebrows.

"Oh." Clearly miffed and confused, Xavier startles momentarily at being pushed aside. He narrows his eyes at me before looking at Vince. "Yes. Of course. Is there something I can do for you?"

"Yes. Give us the privacy I asked for," Vince says, effectively dismissing them and making waves with my boss I'm not exactly thrilled with.

With gritted teeth, I watch them walk away while trying to ignore the feeling of Vince's hand on me. His touch . . . it always affected me differently than anyone else's.

Even now when I don't want it to.

Fear and confusion snake their way up my spine. The two emotions force a decision. They pressure me to react—to choose self-preservation after everything we've been through, or to just accept what's always been between us and cave.

But there is only one option this time.

There is only one way to keep him at arm's length and—*preferably*—out of my life.

It's fight or flight time and I choose fight.

"Are you trying to get me in trouble?" I yank my arm from his grasp the minute we're out of earshot.

"Trouble? With who? That douchebag?"

"*That douchebag* is your new representation and *my* boss. Why the hell did you even sign with him if you don't like him?"

"I needed a change. He's supposedly one of the best." His shrug tells me he's not convinced of that yet.

"You had CMG. They are of the same caliber and better suited to manage you properly."

"Things change."

"Exactly. They change." *I've changed.* I cross my arms over my chest. "And that doesn't explain why you're here in my space, in my company, pushing my boss away, and putting a huge goddamn spotlight on me—and not the good kind. Don't you smirk at me like that."

"Like what?" He holds his hands up, his face a mask of feigned innocence.

"Like that." I shove a finger in his direction. "The last thing I need is to get fired and—"

"I'll take care of him for you."

"I don't want that, Vince. I don't want you 'taking care of him' for me. Not with my boss . . . just not ever."

I know Vince hears my words, the conviction and determination behind them, because his smile fades and his eyes narrow. "You're actually upset with me, aren't you? It's been years since I've seen you—"

"Seven to be exact, but who's counting?"

"Clearly, you are," he murmurs, crossing his arms over his chest and cocking his head to the side to study me. And in that brief moment of scrutiny, my insecurity rears its ugly head. There is Vince Jennings looking even better than the last time I saw him. Tall and tan and by the biceps straining the cuffs of his shirt, still as sculpted as my fingertips remember from running over them.

And then there's me, in desperate need of a good cut and color, the bare minimum of makeup, and a little softer around the edges than the last time he saw me.

Seconds pass that feel like minutes as we wage a visual standoff.

"I thought we were fine with how we left things the last time we saw each other. We agreed beforehand that—"

"I know what we agreed on, thank you very much," I snap at him and then hate that I do. But agreeing to no strings beforehand and then dealing with the emotional turmoil of the aftermath are two completely different things.

But he doesn't know that.

He can't know that.

"Still snarky, I see."

"Still sarcastic, I see." I lift my eyebrows in challenge as his eyes search mine.

"You look incredible, but then again, you always do," he says, knocking the proverbial wind from my sails.

Wind that I needed to keep that wall of mine fortified . . . so he couldn't knock it down like only he knows how to do.

I take a deep breath and close my eyes for a beat. Why can't he see that he doesn't get to say shit like that? Shit that makes it hard to be mad at him when that's the only way I know how to be so I can keep him at a distance?

"How have you been, Shug?"

"Stop calling me that."

He purses his lips and nods, but I'm under no impression that he'll listen to me. Vince always played by his own rules, always got away with it, so it's naïve of me to think he's any different now.

"Old habits die hard. Especially with our history." His smile softens as does his stare and that familiar ache in my chest returns.

"It's just that. History. In the past where we belong," I say harsher than I should as I try to find my footing. To try to not fall under the Vincent Jennings spell. We've had our chances to make things work. It didn't. I've had years to accept it. Years to question *what if?* Years to learn to love the life I've made. The last thing I need now that I'm finally settled is for him to show up and blow my carefully crafted world to smithereens.

"So much easier to say. So much harder to do," he says and takes a step toward me that has me tensing and preparing myself for his touch that doesn't come.

It used to be so easy between the two of us. Effortless. Carefree. Real. Until it wasn't.

And that *until it wasn't* part is what I hold tight to as I look at the man a part of me will always love in some way, shape, or form.

"Don't do this," I whisper.

"Do what?"

"This," I say emphatically.

His chuckle is a low rumble. "What is *this*? Talk with an old friend? Ask her how she's doing? Wonder why she's a—whatever it is your position is here—instead of running this damn company like you should be?"

Shame heats my cheeks. A million excuses for why I'm not where I should be in my career fill my head but remain silent on my lips.

"You know what I'm doing here, Bristol, but you haven't told me what it is that you're doing here."

"Working."

It's his turn to give an exasperated sigh, but he doesn't get to waltz in here and play the I'm-a-god card and think I'm going to answer every question he asks me.

I don't owe him a thing.

"That's not what I meant—"

"Excuse the interruption, Mr. Jennings, but we're ready for you." We both look to our right at a woman we didn't even realize was standing there. Her headset, clipboard, and no-nonsense expression tell me she's the assistant director or first AD or second AD. Some position to that affect where stress is something she thrives off.

"Of course." He gives a polite nod. "Let's get the show on the road. It's going to be a long night. You ready?"

"For what?" I ask, my mind so scattered that I've already forgotten how this conversation started.

"To be my love interest in the video," he says. The way his face lights up has me immediately shaking my head.

"No. You're crazy if you think—"

"Fighting. Kissing. Making up."

"Absolutely not."

"For old times' sake." He shrugs, his boyish grin in full heart-stealing mode. "We used to be really good at it."

I know. Believe me, I know. I chuckle and then take a deep breath to calm myself. *This man is so damn frustrating.* "It's not part of my job description." I take another step back. "And I sure don't get paid enough to—"

"It's a moot point." We both turn and look at the AD when she silences our banter. "Casting pulled through last minute. An actress showed. She's the gorgeous blonde standing over there who fits the part." She hooks a thumb over her shoulder to highlight said woman. And when I look back to the AD, her eyebrows are raised in what I try not to take as judgment but do anyway. "See? You're no longer needed."

Relief rushes through me followed by a slight streak of envy that I have absolutely no right to feel. Or want to feel.

"Perfect," I say with a flash of a smile that I'm more than certain doesn't reach my eyes. "Now if you'll excuse me, I have work to do."

"That's it?" Vince asks, reaching out for my arm again but missing when I take a step to the side. He's not used to women walking away from him. That much I know to be true. In fact, I'm pretty sure that's his forte.

"That's it." My smile is tight. My shrug unapologetic. My heart thundering in my chest.

Is his doing the same?

He nods subtly, and I can't quite read the look he gives me. "Good seeing you, then. Maybe I'll see you around again while I'm in town, and we can have a drink to catch up on old times."

"Maybe." It takes everything I have to turn my back and walk away when it should be the easiest steps of my life.

One foot in front of the other, Bristol. Take the space. Create the distance. Don't let him through your guard.

But I only make it a few feet before I turn back around, conflicted and feeling like I need to say more to him. Out of guilt? Out of responsibility? Out of—never mind. It doesn't matter because Vincent is already walking to where the rest of the room patiently awaits him to begin the long night.

Statuesque blonde all but bouncing on her toes in excitement, included.

I'm not sure why I expected him to be standing there still looking at me. Waiting for me. Wanting me.

Isn't that what I thought the last time we saw each other? That the connection between us would be so strong he'd still be there?

I emit a nervous laugh, the taste of rejection I shouldn't feel a bitter tang on my tongue. A tang I remind myself is necessary when dealing with Vince. *An old friend.*

His label hits my ears again and makes me feel ridiculously stupid and soundly put in my place.

Here I was thinking and worrying while he was staring at me, talking to me, that we'd fall right back into what we've always been. Connected by an undeniable chemistry we never could ignore. That I'd have to stand my ground and tell him I'm not interested.

All that gusto for nothing.

I'm just an *old friend*. Pfft.

A woman among many to him who he had a little more history with.

But didn't I already know that's where I stood? Wasn't that what we agreed to the last time we were together? So why does emotion burn in the back of my throat?

Because a small, foolish part of you held an iota of hope that maybe he thought of you as more. Seeing Vince again only reaffirmed that hope was as ridiculous as me thinking it.

Besides, we live two completely different lives in two vastly different worlds. It would never work. We would never work.

For reasons besides the obvious.

CHAPTER

three

Bristol

NEEDING A MOMENT TO PROCESS THE LAST TEN MINUTES, I PURPOSELY blend into the shadows against the wall.

It's going to be okay.

Vince will be in Los Angeles for a while. He'll do his thing. He'll leave and then go back to wherever he lives now.

Plain. Simple. No need to intermingle our lives again. Problem solved.

I think that yet when I look up, it's clear that Vince has already charmed nearly everyone in this room. It's impossible not to be drawn to him. There's a charisma about him. A playfulness. An edge to him that draws you in and makes it impossible to look away.

And it doesn't hurt he's more than easy on the eyes.

During the next thirty minutes, I busy myself with anything and every-thing that is as far away from him as possible. I've never been more willing to do the meaningless tasks Kevin requests than I am right now. Fresh coffee. A message delivered to the AD. A dictated task list typed up on my phone for him. But like everybody else in the room, when Vince takes the mock stage and begins to sing to the camera, all tasks are forgotten. I stop. I take one step toward the stage, then another, and fall under the trance of his voice.

> Soft heart. Sharp knife.
> This love of ours has ruined me for life.
> Harsh words. Punched walls.
> This pain is raw but fuck was it worth the fall.
> Broken dreams. Scar lines.
> You'll always own this heart of mine.

For a moment, I let myself believe he's singing to me. I allow myself the fleeting fantasy that this had all played out differently.

But only for a second.

Only so I can remind myself why it didn't.

And when I blink away the tears that have welled in my eyes, Vince has his hands shielding his eyes from the lights, and he's looking straight at me.

There's no way he can see me where I'm blending in with the darkness of the room.

There's no way he could know . . .

"Matthews."

I jolt from my trance at the sound of Xavier's voice, and I'm instantly on alert. No doubt he's coming to give me a lecture over earlier. Or fire me. I've seen him fire people for less. It just depends on the mood he's in.

Let's hope he's in a good one.

"Yes, sir?" I ask with cheer I don't feel infused in my tone.

"What's the deal with you and Jennings?"

"There's no deal, sir."

"Humor me with the fact that I wasn't born yesterday. Clearly you know each other. Do I need to worry about anything here?" His eyes bore into mine demanding answers I'm not exactly comfortable giving.

"We went to high school together." While it's true, it's just not the whole truth.

"So you do know him?"

"I knew him, yes, but haven't seen him in years."

Xavier chews the inside of his cheek as he stares at me with narrowed eyes and arms crossed over his chest. "He's yours."

"What do you mean he's mine?"

"I've heard good stuff about your work. Your attitude. Your rapport with the talent. Our client list is overflowing, and while I'm thrilled to have Jennings on board after years of pursuit, it was all a little unexpected."

"Congratulations." It's a lame comment, but it's all I can think to say because I'm dreading what I think he's going to say next.

"Congratulations indeed. He's a great asset. A little unpredictable. A lot unscripted. Everything we as fans would hope for in a rock star, right?" He glances over his shoulder to where laughter rings out over something on set. "And that's why I think it's best I assign you to him."

"Assign me to him?"

"I didn't stutter, did I?"

"No. It's just—"

"You're going to turn down the opportunity every person in your position in this company would kill to have?"

"I didn't say that." I swallow over the lump in my throat.

"Good. I wasn't asking you if you wanted this. I was telling you." His smile is quick and unforgiving. "I'm under no pretenses that he's going to be an easy client for us, but I think your familiarity with him will serve us both well. Thoughts?"

I shake my head because Xavier doesn't want my thoughts. He just wants to hear himself talk and that's fine with me because my head is spinning from the events of the past two hours.

Seeing Vince again.

Getting the opportunity I've hoped for.

Just my luck that I get my first real break in this job—that *the* Xavier McMann has actually noticed me—and he rewards me with an opportunity like this. He rewards me with Vince. The irony is so rich it's not even worth summoning the laughter.

"Perfect. I'll make sure that Kevin gets with you soon on what I expect."

"Yes, sir."

"Regardless of the situation, it's your job to let the client think he's always right even when he isn't."

"Mm-hmm."

"And it's my name you're representing. I expect professionalism at all times. This newfound position is temporary unless you show me otherwise."

"Thank you. I . . ." But he walks off, answering his ringing phone before I can say anything else.

I stare after him for a beat, my adrenaline pumping and my head swimming with a myriad of emotions. Excitement. Confusion. Caution. Trepidation. Optimism. Worry.

It shouldn't be possible to feel all those things at once, but I do.

I can do this. Easy. I'm just an old friend, remember? Keeping my professional life separate from my personal life is something I do every day.

There shouldn't be a difference now.

The director yells action and music engulfs the sound stage once again. The bruising melody of the ballad hits my ears. Another take of words that strikes a little too close to home.

Did you know? Did you care?
I looked up to find you weren't there.
Kid gloves. Holding tight.
I still reach for you in the dark of night.
Shattered hopes. Love undefined.
You've always owned this heart of mine.

Yeah, it should be easy . . . if I don't listen to his lyrics.

CHAPTER
four

Vince

"**F**UCK." DAMMIT. "SORRY, GUYS. MY BAD," I GROAN, HOLDING UP MY hands to peer beyond the stage lights. "I swear I know the words to my own song."

"No biggie," my director says from the darkness. "It's been a long night. It happens to the best of us."

No need to stroke my ego. I'm fucking up and I know it.

"Let's take a break from this scene," he says, his voice coming closer until I can see his shadowed face. "We'll give your voice a rest and move to the fight scene. That way we can get Jennifer wrapped and off set and then move back to this part." He motions to the actress.

"Sounds good."

And before I have a chance to unhook my guitar strap from around my neck, the whole room begins to shift their focus to the right where a mock backstage area has been created for the fight scene. Fucking Hollywood, man.

The place where something can be made of nothing. A set. A scene. Even a rock star. I'm living proof of that.

I hand my guitar to the assistant they've assigned to me, all five foot nothing of her doe eyes and trembling hands, and head for my bottle of water just offstage. My first swig has me wishing it were something stronger. I need something to take the fucking edge off.

And why is that, Jennings?

Why do you keep fucking up? Why is your head so far up your ass you can't remember the words you wrote?

I search the darkness beyond the stage again and come up empty. It's probably for the better. Seeing her will just fuck with my concentration even more.

Goddamn Bristol Matthews.

To say this would be the last place I'd think to see her would be a lie. I'd expect to see her *here*. Just not as a bullshit gofer, whatever the fuck position she has.

And yet I look along the walls for her again.

Fuck this.

"I need something else," I say to my assistant. A little something never hurts. "Something stronger."

The poor kid's eyes grow wide as if she can't believe I'm asking for alcohol. Definite newbie. Alcohol has nothing on some of the shit I've seen asked for—and provided—on set. Onstage. Anywhere, really.

"Um, is that allowed?" she asks.

"My stage. My rules." I wink. "A greyhound, please. Whoever has the alcohol will know what's in it." She just stands there and stares at me.

"You're serious."

"I am." I smirk and she remains standing there. "Pretty please."

"Yes, sir. Sorry, Mr. Vincent. I mean Jennings, I mean—"

"Vince is fine."

It's going to be a long fucking night if her sputtering is any indication.

But she does her job and she does it well, because the drink is in my hand within minutes. It's stiff as hell. Just the way I like it.

"Any questions?" the director asks as he tries to focus my distracted attention on the storyboard in front of me.

It looks like a graphic novel with each square illustrated, depicting what's in the next scene of the music video. It's nothing creatively groundbreaking in terms of music videos—hell, music videos are dying in a sense—but they are a necessity for publicity's sake.

And no matter how many I've done, it's still pretty fucking cool to get to make them.

"Got it. Pretend to argue. Throw my glass against the wall. Jennifer takes a swing at me, and then I pin her against the wall. Kiss her breathless." I nod and take a sip, my smirk lopsided. "You know, just like I do with every woman I meet backstage." My joke draws some laughs, but when I glance back to the storyboard again, something strikes me.

Similar scenario but without the fight.

The last time I saw Bristol, this was how it started. Me. Her. Against the wall in the hotel hallway. Breathless. Desperate.

How it ended was even fucking better.

Christ. I haven't thought about that in years. Scratch that. I have. Off and on. When I write songs. When I see someone who looks like her. When I have an off night, drink a few too many beers and curse why what is, is.

Hell, that night between us was supposed to be closure, but all it did was open wounds. Wounds I then tried to seal shut with superglue, never to be opened again.

Until now.

Until I saw her standing there staring at McMann, and it all came rushing back.

Fucking hell.

Was it the same for her after that night? Is it the same for her seeing me now?

It's not like you'd know, Jennings, since you blocked her number from your cell after that night.

Christ.

I take another long sip of my drink and ready myself for this next scene.

Not like it's a hardship kissing another woman for the sake of a video. Or for any reason, really.

But as we go through the drills—wide shot, close-up shot, detail shot—take after take, kiss after intense kiss, it's Bristol who's on my mind. It's Bristol who is fucking up my concentration.

Is she watching?

Is she jealous?

Is she wishing she were the one I'm kissing?

Mature. Real fucking mature.

Then again, there's no goddamn law that says I have to be.

Jennifer's fingernails rake down my back as her tongue dances with mine. And as much as there are lights and people watching, it's hard not to be turned on by the feel of her body against mine. By the unprofessional hum of her approval against my chest. By the heat of her pussy on my thigh where it's pressed between her legs.

She's sending all the signals that she'd be willing to continue where we leave off after we're both wrapped from the set.

Another time maybe.

Another place.

Somewhere where Bristol isn't, perhaps.

But why? It's not like knowing she exists has prevented me from living my life over the years. I've kissed a whole hell of a lot of women. I've fucked more than I can count. All without giving a thought to how it would make Bristol feel.

I'm a rock star. That's just how it goes.

So why in the fuck is it bugging me now?

"Can you get into it a little more, Vince?" the director asks.

"If I get any more into it, I'll be inside her," I say, garnering a laugh from the crew and the clenching of her thigh against mine.

"Right. Yes." Clearly, I'm not selling it by the director's comments. "Put your hand on her breast. Yes. Like that. Fist your other in her hair. Good." He hums in approval and then I assume he speaks to the director of photography. "Zoom in on her hand twisted in his shirt. Then on his knee between her thighs. Then on their mouths as they move. Yes. Perfect. Believable. Sexy as hell."

We keep going. Making out in a roomful of people—not like that's new to me—but not typically with cameras and bright lights documenting each slip of the tongue.

Is Bristol still an incredible kisser?

Is her taste still as addictive as I remember?

"Cut," the director yells out.

We untangle ourselves from each other, and when I look up, I lock eyes with Bristol where she stands a few feet over the director's shoulder.

Seeing her hits me like a sucker punch, even more than when she turned around earlier today.

She doesn't get to look at me like that. Not with the hurt. Not with the pain. Not with those big brown eyes judging me for doing my job. Those eyes that used to own me.

She's the past. The one who let me walk away. The one who agreed to one incredible night.

She's the one who . . . just stormed out of this sound stage.

Shit.

Damn.

Fuck.

Why do you care, Vince?

I run a hand through my hair and down the rest of my current drink. "I need a fucking minute," I mutter to anyone in earshot, knowing they won't say a word. They're here because of me. Perks of being the star.

A low chuckle hums across the room. They're assuming I've got a hard-on that I need to calm down.

They can think whatever the fuck they want. It's not like I've ever cared one way or another, and I sure as hell don't now as I casually make my way toward the exit doors Bristol just pushed through.

McMann steps in my way. "Everything okay? Need me to take care of something for you?"

I hold up my cell. "Need to make a quick call." It's the only explanation I give.

"Not a problem," he says as I move past him. "Oh, and if you need any-thing, I've assigned our junior associate Bristol to you. She can take care of whatever your needs happen to be."

I've got a whole lot of needs when it comes to her, Xav. You might not want to say that.

"Ten-four," I say and keep moving right on out the door.

CHAPTER
five

Vince

S HE'S STANDING A FEW FEET TO THE LEFT OF THE EXIT. HER BACK IS
to me with her arms crossed and shoulders hunched to ward off the cold
night air.

Why is seeing her again fucking with my head? She was a lifetime ago.
Done and over with.

Have I missed her? Christ, after I walked away the last time, she owned
my mind right along with my breaking fucking heart. She's the only thing
I've ever loved other than music. I hated leaving her, but it was the right
thing to do.

I get that she might still be mad at my chickenshit exit that morning,
but this tension between us feels so wrong. So . . . *off*.

In the past, we'd see each other and the rights, wrongs, and everything
in between would just evaporate into thin air until it left just us again. That
had always been our M.O.

How do I get that back? How do I fix this?

Slow down, Vin. Your time here is limited. Don't start what you can't fucking finish.

"Bristol."

"Please, Vince. Don't do this right now."

"Do what? Since when is talking a crime?"

Her shoulders slowly drop, and then she finally turns to look at me.

Fucking hell, she's gorgeous.

The dark hair in waves down her back. The big, light brown eyes. The pouty, pink lips. The full curves of her body—that she always hated and felt judged for—underneath her black jeans and sweater.

She's still stunning.

"This is not the time or place to rehash our past, okay? I need you to just get back to work."

Beautiful *and* professional.

So why do her words feel like a punch to my gut?

"Sure. Fine. No rehashing. But can you at least explain why you're angry at me?" When she just continues to stare at the ground, I take a step closer. "Talk to me, Shug."

She grits her teeth and meets my eyes. "Look. You have a roomful of people in there waiting on you hand and foot," she says, all business and completely ignoring my question. "You should get back to them."

"According to what Xavier promised me, you're supposed to be doing the same."

I go for the wisecrack and only get her hands fisted at her sides in return. It used to be so easy to make her laugh. What am I missing here? Why is she so closed off?

"I don't wait on *anyone* hand and foot." There's that fire of hers I used to love. "But as the person who's been tasked with making sure you do what's needed, I kindly request that we stop talking so you can get to work. I assure you that everyone inside would like to finish sooner rather than later so they can go home to their families before the sun rises."

"Fine. I will. Right *after* this conversation."

"Why even have it?"

"Because I'm more than certain it's an important one." I take a step closer and instinct, old memories, I don't know what, has me trying to run my hands up and down her biceps to ward off the night's chill. She takes a hasty step backward.

"I don't bite." My chuckle this time earns me an exasperated sigh.

"Vince, you can't just walk in here and act like there is no past between us, but touch me like there is."

"Then maybe we should talk about that past. You're the one trying to ignore it."

Her face pulls tight but her eyes relay that there's so much more than her words are saying. "I can't do a repeat of seven years ago where you play with me while you're in town and then return back to your glamorous life without ever looking back."

Um, wow. Okay. I sure as fuck wasn't expecting that one.

"Play with you? That's what you called what happened last time? Because from where I was standing, you were a more than willing participant."

"*Were.* Past tense." She gives a quick nod of her head. "Rest assured that won't be happening again."

"Who said I wanted it to?" My words are cruel but serve a purpose.

Her reaction is what I needed to see.

The wince in her expression. The flare of her nostrils. The grit of her teeth.

She's bluffing. There's still something there. Always has been. Good to see I'm not the only one who feels it.

And *fuck me* for still wanting it.

Then again, haven't I always despite convincing myself otherwise?

"Keep thinking along those lines," she says, her words betraying the look in her eyes. "There is *no* want on this end either."

"So who is he then?"

Shock flashes through her eyes and lands like a punch to my gut. She's with someone? Dating? Married?

Don't ask questions you don't want answers to, Vin.

My stomach churns at the thought as I glance at her finger, looking for a ring, but her hand is tucked under her other arm and I can't see it.

"That's rich. You thinking the only reason I don't want anything to happen between us is because of another man. Maybe there is one. Maybe there isn't. My life is none of your business."

And why does not getting a concrete answer drive me mad?

"Fair," I say and let a slow smile crawl on my lips. "But c'mon, it's *us* we're talking about."

"There is no *us*, Vince."

"And yet you still think about me." *C'mon. Smile for me, Shug. Once I get that, I know I'll be able to get more out of you. Like why you seem so angry with me.*

"Never. Rarely. It's just . . ." She draws in a deep breath. "It's not that easy anymore. *Life's* not that easy."

"It's only hard if you make it that way."

"Not all of us have choices like that."

"What does that even mean? What happened that I don't know about?" *How about seven years' worth of life, Vin?* The look in her eyes says she's thinking the same damn thing. I shove my hands in my pockets and rock on my heels. "So, how long ago did you make the move out here?"

She looks up at me from beneath her lashes almost as if she's debating whether answering the question will be letting me in too much. The slightest nod of her head says she doesn't think so. "A while ago."

Not all of us have choices like that.

Her words hit my ears again and pique my curiosity. "Is that why you're a junior associate for McMann?"

"Come again?"

Huh. Touchy subject. Maybe if I push enough of her buttons, I'll sneak past that goddamn wall she's put up and get a reaction out of her. A reaction that isn't so measured and guarded. One that will give me a fucking clue into what she's being so protective of.

"You said not all of us have choices like that. What did that mean? What happened? Is *life being hard* why the dreams you had are still just that, dreams?"

"Talking to me for ten minutes after seven years doesn't give you the right to ask that question."

"Maybe it doesn't, but I'm confused why you're with McMann in a job that's way fucking beneath you." Her wince is telling. I just wish I knew what it told. "Being a babysitter for spoiled assholes is overrated, Bristol."

Something flashes in her eyes. It's so brief that I can't read it, but it's followed by a stiffening of her spine. *God, her fire is a turn-on, even now.* "Why did you leave your best friends behind—leave a good fucking thing—and go out on your own? Huh? What happened with Hawke and the guys? With Bent? Did your ego get too big that you thought you didn't need them anymore?"

"Tou-fucking-ché." Got to admire a woman who knows how to hit where it hurts. And that fucking hurt.

Seems like life has given Bristol Matthews a stronger backbone.

"And while we're at it, stick to what you do best. *Domino* was decent," she says, referring to my last single that flopped, "but it wasn't you. There was no edge to it. No trademark Vincent Jennings sound. It was soft. Generic. More like white noise that blended into the background."

"For someone who hasn't thought about me at all, you sure have a lot to say." She's on point about the song. I hate it, but she's right. I wouldn't expect anything less from her.

"Call it professional research."

"Bullshit. You didn't know I signed with McMann until tonight and yet you claim knowing my songs is research. Pretend all you want, but you still think of me. You still follow me."

"And your ego is still as big as Texas."

Among other things.

"So you don't want to talk about our past. You don't want to talk about what you're up to now." I cross my arms over my chest and shrug. "It's going to be a pretty boring conversation standing here, staring at each other, and not speaking at all."

"Then we should get back to work."

My chuckle is laced with confusion as the thought strikes me. "Is it because of last time?"

"Is what because of last time?" Arms still crossed. Finger still hidden. Head angled to the side.

"Why you're angry at me? Do you have regrets?" *And why would it kill me if she says yes?* "That's a long time to harbor something if so."

"It is a long time. That's why I had to accept what happened and move on with my life."

"That's a pretty clinical description for something we both went into willingly." It wasn't a business transaction for Christ's sake.

"You know . . ." She swallows forcibly and shakes her head ever so subtly. She opens her mouth to speak and then closes it just as quickly. I swear there are tears in her eyes, but she looks down so I can't be sure. The problem is that when she looks back up, the emotion is gone. *All emotion is.* Bristol has put her guard up in a way I've never seen before. "Nothing. Never mind. As much as you think we need to talk about the past, we really don't. We've both moved on, and that's okay. We both have a job to do here, so let's just get back to that and let bygones be bygones. Okay? You have people waiting for you, and I have a job to do so I don't get fired."

"Go out for a drink with me. After we're done. We can talk about whatever it is you want to talk about. How much my music sucks. If you still love watching baseball. The fucking weather, for all I care."

She waves me back toward the door. No fucking ring. At least there's that.

But was there one? Is that why she's so guarded? Was she married? Divorced? Was she hurt?

Did he hurt her?

"It's probably better if we don't. Blurring lines and all."

I itch to grab her arm and pull her against me. I spent years wanting this woman only to have one night with her.

Clearly that one night wasn't enough. Fuck.

"Seriously?"

"Seriously," she says and moves toward the door, but my hand is on her arm this time.

Look at me.

And when she does, it's still there. I'm not imagining it. That thing that's always been between us is still fucking there.

Why do I suddenly feel the need to make her see it?

"You know . . ." I say playfully. "I require a lot of maintenance. Me and my ego? We're demanding. Petty. Have a lot of fucking needs." I shrug. "McMann said anything I needed, you'd provide. My bet's on you doing your job to the best of your abilities."

"You wouldn't dare."

I lift my wrist and show her the light pink heart tattooed there. The one that's proof of a dare I made. One we had a whole discussion about the last time I saw her so she knows the meaning behind it. "Actually, you know I would."

"Quit being selfish. People are waiting to finish and go home," she says and then stalks past me. I know she tries to slam the door, but the shock on its hinge prevents her from doing so.

I chuckle.

Nothing like being denied a good slam.

Shit. I scrub a hand through my hair and stare at the door she just went through. The one I should also enter because she's right, everyone in there is waiting on me.

I walked away from her a long time ago without looking back.

I've seen her one time since then, and that one time is cemented in my memory forever.

So why is seeing her again—when I've gone on and lived my life—causing such confusion?

Because your life's in limbo, Jennings, and she was the only real thing you ever knew.

Fuckin' A, man.

If I'd known that Bristol worked for McMann Media, I may not have said yes to their offer.

Who am I fucking kidding? That would have made me sign even quicker.

Yeah, I'm the one who walked away again last time. Who blocked her number from my cell all those years ago. But life is too fucking real right now, and losing myself in her for a while seems like it could be a good fucking distraction.

"I can't do a repeat of seven years ago where you play with me while you're in town and then return back to your glamorous life without ever looking back."

She's right.

I know she's right.

But it doesn't make me want her any goddamn less.

You signed on the dotted line, Vin. You have a job to do. A job you're clearly struggling to get through, and it's only day fucking one.

Do the job.

Do the one thing you've never been able to do when it comes to her—keep your hands to yourself.

Try to forget just how hard Bristol Matthews is to quit.

With a sigh I feel deep in my bones, I open the door with a determination to remember those three things and resignation that I'm probably going to fail at least two of them.

CHAPTER

six

Bristol

"**M**OMMA?"

Jagger stirs beneath the covers as I slide in beside him and pull him against me. He snuggles into me, his face beneath the curve of my neck like he's done since he was a newborn, his hand resting on my heart, and his feet gently rubbing against mine like a cricket.

"I'm here, buddy," I murmur before pressing a kiss to the top of his head and simply breathing him in. Strawberry shampoo and everything that is my little boy weaves into my soul, and I sigh.

His dark hair and light eyes. His olive complexion. His mischievous smile and belly giggles.

As I stood in the doorway watching him sleep, my heart felt like a balloon in my chest, expanding with more love for this perfect little human I created. That I've raised. And all of my mistakes—the ones that have robbed him of things every little boy deserves—made that balloon feel like it was going to burst.

I needed to hold him. To touch him. To pull him in tight. To try and erase the torrent of emotions coming at me one after another.

"I don't feel yucky anymore," he slurs in his sleep-drugged state. It feels like days since he threw up on my shoes and it was less than twenty-four hours ago.

"That's good." I lean back, brush his hair off his forehead, and can't help but smile. His dark lashes and rosy cheeks get me every time.

"School?"

"Uh-uh. Not yet. Go back to sleep." I hold him a little tighter and lightly stroke his back to help him get there. He has a few hours left before we start the morning routine. A routine that will be much easier no doubt since my mom, who is currently asleep on the couch, will be there to help with.

"You're in my bed."

"I just missed you is all."

"Missed you too," he says seconds before his breathing evens out again.

Sleep. That's what I should be doing. That's what I want to do considering I've been running on fumes and caffeine for the past few hours.

Me and my normal ten p.m. bedtime and Vince and his energizer bunny energy that never waned through the entire night and early morning as he shot take after take after take for the video.

And as he made demand after demand after demand of me. Always playful. Completely unnecessary since he had an assistant on set. But demands nonetheless under McMann's careful eye to remind me that my only choice was to do what he asked or risk my job.

Prick.

Then why is there a soft smile on my face? Why did I find myself laughing at the jokes Vince was making with the crew while trying to stay mad at him for personal reasons? Why did I find that anger I was trying to hold on to solely to keep him at a distance, slowly dissolving?

Probably the same reason I need to hold Jagger right now. Because some things are just so natural that they're hard to let go of.

I stifle my yawn, knowing I need to get to sleep. My late night doesn't mean I get to skip work tomorrow.

And tomorrow brings more Vince.

I was naïve to think this day would never come. It was even more ridiculous to think if it did, that I could write it off and it wouldn't matter.

How could I have thought that when my life has been labeled in three parts. With Vince. After Vince. And After *After* Vince. And no matter how much I tell myself I resent and dislike him with every part of my being after everything we've been through, he's always been a part of my life.

Ever since that first day he walked into the tutoring session with a busted lip and a bad attitude my freshman year.

The memories hit. One after another. The good. The bad. The ugly. And the one incredible thing that I got from all of this despite the pain and the doubt and the hardship.

But then there's the guilt, still there after all this time. Still making me wonder and question if I've done the right thing. *Will Jagger hate the choices I've made for him?*

Surely it's better not to know your father than believing you're unwanted. The question I've often asked myself is whether Vince still feels the same. That the last thing he'd ever want is to have someone carry on the Jennings name.

Do you have regrets? That's a long time to harbor something if so.

Regrets? No. That night gave me the most important thing in my life.

But I've done this alone. Right, wrong, or indifferent, when he cut off every means of communication with me without knowing why I needed to get ahold of him, I made decisions that to this day, I'd make again if I had to.

When it came down to it, he shut me out and moved on with his life while my whole world shifted and then spun onto a different axis.

And regardless of his crooked smile and witty charm, I need to remember this.

I was the one who reached out. Who tried. Who was rejected.

I thought I'd made peace with my decisions and buried the hurt that came with it. Now I'm not so sure . . . about anything really.

Besides the shock of seeing Vince again, today brought so many unknowns to the surface. Unknowns that I need to figure out answers for. Unknowns that could turn my perfect, chaotic, carefully crafted world upside down.

Unknowns that once seemed so concrete and now seem extremely selfish when I never thought of them as being that before.

"Oh, Jagg," I murmur into the darkness, pulling him even closer against me. "What am I supposed to do now?"

CHAPTER
seven

Bristol

STRIDE INTO THE BURBANK OFFICE WITH AN ESPRESSO IN ONE HAND, two bottles of liquid energy shots in my purse, and thoughts of how quickly this day can pass so I can catch up on my sleep.

Because the little sleep I finally got wasn't enough. Dreams plagued my sleep. Ones that rewound time and reminded me of things I'd long forgotten.

But I'm on more sure footing today. I took the extra time I didn't have to do my hair and makeup when normally it's a topknot and a brush or two of mascara. I think that's maybe why I felt off-kilter last night when it came to seeing Vince—well, besides the obvious reasons. So today, I figured I'd fix what I could on my end to make sure I didn't feel that way again.

As I make my way through the cubical maze of junior associates' desks, heads pop up like whack-a-moles, glancing toward the conference room, before sitting back down just as quickly. There's more of a low buzz of conversation than normal.

The last time the office was this distracted was when senior associate,

Lilah Glasnow was fired for sleeping with her client. The last thing McMann wants is for his firm to appear unprofessional, and when those rumors started flying, her walking papers were typed up. She didn't go without a fight. There was a shouting match with insults hurled and threats made while we all sat with our heads down, listening to every single, deliciously scandalous word of it.

I look for Simone in her cubicle, knowing she'll give me the scoop, but she's not there. However, I find her sitting in my chair, at my desk, with her arms crossed, her eyebrows raised, and her feet propped up on my desk.

"Make yourself at home, why don't you?" I say, noticing she's pushed aside my frame so that my collage of Jagger is facing the wall of the cube.

"I have. Thanks." She places one of the peanut butter cups I leave in a dish on my desk in her mouth and smiles while chewing it, her eyes never breaking from mine.

"What?" I ask, already on the defensive because I know that look.

"I didn't even garner a phone call?" she says.

"For what?" But I already know.

It's why necks are craning toward the conference room. Why the chatter is muted but still excited. We're used to celebrity sightings around here. It's what our company does, but not every celebrity holds the same mystique as the man I'm more than certain is sitting in said conference room.

"Vincent freaking Jennings?" Simone says, confirming my hunch. "First, you find out who the hush-hush client is, and you don't say a word." She points to one finger. "Second, you've been assigned as his handler—a freaking promotion—and you neglect to call." She points to another. "And lastly, let me reiterate, Vincent freaking Jennings." She throws her hands up. "I thought you were my girl, but nope, you leave my ass out in the cold and don't say a damn word."

"I didn't get home till after three in the morning, *and* I was under the impression that your ass was otherwise occupied." I cross my arms over my chest and lean against one of the gray fabric, portable walls.

"I was, oh was I," she murmurs, her eyes alive with suggestion, "but that doesn't mean a girl isn't going to check her texts during that post-coital glow period."

"Jesus." I roll my eyes.

"I mean, I hand you this gift, and I don't even get a smoke signal to tell me what's going on. I had to show up today and be knocked on my ass when that . . ."—she mock shivers— "gorgeous beauty of a man stepped into the elevator right before the doors closed. I mean he was close enough for me to touch. To stealthily stare at the very intricate designs of his tattoos. To smell his cologne."

"Simone—"

"There needed to be a 'clean-up on aisle five' from the puddle of . . . me, that was all over that elevator floor."

"Whatever."

"But you already knew how good all of those things were because you spent the whole night with him. Beside him. Listening to him." She puts the back of her hand to her forehead and pretends as if she's fainted. Dramatics are definitely her strong suit. "Lusting after him."

"Refilling his drink and getting him whatever he asked for."

"Please say he asked for me." She holds out her hands as if they are hand-cuffed together. "You can serve me up on a platter to him."

"Says the girl who was otherwise busy getting laid."

She bursts out laughing and puts her feet soundly on the floor. "You know I'm just fucking with you." She sighs loudly. "But hell if I'm not mad at myself for picking sex over work and jealous of you in all the best ways."

"I know. For what it's worth, Xavier made it sound like the promotion was temporary and only because we're short-staffed at the moment. And Vince? Vince is . . ." A prick? Demanding? A diva? I think of the dozens of things I could say to make her feel better about missing the opportunity she gave me, but I can't find it in me to lie.

"He's what? Gorgeous? Mysterious? Sexy? I mean—"

"Matthews." We both jump at the sound of Kevin's voice from across the room.

I glance at her with wide eyes before grabbing a pad of paper I don't know if I'll need or not. This whole beck-and-call thing for a client instead of my immediate boss is all new to me. "Coming."

I can feel the stares from the other junior associates as I make my way across the office floor. I've been where they are—watching someone get the opportunity they so desperately want—and am under no pretenses that that won't be me again in a heartbeat if I don't impress Xavier with whatever I'm supposed to be doing for Vince.

I enter the conference room, empty save for the man across from me.

Xavier stands with his ass against the glass wall of windows, his arms folded over his chest, and his head angled to the side as he studies me.

I've squirmed under less scrutiny, but I actually have his attention now, so I meet him stare for stare.

"What can I do for you?"

"We're brainstorming today. Marketing is meeting with us on the tenth floor shortly."

"Okay." I glance toward Kevin and then back. "Do you need paper or coffee or me to set things up—"

"We need you."

Both Kevin's and my head whip up in unison. "Me?"

Junior associates are typically on the outside of these glass walls looking in. Unless of course, they're asked to fetch something trivial to which they're invited in and then promptly ushered out.

"Yes," he says but for some reason doesn't seem too happy about it. "Sit."

"Okay. Why—"

"I told them you had some great ideas last night and that I wanted you in on this." The punch Vince's voice packs didn't lessen overnight. Not that I thought it would.

I turn to look at where he's just walked into the room. He has a pair of dark sunglasses on even though we're inside, his hair looks like his hands have been running through it nonstop, and his lips are pursed in that way of his that tells me he's studying every single thing about me.

Not to mention the fact that he just lied through his teeth about me having good ideas last night. About what? About how I don't want him here? About how I told him his last single wasn't great?

"Yes," Xavier says before I can speak. And I know exactly why he looks miffed. Xavier McMann doesn't like having his hand forced when it comes to anything. And it's clear that he's appeasing Vince's request to have me here.

Sure he's keeping his newest client happy, but it's also putting me in a very precarious position.

"Do you mind sharing some of those ideas?" Kevin asks.

I look from him to Vince and then back again. "I—"

"She let me know why my last single flopped. Explained the reasons for her opinion."

"Now you're a music critic?" Xavier asks, the tendons in his neck taut as he reins in his temper.

Why do I feel like I'm in the middle of a fight for control that one has a hard time ceding and the other's having fun testing?

"That's not what I meant. I was simply telling Vince that this new song he was singing—"

"*Heart of Mine.*"

"Yes, is more in line with what his audience expects. And if he's breaking away from Bent and trying to establish himself then—"

"He's already established himself just fine." That fleeting, tight smile is flashed my way. The one that says clearly, I don't know what the hell I'm talking about. "I assigned you someone. It's your job to know this information."

Talk about unrealistic expectations considering he paired me with Vince on the fly yesterday. There's a reason people say if you can survive McMann, you can survive the industry.

"Because this is a career for you, right? Not just some job to fill the time as you figure out what to do with your life while gaining bragging rights that you have access to the famous? Like it is for most of the associates out there? If it were, you would have found the time to know everything about our newest client so you could anticipate outcomes, mitigate expectations, and assist in planning for his future."

He has a birthmark on his inner thigh. How's that for knowing your newest client inside out? Choke on that, you asshole.

"Only then do any of us want to hear your opinions on Mr. Jennings's career. And if you're not willing to put in the time and effort, there are a dozen more in the room behind you waiting to take your place."

Embarrassment heats my cheeks over letting him berate me like this in general, but also in front of Vince. I know I'm better than this, but I also know I have to pay my dues to move forward. Unfortunately, sucking it up and swallowing my pride is what's needed for the time being.

Apparently, each step up the rung comes with a little more respect. Or at least, so I'm told. Right now, the rung I'm on isn't exactly feeling that way.

My smile is placating despite the stiffening of my spine. "I assure you that—"

"She was just giving me the honest feedback I asked for." Vince steps farther into the room, his shoulders squared as he shrugs and his tone impenitent. "Truth be told, she was right on the money."

"It wasn't her place to opine," Xavier says.

"Well, I prefer it actually. Most people tell me what I want to hear, kiss my ass because of who I am. I respect that she had the balls to say the truth versus sugarcoat it." He looks from Xavier to Kevin and then back. "That's why I asked that she be a part of my brainstorming sessions."

Vince looks my way, his expression impassive, but his eyes ask questions I don't want to answer. Why do you put up with this shit? Why do you let him treat you like this? What happened to that headstrong girl I used to know?

She's still here. She just got sidetracked for a while, made some sacrifices, and needs this job to get where she wants to be.

"Understood," Xavier says with a curt nod. "Kevin will make sure that she's kept in the loop on all of those types of meetings."

"Preferably all meetings," Vince says in this unspoken tug of war.

"That's not exactly the hierarchy we have set up here," Xavier says.

"Then make the adjustment," Vince says, clearly aware he has the power in this relationship.

"Of course. I'll make an exception for the next couple of weeks while you're in town and we're sorting through our plans for you."

"Great. Make sure you do." Vince takes a seat and unceremoniously props his combat boots on the conference room table as if discussing my fate and my job duties are something he has a right to do. My hands fist over this sudden helplessness I feel. "Now that that's settled, let's get this boring shit over with. I have studio time we're cutting into, and my muse is speaking to me."

"Of course." Xavier's mouth pulls tight momentarily. "Bristol? Why don't you give us about thirty minutes to go over some things, and then you can show Mr. Jennings down to the meeting with the documentary team." He looks to Vince, clearly unhappy to be asking his next question. "If that's okay with you, of course?"

Vince nods. "It's fine."

"We'll let you know when you're needed again."

"Sounds great." My smile is quick but relief even quicker as I swiftly exit the conference room.

I'm beginning to think I'm going to need something stronger than coffee to get through today.

CHAPTER
eight

Bristol

I'LL GET IT TO YOU BY TOMORROW MORNING. I HAVE A FEW MORE things I need to add to the list before it's ready to go," I say to Bianca as Simone and I pass her cubicle.

"Sounds good. At least I know when you say it'll be done, it'll be done. Unlike some others around here," she says a little louder than necessary to which a coughed bullshit is heard from the other side of her cubicle walls.

We both laugh, and I schedule a reminder on my phone for later today so I don't forget my promise to her.

"So what gives then?" Simone whispers. "Why is he using you as some kind of leverage against Xavier?"

"Hell if I know."

"Girl, were you doing more than just serving the man his drinks last night? Is that why he's demanding your presence at every meeting?" she teases. "Because if you're skipping out on telling me those details, we are no longer friends."

"Will you shut up?" I look around to see if anyone could have heard her. I know she's joking, but the last thing I need is rumors flying around.

"Oh please." She laughs.

"I'm serious. It's like he's put a huge target on my back with McMann," I say as we reach my cube.

"Who's put a target on your back?"

Simone yelps quietly at the sight of Vince sitting in my chair, one ankle resting over the opposite knee. His large frame eats up what's left of the small space that his presence doesn't already own.

"Oh. My," Simone murmurs under her breath before giving one last look and then walking off.

And while she may be ogling, the suppressed confusion and anger over how Vince used me as a pawn in his power play with Xavier returns.

And then it dies a rapid death as one thought permeates all others: my pictures.

I have a few seconds of abject fear until I see that the frame that displays Jagger in all his goofy, adorable glory is still facing toward the cubicle wall where Simone's feet had knocked it earlier.

If Vince were to see a picture of Jagger, he'd know. There's no way he couldn't.

The relief that floods through me is short-lived as my scattered emotions struggle to find footing.

"What are you doing here?"

He shrugs in that cocky, casual way of his. "Trying to figure out what that look on your face is for."

"What look?"

"The one that says you've seen a ghost." His eyes narrow as he studies me.

"No ghost." I keep my eyes on him instead of scanning my space like I want to, just to make sure there are no other visible personal effects. I have a lot to figure out, and right now isn't the time to do that.

Clueless to my personal war, Vince angles his head and simply stares at me. It makes me feel like he can see right through me. "Then what is it, Shug, because there's something you're not telling me."

My nervous laugh flits through the air. That's the good and bad of being so connected with someone. They see everything when you want them to . . . and even when you don't want them to.

"Not telling you?" I snort and divert. "How about you stop using me to piss off my boss."

"Again with the anger? I thought we brought it down a notch last night. What? Did you go home and decide you hated me again and figured you'd make sure you put your foot down today and really let me have it?"

"Are they ready for you downstairs?" I ask.

"You're not answering my question," he says completely unfazed. "Was this a predetermined reaction this morning or does seeing me just bring out the best in you?"

Why is everything so casual for him, so easy, when it comes to interacting with me when I feel like I'm tiptoeing barefoot around shattered glass?

"It's cuz you missed me so much, isn't it?" he continues.

"I'm not doing this with you."

"It seems you don't want to do a lot of anything with me." Vince stands to his full height while I look around fervently, hoping it will prevent people from hearing this conversation. When I look back, he's scratching just above his waistline, fingers holding the black T-shirt up so that I'm greeted with a glimpse of his happy trail.

"This right here."

His groaned gasp as I playfully nip the dent of muscles is a seduction in and of itself. "What about it?"

"I could lose myself here all night." I look up the plane of his chest and meet those pale eyes. His lids are heavy with arousal as he stares intensely at me.

His smile is crooked. Arrogant. "By all means, Shug. Take all the time in the world. You won't find me complaining about it."

The memory hits me out of nowhere. Hard and fast and so very real and, by the smirk on his lips when I meet his eyes, he's remembering it too.

"Let's go," I say, tearing my eyes away from him and his happy trail.

"Where to? For that drink you promised me? Good idea." Frustrated and exasperated, I grab him by the arm and pull him out of my cubicle, his low, rumbling chuckle grating my every nerve. "God, you're so easy to rile up."

I stare at him for a beat, no doubt my cheeks are flushed, before stalking through the maze of cubicles toward the back elevator on this floor. The hall leading to it is closed door after closed door behind which are various stored items. Files. Furniture. Electronics. Places where no one should be, and therefore, whatever flirtatious taunts that Vince may throw my way won't be heard.

His footsteps fall heavy behind me.

At least he's not arguing with me about that.

But he's chirping little comments as we go. Comments made to irritate me further but that I try valiantly to ignore.

If there is such a thing as ignoring Vincent Jennings.

"Where are you taking me? This isn't the elevator I came in on," he says as we reach the end of the long hallway.

"You're right. It's not. It's the cargo elevator." I turn to face him to find his brow furrowed as he studies me. "Oh, wait. I'm sorry. I forgot that you need to have everyone staring at you to feed that giant ego of yours." I roll my eyes. "Forgive me for not thinking of your needs first."

"There's that animosity again."

"You're goddamn right it's there," I grit out.

Vince steps into my personal space. Space I want to step back and reclaim, but that would only prove to him that he's getting to me when I don't want him to know that. "What is your problem because last time I checked, my presence excited you and it wasn't in this way."

His comment was meant as a joke. That crooked smile and sheepish eyes say so. But all it does is churn up confusion I don't want to feel and cause all the cylinders of my temper to fire.

I step into the elevator that has just opened, keeping my back to him until the doors shut. And the minute they do, I whirl on him, finger pressing into his chest and anger spewing.

"If you want to have a pissing match with McMann, then have one. Keep me out of it. I need this job, and when you leave, whenever it is you're leaving, I still have to be here. I still need the job. The income."

He stares at me, jaw ticking, eyes flaring, but he doesn't say a word.

"Why are you here at McMann anyway?" I ask. "Clearly you have issues with Xavier, so why'd you sign with him?"

"I don't have issues with him."

"Could've fooled me. Why'd you leave CMG?" I ask of his previous management company.

And it's that fleeting grimace, the one he tucks away just as quickly as it comes, that tells me there's more to the story than I thought.

"He's a prick, I'll give you that, but he's good at what he does," Vince says evenly.

"So you hired a man you hate?"

"Hate's a strong word."

"How about dislike? Is that better?"

"It is." He gives a measured nod followed by a slow crawl of a smile. "You know me, I'm not exactly a fan of being told what to do."

"Then McMann was the wrong person to hire." I snort.

"I needed the change of scenery and someone who knows the playing field. He's one of the few who fits that bill."

"Yeah, well, I hate to break it to you, but you're just as bad as him."

"Yep, sure am." The roll of his eyes pisses me off.

"Well, he talks about me like I'm his property. You did too."

"Then start acting like you're neither to either of us. That would be a good place to start."

I stare at Vince with wide eyes and a blank expression, uncertain what to say.

I hate that he's right.

"You don't understand. McMann eats junior associates for lunch, and you just served me up on a platter by telling him I offered my opinions."

"The Bristol Matthews I knew didn't let anyone tell her what to do. I was hoping she was still around."

"That's not fair." My words are all but a whisper as my ego takes a hit, and we stand there staring at each other. This job is my sole source of income. It barely covers my bills, a few extras for Jagger here and there, and the interest of my deferred student loan payments, but it gives me the experience I need and the free time for studying. Losing it is the last thing I need, and Vince being here, pulling his chest-thumping bullshit like he did in the conference room, makes that a possibility. I refuse to let him be the reason everything changes in my life. *Again.*

"Bristol?" he finally says.

"Hmm?"

"You need to push a floor, sweetheart, or we're not going anywhere."

"Oh. I didn't—"

But I'm silenced as he leans past me and pushes the button for the tenth floor. It just so happens that to do so, his entire body presses against mine.

And this elevator, the one that's used for cargo and is larger than normal, suddenly feels so damn tiny with Vince occupying what feels like every inch of space and breath of air in it.

When he pulls his arm back, he doesn't move his body. All six foot plus of him remains firmly against mine. His cologne is subtle. His breath smells like mint. And when I dare to meet his eyes and the intensity in them, it's my own breath that sucks in.

Seconds feel like minutes.

Minutes that need to end but that history has me holding on to.

"Do you remember how good we were?" he murmurs. His breath feathers against my lips as he runs the back of his hand down my cheek.

Chills chase over my skin as my head and my body battle for control of the narrative. One that knows this can't happen. The other that craves for it to happen.

"Vince." It's barely a whisper as his hand slides down my neck to the curve of my shoulder so his thumb is resting on my jawline.

"I know. It's crazy it's still here after all this time."

"We can't—"

He runs his thumb over my lips to stop me from talking. His thumb . . . when all I want it to be is his lips.

He rests his forehead against mine, his mouth a whisper away, and we just stand like this for a beat.

My pulse thunders.

My chest constricts.

But my head knows so much better than to start this.

And when the elevator dings, I'm not sure if the sigh I emit is in relief or defeat.

CHAPTER
nine

Bristol

FOCUS IS A STRUGGLE.

And it's not because I'm past the point of exhaustion where coffee usually works.

It's the elevator that I can't get out of my head. Vince's hand on my face. The way his words made me feel.

And the confusion both created.

How can I hate a man *and* be tempted by him? How can I have spent years telling myself that Vince Jennings doesn't mean a thing to me, and then the first time I see him, feel my heart tripping over itself to ignore the scars he previously left there?

Vince's words come back to me: The Bristol Matthews I knew didn't let anyone tell her what to do. *Where was she earlier?*

The problem is, I thought I knew who the new Bristol Matthews was. The After *After* Vince one. Now I'm beginning to worry that I don't even have a clue. That I'm nowhere near as strong as I thought I was.

Deep-seated disappointment in myself hits hard. But not as hard as the punch of Vince's deep tenor reminding me just how good we used to be.

Neither thrill me.

And yet there I was acting like a giddy schoolgirl pining for her ex like she forgot all the bad that's happened.

But I'm not in high school.

And there is so much more at stake than my reputation this time around.

But the question that remains is why? Why did I want him to kiss me? Why am I still thinking about it?

For nostalgia? For old times' sake? For unadulterated pleasure? To prove *I* could kiss him and walk away and be in control of it rather than devastated by it?

But those are all games. Games I'm too old to play and don't really want to play anyway.

"*I know. It's crazy it's still here after all this time.*"

Attraction. That's all he was talking about. Our chemistry. The way our bodies react to one another's without thought.

Isn't that who Vince is though? He was always good with words. With making me feel wanted.

But that's where he stopped at everything else. He loved me till he didn't. He needed me until he didn't. He wanted me until he didn't.

"Right?"

I smile reflexively as I look up to find four pairs of eyes looking at me. Vince's, the director of the documentary, Will, his assistant who is taking notes, and the person who will be interviewing him on camera, Jasmine.

"I'm sorry. I got caught up thinking about something else. What did I miss?" I ask.

"I was just saying how perfect it was that you work here since you knew Vincent way back when," Jasmine says. "You might be able to add some additional insight when we head back to your hometown next week."

"Next week? What?"

"It's on the schedule in front of you," Vince says with a motion to the paper on the table. His smile is unapologetic. "Just for a few days."

I nod, my smile strained.

I don't like the unexpected. I like plans and schedules and having time to digest what's expected of me. While someone like Vince thrives on spontaneity, it gives me metaphorical hives.

To say I feel like I'm being thrown into the fire is an understatement. Now I'm being forced to travel with the man I'm currently tying myself up in knots over. In addition, now I need to ask my mom for more help with Jagger when she already does a ton.

He's my child. He's my responsibility. I'm the one who should be and wants to be watching him, not my mom.

"Give her a sec," Vince says. "She's a planner so this is going to throw her for a loop."

Everyone at the table chuckles while Vince winces when my shoe connects with his shin.

"Next week. Noted," I say and offer a sugary-sweet smile his way. No doubt that's going to leave a mark. "And no worries. I'll have plenty of anecdotes I can throw your way to enhance Vince's documentary."

"You wouldn't dare," he says, mischief in his eyes.

"Try me."

The whole table erupts in more laughter, but Vince's gaze remains on mine as his lopsided grin grows.

My threat rings hollow to my own ears though, because I know that revealing too much about Vince's past will only put me in the spotlight. And the last thing I want anyone to do is to look closer at me.

"So we'll get started then," Will says. "The point of this pre-interview is so we can weed out the normal, everyday things and maybe find a nugget or two to focus on. Something that will hook the public into wanting to know more about."

"There's not much out there that people don't already know," Vince says.

"There always is." Will's smile says he's determined to find something. "Whatever we decide to talk about during the actual filming will be given to you ahead of time so you're not taken by surprise."

Vince shifts uncomfortably, his eyes focused on the paper in his hands for a beat before he slips the public mask on and grins. "Hit me."

But it was there. That small slip. Just like he had last night when talking about Bent. Clearly whatever is going on, he's determined to keep it close to the vest.

"Perfect," Jasmine says. "Let's cover some basics. Mom. Dad. Brothers. Sisters. Normal childhood. Troubled childhood. That kind of thing."

"Normal childhood." Vince's tone is flat and the glance my way, the one with piercing eyes, reaffirms his lie.

"Okay." She makes a note. "What about your mom and dad?"

"Dad." It's all he says, and it causes the room to pause briefly.

"Okay." She gives a slow nod before painting an encouraging smile on her lips. "Tell me about what happened to your mom. Give me more info on what it was like growing up in the two-man Jennings household."

I squeeze my clasped hands harder knowing what seemed to be a simple conversation just became quite prickly.

"My mom left before I turned two. That's all I know and there are not many details a person can remember from that age."

Another slow nod from Jasmine. "I'm sorry."

"Don't be." Vince's voice is gruff despite the nonchalant shrug.

"And your dad?"

Vince's lips pull tight. "He was a dad and not a great one at that. Next?"

"There's nothing else you'd like to say on that? This could be your time to talk, to control the narrative and explain your childhood. Why you are who you are," Jasmine says.

"I am who I am because of me. My drive. My desire. My need to be anything other than him. The sacrifices I made to be the man I wanted to be. That's the only explanation you're going to get from me on this."

"Vince. I understand your position, but showing the public what and where you came from will make you more sympathetic to—"

"I don't want anyone's sympathy. Understood? This isn't let's talk about how bad poor little Vinnie had it. It's not a way to excuse away some of the shit I've done. My dad was and still is a prick. There's not much more to say."

Jasmine glances at Will and then back to Vince. She's just about to open her mouth when Vince shoves out of his chair. "What else do you want to know? Do I have a girlfriend? No. Have I ever been in love? Just once." He stops at the windows. His thumbs hooked in his pockets, his back to us as he watches the cars march like ants on the always jammed 110 freeway. "Do I want to get married someday? I don't fucking know. Do I want kids? That's a hard fucking no." He shrugs dismissively. "Does that give you the basics that you need? Is that juicy enough for you? Because there's a whole treasure trove more of where that came from after I made it big that you can dig through. I guarantee that shit's a lot more fucking interesting."

Will swivels in his chair so that he's staring at Vince's back. "Look. It's not fun for us to ask you about things that you clearly don't want to talk about. We get it. We've done these documentaries enough times to know that everyone has a hot spot. But we need to brush over these things quickly for those who may be familiar with Bent on the whole, but not you in particular."

Vince rolls his shoulders before turning around and facing us. "Got it."

"Before we move on, I'd be remiss if I didn't mention that while poking around in your hometown, your father did reach out to us. Said he'd love to be interviewed."

"He will not be a part of this."

"Okay, but he—"

"If you want me to be a part of my own documentary, then you'll make sure he isn't. Clear? Are we done here?"

And before they can answer, Vince storms out of the office without another word. I fight the urge to go after him. To comfort him. To give him what I would need if I were in his shoes, but I know better.

It seems the man now isn't much different than the teenager I once knew. Keeping everything in. Bearing the brunt of a shit hand dealt to him all on his own. A burden only he's ever really known.

He never talked about his mom.

His dad and whatever happened in his house has always been off limits. In high school, from the outside looking in, it appeared he lived alone. Like he made his own rules and had the life every other teenager envied.

But I was close enough to Vince to see the fading bruises. I knew they appeared after he was conveniently sick from school or ditched for a few days. I was well aware of his moods and his determination.

Of course, I know because I was a casualty in it all.

"I'm sorry," I murmur, attempting to ease the tension he mostly took with him when he left. "I knew Vince back then, and he never talked about family stuff. He kept it close to the vest."

"No need to be sorry. We're used to this. Not everyone wants their life peeled open like an onion," Will says.

"Speaking of that," Jasmine says, her expression softening. "After cross-checking names with our research, is it true that you and Vince dated in high school?"

I attempt to keep my face impassive. If Vince wanted them to know this, then he would have mentioned it already. Besides, the less said about me the better. The last thing I need is a spotlight on me so that people look closer.

My chuckle is dismissive. "You know how it goes, giving someone a ride home after class can be considered dating in high school."

"So you didn't date, then?"

I blink rapidly as I try to figure out the answer Vince would want me to give. There are pictures of the two of us in a yearbook somewhere. Classmates could talk. But at the same time, no one cared much or probably took much notice about the nerdy wallflower and the loner, wannabe musician at Fairfield High. I give the biggest non-answer-answer I can think of. "We went on a few dates. But Vince dated a lot of people back then. He wasn't big on commitment."

"Seems like he isn't now either." Jasmine chuckles as she finishes making a few notes on her pad of paper.

I glance toward the door that Vince just stormed out of and wonder why he demanded that I be here. There were no opinions needed. No advice to be had. He's never been one who needed his hand held, so why ask me to be here?

But my mind keeps going back to the one off-the-cuff line of his. The one that stuck out to me above all the others.

The one that makes me feel like a selfish asshole since there were so many other important ones.

Have I ever been in love? Just once.

You're stupid to think he was talking about you, Bristol. He lived a lot of life after you.

Just like you have.

But why do I hope it was me?

CHAPTER
ten

Vince

"**T**HIS IS BULLSHIT." I SET MY GUITAR DOWN AND PACE THE CONFINES of the small room.

"Is it the guitar? Are you comfortable with it? I can play it if you want to pick up the bass," my producer/songwriting partner, Noah, says and sits back, crossing his arms over his chest.

"I've been playing both my whole life. It's not the fucking guitar."

He chews the inside of his cheek and just nods, more than used to the tantrums of frustrated rock stars. "You said your muse was talking to you."

"It was. Now it's not."

Fuck.

I run a hand through my hair, the restless energy I've felt since the elevator and then the conference room has thoroughly screwed with my concentration.

One was welcome.

The other not so much.

"What gives?" he asks as he pours himself a double and takes a long pull.

"Nothing. Everything. Fuck if I know."

But I do know. It's the documentary bullshit and the questions about my dad. It's the stuff about to be dredged up from the past to make people overlook the crap I've done recently.

It's the damn elevator ride with Bristol. The feel of her body against mine. The hitch of her breath. The want to start something with her, to use her body, to simply get lost in the past for a bit. Solely to drown out the bull-shit that won't seem to quiet anymore.

A temporary fix to a permanently fucked-up situation.

The issues with my dad will remain. Being alienated from Hawke and Gizmo and Rocket won't change. And I'll have to walk away no matter how good it feels to be with Bristol again.

There was a reason you walked away from her before. That same reason still holds true now.

You did this to yourself, Jennings. No use bringing her down with you.

"We can take a break," Noah suggests.

"I don't want to take a fucking break. I want to figure this out so we can lay it down and move on."

"So just the music? Have you given up on the lyrics?"

"Just . . . just record and we'll see what happens."

"Whatever you say, boss, but give me a few." He shrugs and stands to stretch his legs. We've been going at this for so fucking long that it's begin-ning to feel forced.

And "forced" turns out shit music.

My sigh is heavy as I play back the last take. It's shit. Great. All of this . . . pent-up everything, and I have nothing to show for it.

Emotion used to help me write better. The demons I wrestle with added that edge. But this . . . this is utter garbage.

"The guys were in here the other day," Noah says casually while the words hit like a rusted dagger to my chest.

I grunt in response. To the world, we're on a break for individual proj-ects. Not an ill word has been said publicly. It was in private where our words were used like weapons. Where what came out of my mouth fucked up so many things.

"They sounded good. Not the same without you, mind you, but still good. They had some new stuff that's going to kill it."

"Good for them."

Jealousy is a bitter bitch, especially when it's felt about your best friends.

Then again, what right do I have to even call them that? To assume they still think of me as the same?

"Are you joining them again when you're done with this album? Or is it too hard going from background to front man then back to the background again?"

I open my mouth to speak and then close it. Hasn't all of this taught me some things are better left unsaid? Because if they are, then there's no need to take them back.

A tight smile is all I offer in response and a lift of my chin toward the table and the bottle of Jack. The only vice left that I'll allow myself. "Pour me one, will you?"

Noah does as I ask without a word and holds the glass out to me. I down it in one long gulp.

I welcome the burn and hope for some clarity as a result before grabbing the neck of my guitar and positioning it on my lap as I take a seat. My fingers begin strumming automatically. A habit ingrained in my every fiber. A way to calm the riot inside. A mechanism to soothe the chaos I've lived my whole life with.

My fingers change to plucking the strings and create a melody that I can't shake from my head. There's a hard edge to it underlined by a haunting melody. The combination of the two sends chills over my skin, a sure sign that I'm on the right track.

I close my eyes and keep playing, keep experimenting, knowing we're recording this on our phones so I don't have to stop to write it all down.

Words come to me. Some I sing aloud, others I hum to be filled in later. I repeat the process.

Over and over.

Again and again.

The problem? When I drown out all the outside noise, when I really try and step into the song, it's Hawkin's voice that I hear singing it. It's his unique grate I expect to hear jump in and take over just like we've done countless times before.

We always were a damn good team.

But there is no Hawkin to do that. No Rocket to tell a joke and ease the tension when we get frustrated and start taking swipes at each other. No

Gizmo to experiment with some riff totally out of the blue that we'd never think of but that is absolutely fucking perfect for the song we're building. No Bent to make this experience what I know it can be. What I've come to expect it to be.

It's just me.

It's just Noah.

Just a lot of loneliness and acceptance that it feels hollow without them.

And a whole shitload of unresolved bullshit that's unfixable in between.

I mix the chords up. "Fuck." And then pat the strings to make the sound stop. When I hold my glass out, Noah refills it without saying a word.

I've cut back.

I drink less now. For a musician anyway. But it's going to take a hell of a lot more than a glass of Jack to find out what I feel is missing. The liquid courage might solve a lot, but it's not going to fix the damage I've caused.

CHAPTER
eleven

Vince

One Year Ago

"I F YOU DON'T LIKE IT ANYMORE, THERE'S THE FUCKING DOOR."

I stare at my best friend, the room spinning as I tilt the bottle to my lips, drinking until the last of the Jack is gone. The burn is better than the response I'm afraid I'll give.

"Don't tell me what to fucking do, Hawke," I say through gritted teeth. His chuckle is condescending as fuck. On the other side of the studio, his ass is resting against the front of the soundboard, his arms are crossed, and the shake of his head only serves to piss me off further.

Hawkin Play. Lead singer for our band, Bent. My brother from another mother. The person who knows all my secrets. All-around good guy. And apparently, by the threat he just gave, a newly minted ball-buster.

Fuck that.

I toss the empty bottle into the trash across from me, and the sound of glass hitting the metal ricochets around the room.

"Don't tell you what to do?" He emits that patronizing, bullshit chuckle of his again that grates on my every nerve. "I don't have to tell you shit, brother, because it seems you're content on doing the damage all your fucking self."

Here we go again.

"Let me guess. Rocket and Gizmo set you up to do this," I say of our other bandmates. Of our friends. The family I made for myself. The men who hightailed it out of here after our session most likely so Hawkin could read me the damn riot act. "What? Did you have a fucking kumbaya session over how to wrangle Vince and protect Bent's precious goddamn image?"

"Image?" Hawke shouts, throwing his arms out to the sides. "We're rock stars. The drinking and drugs are expected. Par for the fucking course. What's not the norm is being so goddamn high you all but fuck Rocket's girl." He looks at me with wide eyes that sure as hell probably match mine. "Jesus Christ. You don't even remember that, do you?"

"Didn't we fight about this last week?" I say drolly, trying to rack my brain if what he's saying is true.

But he's right. I can't remember.

I didn't do that, did I?

"Yep, and we're going to talk about it again. Shit, Vin, you almost missed our performance on *Saturday Night Live* because you were off doing who the fuck knows what."

"I know what I was doing and damn, she was incredible." It's a lie. I was high as fuck and lost track of time. But at this point it seems like the lie will fare better for me than the truth.

"Class act. Way to go."

"Fuck off."

"You probably wish I would, huh? Then you could circle the drain all by yourself and prove your dad right."

"Do *not* mention him again," I warn.

He sees me. He hears me. But he clearly doesn't fucking care about the warning because that chuckle is back and so is the disappointed shake of his head.

What he doesn't know is that I've disappointed everyone my whole life, so why start changing that shit now?

"You made us a promise, Vin. You made me one. From the get-go, we agreed that *we* come first—the band and its best interest does."

"Your point?"

"That sure as shit doesn't seem to be the case anymore."

"Well maybe it's time for a fucking change, then, huh?"

"Not on my watch."

"Oh, Jesus. Are you listening to the egotistical bullshit you're spewing? *Not on my watch*," I mimic.

Fuck. I need another drink but turn around to find my second fifth that I put on the table is empty already. Did I do that? Did Hawke pour it out?

"You're still nothing, Vinnie. Always have been. Always will be. You couldn't hack it on your own even if you tried, because you sure as hell aren't good enough with your mediocre talent and lack of drive."

"Management isn't happy," he says softly.

"Screw them. They're never fucking happy with us, and yet it's us who're lining their pockets, so I don't give a rat's ass what they think."

"You're fucking up, man."

"So you've said."

"Onstage. In the studio. In public. In private. Not many more places you can."

"I'm sure I'll figure out how to." Sarcasm drips from my words as my best friend stares at me with a disdain I don't understand.

"I'm worried about you."

My throat feels like it's closing up. I shake my head, rejecting Hawke's words. Not being worth enough to be cared about. "Like you give a flying fuck about me." Drown him out. Shut him up. "All you care about is your own pristine image. But I know, Hawke. I know about your fucked-up brother and the shit he did. The shit you hid and protected him from. I know you're nowhere near as perfect as the public thinks you are," I say, trying to throw the whole kitchen sink in.

Wanting the argument.

Needing the argument.

"You're right. I'm far from perfect. But just like you helped me then and every other time, I want to help you now."

"Fuck you and your placating tone. I don't need shit from you." I shove a hand through my hair and pace the small space. Back and forth, hands fisting as the anger burns a pit in my stomach. "God, I need a fucking drink."

"Cuz that's *just* what you need."

"You're right. A bottle would be better than one drink if I have to listen to more of this." I turn and look at him. "Since when did you put that stick up your ass? Huh? What are you? The fun police now?"

"Yep. Sure am. And I started being it when you decided to slowly start killing yourself."

"Whatever."

"Cut the crap, Vin. It's me here. I just want to help. What's going on that you're not telling me about? What are you trying to dull? I've known you for too damn long to know that something's wrong."

"How did I raise such a pussy, huh? A real man wouldn't need to hide behind his best friend to make it. A real man would be able to do it himself."

"Fuck you, Dad. You don't know—"

"Ah, but I do know." His laugh is grating. His words a reincarnated repetition of the same shit I've been hearing for over a decade. "I know your mom left because she didn't want you. I know I've fought for years to give you everything so you can what? Be in the background because you're too much of a pussy to take center stage yourself? I would have killed for that chance, and clearly you just don't have it in you. A real man would, but then again, it's you, right? Can't expect too much from you when you never were much to begin with anyway."

"Nothing's wrong," I mutter.

"I call bullshit."

"Fine. Call it." I shrug. "Does it make you feel better?"

"This isn't a joke."

"Who's laughing?" I ask.

"You're not taking me seriously."

"I pride myself on it."

Hawke pinches the bridge of his nose and sighs. "Look. You fucked up big time last night."

"Nice change of tactic. You've always been the one who tried to keep the peace."

"Last night?" He raises his eyebrows and demands an answer that I don't have a good enough answer for.

"The fucker had it coming to him," I say of the reporter I chewed out on the red carpet. On live TV. "Ask stupid fucking questions like that and—"

"They're only stupid if they're not true."

"I didn't touch the woman. The kid she's claiming is mine, isn't. I'll never chance my fucked-up genes in a next generation."

"C'mon. Talk to me. Maybe I can help."

"I don't need your fucking help, *Doctor Play*. I just need . . ." I don't know what the fuck I need, but I'm sure it can be found on the other end of a vice.

I brace my hands on the soundboard and look at the empty studio beyond. The one we were in thirty minutes ago. The one that gave me the only reprieve I seem to have these days—music.

My friend's sigh is as heavy as the weight on my chest. "So this is how it's going to be?"

"How what's going to be? You trying to control me? I like handcuffs, brother, but only when they're used during sex."

If I keep pushing, maybe he'll just walk away. Maybe he'll just leave me the fuck alone.

"I'm just trying to help, Vince."

The minute his hand touches my shoulder, my temper snaps and arm is cocked back, ready to fly.

He stares at me, eyes daring me to land the punch and begging me not to at the same time.

He doesn't understand.

No one does.

How do you hate someone and love them simultaneously? Even when they do nothing but tear you down? Especially because they're the only person who didn't leave you?

"I'm dying, Vinnie. Liver cancer. Stage four."

My dad's words come out of nowhere. The fuck?

"A year, maybe."

I keep my head down and just nod. What the fuck am I supposed to say?

"Just thought you'd want to know."

I grunt. Is it normal not to feel a goddamn thing hearing that?

"What? No comeback? No sweet words from a son to his father?" His chuckle is cruel. "Don't worry. I didn't expect much from my total loser of a son. Perhaps the shame I feel about you will kill me before the fucking cancer does."

I lower my fist, the need to throw it still vibrating through me. Still owning me. Still begging for the release I can't seem to find. *Fucking great. Way to be just like your old man. Come out swinging when you feel backed into a corner. You're an asshole, Jennings. A total fucking asshole.*

"That's how it's going to be? You don't want to hear the truth so you're going to fight your way out of it?" Hawke asks.

Instead of answering, I move around the room again, looking for a bottle of something, anything, to numb the pain. "You forget, brother. I never had a mom, and I sure as hell don't need one now."

The vial. I forgot I had some feel-good powder with me. With my back to Hawke, I pull it out of my pocket, pour a little powder on the tip of my finger, and wipe some on my gums. The kick is almost instant. The feeling that all is right with the world. The euphoria that lets me breathe again. The ability to forget for just a moment.

"Want some?"

"Fuck no," Hawke shouts, knocking the open vial out of my hand before I can barely finish my question. It falls to the floor and spills out. "What in the hell are you doing?"

My laugh is loud. My head like a balloon floating and attached to my body by a string. "Like I said, Pretty Boy Play is too good for me now."

"Dammit, Vince. This isn't you. This isn't—"

"Like you've fucking looked close enough in the past few months to have a right to say you know me."

"What the hell, man. How dare you say—"

"Whatever." I wave a hand his way. "I don't need you. I never have. I never will again. Go back to your shitty singing, your precious band, and your pretentious, fucking wife. I'm sure you'll be better off without me."

Hawkin stands there dumbfounded, head shaking and teeth gritted. The fist I expect to fly over my insult of his wife, the blatant lie, doesn't come. Hell, it never even clenches. "That's how you want this to go, huh?" His words are measured.

"Pretty sure it doesn't need to go anywhere when it's already been done and gone for some time."

"What are you saying?"

"Doesn't need to be said, does it?" I look around the studio, shake my head, and say, "Fuck this," before heading toward the door.

"You're quitting? Just like that, after everything?"

"Just like that. I'm better off without you. Without this. Just you wait and see."

"You're going to regret those words." His statement stops me in my tracks, hand pressed against the open door.

I hang my head for a beat and chuckle softly despite the pang his words create. "No, what I regret is letting you tear me down for so long that I actually believed I was less than you."

I'm drowning in alcohol, in regret, in words I know we've spoken that I can't take back. That I'm not sure I want to take back because fuck, does it feel good to say them. To tell my best friend how much I fucking resent him for being him when I have to be me.

There's the fucking proof. Money doesn't fix the fucked-up shit in your past. Fame doesn't fill the voids others left behind. "Friendship" doesn't overshadow abandonment.

But alcohol helps dull it all.

Coke helps to forget even more.

Do I still love him and Rocket and Gizmo?

Fuck yes, I do. More than anyone I've ever known save for one person. But I also hate them.

And when I walk out the door, shoving it so hard it slams against the wall behind it, a bitter taste is in my mouth over words I'll never be able to take back.

I glance back and see Hawkin standing in the darkened studio, his shoulder resting against the wall, and his face an expression I hope I never see again.

Disappointment.

Worry.

Pain.

Pity.

Fuck you, Hawke.

Just fuck you.

CHAPTER
twelve

Bristol

"**H**E'S GETTING SO BIG," I murmur to no one as my mom collects her things behind me and gets ready to head back to her place. Jagger is on my apartment's small back patio. He's set up a makeshift track and is "driving" his trucks around on it and occasionally smashing them into each other with the sound effects to go along.

"It goes by in the blink of an eye, doesn't it?"

"It feels like it."

"Just yesterday you were that age and now look at you." Her chuckle is bittersweet, much like how I've felt over the past few days. "He brought up wanting to learn how to play the guitar again today."

She says the words as if she already knows what I need to tell her. As if she already knows Vince is in town.

"I'll have to get him lessons." I sigh. "Just another thing to try and manage, another expense to figure out . . . and another thing I don't want to deprive him of."

She slides her arm around my shoulder and pulls me against her. "If you weren't so damn stubborn and independent, things could be easier for you, you know. Less stressful. Living with me would mean a bigger yard for Jagg. Less work for you because we'd halve our expenses. A built-in babysitter that you don't have to stress about asking to stay over because this or that got crazy at work—or God forbid, you had a hot date and wanted to get a little action. I've heard that relieves stress now and then too."

I laugh as she bumps her hip against mine, but it sounds as distracted as my thoughts.

She deserves to know, doesn't she? After all, she has been through all of this with me. Finding out. The aftermath. The heartbreak. The decision.

And yet, I'm hesitating.

Shit. Here goes nothing . . .

"Talking about stress, I need to talk to you about a few things, Mom."

"Are these good things or bad things? They better not be you're moving out of state and away from me type of things."

"No. It's nothing like that. It's more like, I've gotten a temporary promotion at work."

"You did?" She screeches loud enough that Jagger looks up from his demolition derby, offers an *I'm glad you're laughing but my cars are more interesting than your conversation* smile, and then goes back to making a crashing sound. "That's awesome, Bri. Tell me all about it. What are you doing? Why is it temporary? Does this mean that that McMann guy finally figured out what I already know? That my daughter is an absolute force to be reckoned with, and he's missing the boat if he doesn't utilize her full potential?"

I take a step away from her and motion in the calm down gesture. It doesn't mean that the praise doesn't feel good even if it's your mom saying it. "It's mostly because of a client. The one I had to stay late for the other night. McMann wants me to hold the guy's hand while we're working on repackaging him to the public, so to speak."

"Please tell me that doesn't mean the client gets to treat you like shit. McMann does enough of that already." To say my mom hates my boss is an understatement. But then again, I don't exactly like him either. To me, he's a stepping-stone to get where I want to go.

"Actually, the client has stuck up for me numerous times thus far."

"I like him already. Are you allowed to tell me who it is?" she asks. I always tell her though, even when our client's identity is supposed to be kept confidential.

"Well, that's the second part of what I wanted to tell you."

"Oh?" She takes a seat on the couch, distracted by straightening the pillows on either side of her. But when she glances up and notices my expression, she pauses. "What are you not telling me?"

Rip off the Band-Aid, Bristol.

After a quick glance to Jagger, I confess. "It's Vince."

Her mouth falls into a shocked O. "Bristol." My name is a warning, a question, *and* an exclamation.

"I know."

"You knew this day might come someday."

"I'm well aware of that fact." I don't know why I suddenly feel on the defensive, but I am.

"I don't even know what to say or ask."

"Neither do I, if I'm honest." And I'm not sure why it suddenly feels like a weight has been lifted off my chest, but it does. I've been stewing on this for the past couple of days, worrying about this, and now I feel like I finally have a sounding board.

Albeit a very opinionated sounding board, but one nonetheless.

She glances toward Jagger and smiles softly. "Are you going to tell him?"

That's the question, isn't it?

"I didn't intend to." *Do I want kids? That's a hard fucking no.* His words the other day struck me hard and reaffirmed my decisions. Then and now. "He didn't want kids back then, and he still feels the same. Who am I to upend his life for a decision I made and would make again if I had to?"

"That's one school of thought. The other is that he has every right to know. That maybe he'd feel differently once he met his incredible son." She purses her lips. "You could get some financial support then, and you wouldn't have to work your fingers to the bone—"

"I don't want money from him."

"You have a right to it."

"I have a right to a lot of things, but that doesn't mean I take advantage of them."

She nods but her stare is weighted. "Why did you tell me if you don't want any of my advice?"

"I do, I just . . ." I blow out a heavy sigh and move around my place. It may be small, but it's mine and filled with so much love for Jagger that it makes me happy. "It's complicated. My feelings. My thoughts. Just everything is complicated."

"Anything to do with a child is complicated. I mean, look at Dad and me. We waited to divorce until you were nineteen because we feared how it would affect you. And even then, it devastated you."

"We're talking about apples and oranges," I say but understand her point.

"We're talking about your son and what you're going to do or not do when it comes to his father."

"I worry that I'm hurting him every day because he doesn't have a father who's present. You know that. I know that. But wouldn't it hurt him more to have a dad who knows about him and rejects him than to not know him at all?"

"Telling Vince isn't the same as Jagger knowing."

I force myself to stop moving and sit down. She's right. Maybe it's my own heart I'm protecting. Maybe I'd be devastated if I did tell Vince and he rejected Jagger on the spot. That would be worse than ripping my heart out and stomping on it.

"I did tell him I was pregnant. Or tried to anyway but was railroaded by the manager. And then he wouldn't answer my calls. Then he blocked them. I mean . . . that told me enough in and of itself." I pinch the bridge of my nose. She knows all of this, but it's almost like repeating it makes me feel better about my decision. "Maybe I didn't try hard enough. Maybe, even though I was scared and heartbroken, I was worried Vince would try to talk me out of having Jagger when I knew I wanted him more than anything in the world."

"Maybes aren't going to give you your answers, sweetie."

"I know. Believe me I know." I rest my head on the back of the couch and look at the ceiling. Those fairy-tale visions I'd had in the past come back. The ones where Vince and Jagger are sitting on the floor playing. Where Vince was shirtless and holding our newborn son. Where Father's Day is celebrated instead of being a day where I try to fill in for the things Jagger is missing out on.

"Have you had a chance to talk to him? Really talk to him? Or is that connection not there anymore?"

"It's there." I shake my head as if I don't want it to be there. "But that doesn't mean anything."

She twists her lips in the way that has me wanting to know what she's thinking. "Then I guess that means there hasn't been any time for you two to talk about . . . things."

"Like how we left it that last time we saw each other? Me waking up and him being nowhere to be found? Me calling him over and over without a single response? Being railroaded by his manager and being put in my place so I knew I was just one in Vince's long list of many? You mean that talk?" I snort. "I'm pretty sure we're either both avoiding it, or it only really mattered on my end because of what resulted from it."

"You slept together. I'd think that would matter to both of you."

"Mom, he's a rock star. I'm not naïve enough to think that he doesn't have women lined up outside his dressing room before and after every show."

"And that doesn't bug you?"

"I'm not with him, am I? It's his business what he does. He's a big boy."

Her eyes hold mine, and her smile softens some as she sees what I've been trying to hide all along. Maybe even to myself.

"You never stopped loving him, did you?" she murmurs.

My throat burns with emotion. "Don't be ridiculous."

"You didn't answer my question."

"Maybe I don't have an answer to the question."

"And maybe you're being evasive like you are when you know the answer but fear it's going to upset me." She glances back to Jagger, her eyes steadfast on him when she speaks.

"Upset you? No. But, I mean . . . look at him and look at me."

"Meaning?"

I tilt my head to the side and simply stare at her as I hold my hands out. "He's ridiculously successful while I'm still in school and working toward getting accepted to law school and eventually passing the bar exam. He's lusted after by millions, and this body of mine isn't exactly in prime shape."

"First, yes, you're working toward the bar. Do you know how many people would have given up their dream? You haven't, so I don't want to hear a word about that. And second, do you really want to get me started on how you see yourself?"

"Noted. Never mind." I laugh it off, but it doesn't take away my insecurities.

"No. Not never mind. You asked it, so I'm going to say it. What's wrong with your body? So your curves are more pronounced than they were in high school. That's called being normal. That's called maturing. That's called having a baby. That's called being a voluptuous woman."

"It's called having stretch marks."

"And every damn one of them gave you that beautiful boy outside so I'm not going to hear it. Besides, I never remembered Vince being a shallow man. He did love you even when you had braces. Then that permed hair phase where you looked like a poodle." She shivers. "Oh, and even the white, sparkly eyeshadow phase. I mean—"

"Yes. Okay. I get it." I chuckle. "But that didn't mean that seeing him again made me feel less than when he's become so much more."

"And he made you feel this way? He said oh, wow, you have Marilyn Monroe curves and a nice ass, and I don't like that?"

"Seriously, Mom?"

"Did he?"

"No. Of course not."

"Point made." She gives me a resolute nod and then a smug smile. "Now that we've debunked that myth, I'm going to say this. Vince is the only man I've ever seen you upset over. Twice. That says a lot, which is why I asked if you ever stopped loving him."

Her comment opens a door I'm afraid to step through. If I don't give her an outright answer, then I don't have to acknowledge it myself.

Who am I kidding, though?

I knew it from the moment I heard his voice that first night at the sound stage.

"I think a part of me will always love him," I finally admit.

"Mmm," she says in that way that makes me feel judged. No one ever wants to feel judged by their parents.

"I'm older now. I'm wiser," I say, feeling the need to justify my comment. "I could love him all I want, but that isn't going to make him stay. And I deserve that. Someone who will stay and make a life with me. Not someone who refuses to put down roots. He can say all he wants that it's because of his lifestyle—touring and whatever—but I know it's because of his parents. If you don't put your feet down, you can't get attached, and therefore you can't get hurt. You can't get left behind."

"You've thought about this a lot."

"It's all I've been thinking about. Then and now. Besides, I've internally justified my decisions a lot over the years."

"Unnecessarily, but I understand." She takes a sip of her water. "So what now? If that connection is there, who says he isn't going to ask you out while he's here?"

"I know deep down that anything with Vince would be fleeting." The almost kiss in the elevator fills my head. I haven't stopped thinking about it or him, to be fair. "The problem is I'd get attached. He'll move on to the next city, the next woman, the next whatever, and I'd be here hurting. I've already let the man hurt me more than enough."

"No one ever said love always felt good."

"Then why feel it at all?"

"Because it's not a choice. It's just something that happens even when you don't want it to."

"Why do you sound like you're encouraging this?"

"The only thing I'm encouraging you in is whatever decisions you make."

CHAPTER
thirteen

Bristol

"WHAT DO YOU MEAN YOU DON'T KNOW HOW THE RECORDING sessions are going? Aren't you supposed to be keeping tabs on him? Making sure he has everything he needs? Is this job too much for you, Matthews? Do I need to put someone else on Jennings?"

Xavier's words run on repeat through my mind. His barked words through the telephone that I luckily answered, even though I was in the middle of a spin class.

The one and only spin class I've been able to make in the last month and of course, my boss interrupts it, once again reinforcing how much of a life I don't have. He thinks mine should be lived solely for him.

But I asked "how high" to his proverbial command to *jump*. Of course, I did because I'm standing at the door to Bellinger Studios where Vince is supposedly inside. I didn't know the answers to Xavier's questions because I've been avoiding Vince.

Not exactly an easy feat when I'm supposed to be tending to him, but a few doses of my own reality—Jagger falling off his bike and skinning his knees, a professor telling me that he expected more from me on the paper I turned in, my car acting up so much that I'm afraid of what the mechanic will say when I take it in—were all the reminder I needed. This is my life, and Vince's is the polar opposite.

The question is, what do I intend to do before that day happens?

"Here goes nothing," I mutter to myself and pull open the nondescript door to the building in front of me, hoping like hell I'm in the right place.

The walls are dark and the lighting dim, and there is no one manning the front desk. Nor does it look like anyone has manned it in some time by the large stacks of various things covering its surface.

Fearful of calling out and messing someone's recording session up, I stand there for a few minutes debating what to do. I could always text Vince and let him know I'm here, but then that would give him my cell phone number and I'm not certain I want him to have that yet.

Ridiculous, *I know.*

Standing in indecision, I startle at the sound of a door opening, closing, followed by footsteps down the hall.

"Hey. Hi. Who are you here for and do they know you're coming?"

I flash a smile despite feeling way out of my element. "I'm Bristol Matthews with McMann Media. Here to see Vincent Jennings and no, he doesn't know I'm coming."

He angles his head to the side and narrows his eyes as he studies me for a beat before breaking out in a slow crawl of a smile. "Maybe you can put that surly fucker in a good mood for once. Fuck, man. All I've been getting is Asshole Vince. And I can deal with Asshole Vince, but it sure would be nice to have Normal Vince back for a while."

"That bad, huh?" I ask.

"Down the hall. Last door on the right." His pat on my back and chuckle are the only answer he gives me. "Good luck. I have to pick up my daughter from school. I'll be back."

"Wait, you're leaving me alone with him?"

His laugh is even louder as he pushes the door open and steps outside.

Surly.

Asshole.

Great. At least I know what I'm walking into.

When I open the door to the darkened room, there's a glass window in front of me, soundboards at the bottom with all kinds of buttons and toggles lit up. I hear someone fiddling with a guitar, the same string over and over, followed by a barked out and very frustrated curse.

And there he is.

I involuntarily suck in a breath when I see Vince. He's in a room—white walls lined with industry recognition—sitting on a stool. His guitar is resting across his lap, his back hunched over, and his fingers are on the frets. His eyes are closed, and some of his hair is falling over his forehead that's scrunched in concentration.

Sure he's a devastating package to look at, the kind of man who makes you stop to look twice and try to figure out if he lives up to the bad-boy vibe he exudes, but when he opens his mouth to sing, he's heart-stoppingly beautiful.

At least he always has been to me.

I stand there mesmerized as he works through guitar chords and mumbled lyrics. They don't make any sense but somehow still have a rhythm to them that causes chills to chase over my skin and my body to sway back and forth.

During my brief time in spin class, I had made the determination that I was not going to let Vincent Jennings wear me down in any way, shape, or form. No catching up over coffee. No reminiscing about how good we used to be together. No kissing just once for old times' sake.

Complete and utter self-preservation.

And yet standing here, watching and listening to him, I hate the old feelings that are being stirred up like dust particles. The kind that dance in the stream of sunlight so you can see them, so you can study them, so you can wonder where they came from when you never realized they were there in the first place.

The same dust particles you never notice when you're in the dark because they no longer seem to matter.

The question is, do I leave them settled in the dark or stir them around and bring them to light for a bit?

And right now, they're in the dark. Do I stay here and phone it in to Xavier that Vince is doing what he should be doing—working on his new album—or do I step into the light and let Vince know I'm here?

Still undecided, I stand and watch Vince without him knowing. He's where he belongs—in a studio with a guitar on his lap and a beat as much a part of him as the blood flowing through his veins.

"Noah? You still there?" Vince calls out seconds after the music stops, and his hand taps over the strings to stop them.

Keep them in the dark or bring them to light, Bristol? What will it be?

I open the door into the studio, my mind suddenly justifying my actions by acknowledging the recording studio is dim, and therefore, I'm not exactly making a concrete decision yet.

"Noah's gone. Went to do the school pickup thing even though he doesn't look much older than twenty."

Vince lifts his head slowly, that lopsided grin doing nothing to abate the intensity in the depths of his eyes, but it definitely brightens up the room.

"Forty, but yeah, you'd never know," he says as he sets his guitar down, folds his arms, and leans back in his chair. He studies me in that disarming way he has. The way he did when I met him during my freshman year that feels like his gaze is scraping over every single inch of you. It makes you stand a little taller and hope he likes what he sees. "This is a nice surprise. I thought you were ignoring me at all costs."

"I never said that."

"You didn't have to. You forget, I know you."

"You *knew* me. Past tense."

I have just enough time to catch his nod before I turn to take in the room. His chuckle follows me as I do. It's a gentle rumble that I swear I can feel in my chest even though that should be impossible.

"You can say it all you want, Shug, but that doesn't mean either of us is going to believe it."

I tickle my fingers over the keys of the piano then move to the drum set on the far side of the room and tap my fingernail against it.

Vince has moved from his seat because I can feel him behind me—watching, following, waiting.

"I've been summoned to provide an update on what you've been doing and how the songwriting is going. McMann needs to be kept in the know."

When Vince doesn't respond, I turn to find him a few feet from me, hands shoved in the pockets of his jeans, shoulders resting against the wall at his back.

"What?" I ask.

"You don't have to lie to get in here. It's okay to admit that you miss the shit out of me and needed to see me again." There's that grin as his eyes draw down the length of me again.

"Yes, that's exactly it," I say wryly.

"Well, let's see. You could have picked up the phone and called or texted to get your answer, but you didn't. You came here instead." He shrugs. "That indicates a whole hell of a lot to me."

"Yes, because the last thing I wanted to do today when I finally had a few moments to myself was leave my spin class twenty minutes in and run over here to babysit you."

"We'll get back to that in a second."

"What does that mean?" I ask, already irritated by his nonchalance.

"You could have told good ol' McMann if he wanted to see how I was doing, he could have come here himself."

"Then there would be no need for me and my job, so not the best advice."

We stand a few feet apart and simply stare at each other, almost as if we're preparing ourselves for a war that is coming but that we're unaware of.

"True," he finally says. "But I have better things to talk about than Xavier McMann. Like that spin class of yours."

"What about it?" It's my turn to laugh now.

He pushes himself off the wall in his signature unhurried way. "That's a good look on you."

"What is?"

"The leggings. The tight top." He emits a feral groan deep in his throat that erases every ounce of my self-consciousness. "Jesus, are you trying to kill me?"

"Whatever," I say with a wave of a hand and a blush of my cheeks, more than thankful that today of all days, I decided to wear my super support leggings that hold everything where it should be.

But that doesn't make me feel any less self-conscious with his eyes assessing my every inch and what I feel are flaws.

"Not whatever," he murmurs. "You always could knock a man to his knees. Good to see some things haven't changed even though you keep saying they have."

"Flattery won't get you anywhere."

He chuckles again. "That remains to be seen."

I have a dozen quips on the tip of my tongue, and yet they all seem to have died just like the dust particles left smothered in the darkness.

The silence settles. Electricity snaps between us like it's a live wire. If I can feel it, then I sure as hell know Vince can. The look on his face—the muscle in his jaw ticking, eyes narrowed, lids heavy—tells me as much. Nerves dance with the goosebumps that seem ever present when he's near.

How silly was I to think the dim light would allow me to stay in limbo over what to do when it came to him?

I clear my throat. "Look, I've been thinking a lot about this."

"About what?"

"About how we can work together despite our history."

"I didn't know our history was a problem."

"It's not. It is." I hang my head and draw in a deep breath before meeting his eyes and holding my hands up. "I call a truce."

"A truce?" His eyebrows lift. "I wasn't aware that we were fighting."

"We're not . . . it's just . . ."

"It's just that you still want me, and this is your way to justify why you're angry at yourself for depriving yourself of me."

"It's not always about you," I bark, frustrated before I regroup. "We have a habit of falling right back into what we were—"

"Just the once."

"It's the only other time we've seen each other since high school," I say. *Just the once.* "This has to remain professional. I have a job to do."

He nods with humor alight in his eyes that only serves to frustrate me more. "So there will be no wearing you down? No pressing you against the wall and kissing you breathless? No seeing if you still like being kissed on that spot on the inside of your thigh? No getting to know the current Bristol Matthews? No nothing?" he asks while I shift my feet. "Just a simple truce."

"Yes. A working relationship where we mutually benefit each other."

He snickers.

"Professionally," I warn despite my mind flashing back to that night we were together. "I need to give my boss an update." He just continues to stare and smirk as if he knows where my thoughts are, so I turn and study the gold records lining the walls because they're easier to look at than him. "How the writing is going? If you're having any trouble or have any requests for Will and Jasmine? If you've seen the rough cuts of the *Heart of Mine* video and have any feedback?"

"I love it when you're all business."

"I'm all business because it's my job to be."

"Do you know what this reminds me of?"

"No clue." I read the names on the placards of each record. A pop princess. A Latin superstar. A boy band who's endured.

"Tutoring. Your freshman year. My sophomore. I could care less—"

"Couldn't care less." I chuckle. "Clearly I didn't do a good job tutoring you."

"No, you did, but like I told you, when was I ever going to know the periodic table or the correct use of past participle or whatever it's called? It's just that I was more distracted by my pretty, strait-laced tutor. She sat there every day trying to help a kid who couldn't focus because he was too busy trying to figure out how to get her to notice him."

His words cause a smile to spread on my lips he can't see.

"I never charged my computer so I was forced to sit next to you and use yours. I may have flunked a few tests on purpose so I had to keep seeing you. I might even have driven you crazy playing a beat on the table with my hands so you'd be forced to reach over and grab my wrists to stop me." He laughs. "And that touch might have made this sixteen-year-old hard as a rock under the table where we were sitting together."

The memories are bittersweet. The fact that he remembers them even more so. And despite all that has happened, they were such good ones.

"Then one day over *The Catcher in the Rye*—"

"*To Kill a Mockingbird*," I correct.

"I leaned over and kissed you." His last words are whispered in my ear from behind. The warmth of his breath tickles my cheek. I have to actively restrain myself from leaning back against him as the good memories assault me.

I stay focused on the gold records in front of me. A rock icon. A jazz singer.

"We were good together, Shug. What happened to us?"

"You left. Remember?" I try to keep my voice light, unaffected, but I'm anything but.

A hip-hop artist.

"No, not after high school. I mean the last time." He puts a hand on my hip. His guitar-roughened fingers tickle ever so gently as they rest on the strip of skin between my top and leggings. The heat of his body is at my back.

Focus, Bristol. Get the answers McMann wants. Leave promptly. Save yourself the heartache that is Vince.

"How'd we let that escape us? How'd we walk away from us?"

"I wasn't aware there ever was an us?"

A rock band named Bent. A picture of the four of them—Hawkin, Vince, Rocket, and Gizmo—beside the platinum record in the frame.

Remember how bad he hurts.

"Why'd you leave the band?" I ask, grasping at straws, at my sanity, from giving in to his seductive voice and the feelings I can't erase.

His hand tenses on my stomach. It's brief, but I feel it. "Why do I make you nervous?"

"You don't. And I asked you a question."

"I do, and I asked you first, but you're avoiding this discussion. It seems that's something you've mastered."

"Hey—" But when I spin around to face him, *to argue*, I flinch, because now we're face-to-face and well within each other's personal spaces.

Kiss me.

The minute the thought hits my mind, I take a huge step back as if to chastise myself. Vince reaches out to prevent me from falling against the wall. I immediately shrug out of his grasp.

"Don't touch me." It's my only line of defense—and it doesn't work because his hands are back on my biceps and his mouth is inches from my lips. "What are you doing?" I ask when he doesn't move.

"I'm letting you get used to the idea that I'm going to kiss you. It's inevitable, isn't it?" He leans forward and brushes his lips ever so slightly against mine. It's the faintest of touches, but there's beauty in its simplicity. Tenderness that is so unexpected from a man who is all or nothing. An undercurrent in both of our unsteady breaths that follows it. A burning through my body to want more, to take more, to have more.

"I can't—we can't do this," I manage to get out. My mind races a million miles an hour while my feet don't want to move. "We called a truce. We agreed—"

"You called it. I didn't agree to shit." He reaches out and tucks an errant piece of hair behind my ear. "You always were addictive, Bristol, and that's a bad thing for a man with an addictive personality like mine. One taste is never fucking enough."

Take a step back.

"It's going to have to be." My jaw is clenched. My resolve is front and center. *Truce. Truce. Truce. Dodge. Divert. Deflect.* "Why'd you leave Bent?"

CHAPTER
fourteen

Vince

"**F**INE." I LET A SLOW SMILE CRAWL ON MY LIPS. *TRUCE, MY ASS. SHE* wants me. It's plain as fucking day.

So much for my resolve to keep my hands to myself, but fuck if it isn't hard when she's dressed like that.

So I'll humor her for a bit. I'll play her game of not wanting me when every damn thing about her says she does. Then I'll take what I want. "We'll play your way. Then we'll play mine."

I want more of those lips. Of the taste of her. *Of just her.* Definitely even more than the sixteen-year-old did for that first kiss, years ago. And sure as hell more than the twenty-three-year-old me did the last time.

I forgot what it was like to have to work at getting a woman. The thrill of the chase. The desperation for the victory.

Ironically, it's only ever been Bristol I've had to chase.

The woman standing before me with cheeks flushed and eyes skittish as she tries to deny she wants me just as much as I want her.

"There is no playing anything other than the guitar," she says.

"The lady has jokes."

"The lady has a job to do."

"Ah, yes." I watch her ass as she walks across the room. It's hard not to, especially when she moves to avoid looking at me. "The never-ending questions. *Christ*. Tell McMann that the writing is what it is. My muse is silent— or maybe she died. Who the fuck knows. Art is tragic or some shit like that. No doubt, he'll hear that sound bite and have people rushing in to try and fix shit that can't be fixed."

"Sounds promising." She looks over her shoulder and lifts her eyebrows in challenge.

"A documentary isn't exactly my thing. You know that. I know that. They know that. But apparently, it's a necessity to polish my tarnished image. An image that I could give a flying fuck about."

"You care," she says and turns to face me, those intelligent eyes of hers studying me. Looking closer than I want them to. "You care more than you let on."

"I don't need to be a media darling. Never have been. Never will be."

"And yet you still care."

"Only to the extent that people still buy my music."

"Is that why you're solo? You need to chase a new high?"

"Meaning?"

"Meaning you left something good once before to chase the high. It seems only fitting you'd do the same again."

There's the dig. The subtle reminder that I walked away from her but no acknowledgement over my lack of options. It was my dad's fists, his disapproval, and staying with her, or leaving it all behind and trying to make something of myself.

There is no correlation between back then and what happened with Hawkin.

No connection other than my dad fucking things up for me once again.

But he doesn't belong in this moment. In my head. Not when the woman I've thought about more times than not over the years is standing before me, tempting me with her sass and her grit and a body that I'm more than itching to touch.

It's amazing how easily you can disregard how connected you are to someone when there's so much other than noise in your life. *But I've never forgotten Bristol.* She's everything a sane man would want. She's the ultimate prize, but I've never been in the running. *And I never will be.*

"I'll give you that one dig, Shug. But how come you're allowed to bring up the past and I'm not?" I take a few steps toward her, the urge to touch her stronger with each passing second. "I mean, if we're going to go there, then let's talk about the last time we saw each other."

She stares at me with what feels like a million unspoken thoughts in her eyes that I wish she'd voice. "There's nothing to talk about."

Liar.

"No?"

"We knew what we walked into that night. We did it willingly. We did it knowing we were going to both walk away with a bit more closure than we had before. I woke up. You were gone." She swallows forcibly but keeps her chin high as her words hit me where it hurts. "You made it more than clear that's all there was to it. Even picking up the phone was too much for you. I wasn't just some groupie, you know."

The hurt in her voice hides beneath the bravado. "No one ever said you were."

"You didn't have to say it, Vince. Actions spoke loud enough."

I sigh. What did I expect her to think? "I had my reasons. Ones that—"

"Save them. I don't care."

"That's not fair." Fuck. I run a hand through my hair, wanting a drink but needing to have this conversation without it. I purse my lips and shake my head. "Guilty as charged." I hold my hands up. If only she understood the *why* behind it. "Walking away is something I've seemed to have mastered and mastered well."

"We called a truce. It doesn't matter anymore." Her smile is shaky, but there nonetheless. "See how that works? How easy it is?"

She says the words but for the life of me, I don't believe her any more than I believe myself.

"Nothing is ever that easy, Shug."

Our gazes hold. "True." She lifts her chin at the platinum record on the wall for *Make Me Fall,* Bent's massively successful single. "Why'd you leave Bent?"

"It's a long story." I point to my guitar. "And McMann wants progress that I can't make if I'm telling it."

"You're so full of shit. You said yourself that your muse is dead." She lifts her eyebrows.

Christ. Do we really have to do this? There are much better things I'd rather be doing than talking about this shit.

"Like I said, it's a long story."

"Most are." She shrugs. "What happened?"

"Hawke and I got in a fight. Words were exchanged. Threats were made. A lot of things were said that can't be unsaid. Happy?"

"No, because it doesn't seem that you are. What did you fight about?"

Nothing. Everything.

I've been asked this question a hundred times and never wanted to talk about it. Why do I want to talk about it with her?

I lace my hands behind my neck and sigh. "Look. I was in a bad place and said a lot of shitty things. I made my bed and now I'm lying in it."

"It's easy to take words back. Even easier to say you're sorry for what you did."

I meet her eyes and feel like she's talking about more than just Hawkin right now.

"It's complicated." My answer stands for the fight and how I left things with her last time. I wonder if she knows that.

"Misery often is."

"Who said I'm miserable?"

She crosses her arms over her chest. "You forget that I know you too."

And isn't that the fuck and the fight of it? She knows me, and as much as I like that, it also means she can see right through me.

"You're right. You do. And that means you know the only thing on my mind right now is how I don't give a flying fuck about truces."

"What do truces have to do with anything?"

"They don't. Not when all you want to do is talk about shit that doesn't matter while I stand here obsessing over how much I want to kiss you again." Her cleavage is looking pretty spectacular with her arms crossed like that, and I'm desperate to stop talking about futile crap.

"Vince. I'm serious. Clearly you're—"

"I'm serious too. I've humored you. Answered your questions even. Studio time is precious and we're wasting it, so now it's time to get back to what I want to talk about."

"And that was what?"

Jesus. She even has to ask? I stride the three steps forward and grab the back of her neck. I've had plenty of women, I won't lie. But there has always been something . . . magical about Bristol. Her intelligence, her beauty, her presence. It seems like anytime I'm near her all I can think about is *want*. So I say the words that need no further explanation. "*This. Just fucking this,*" I say before slanting my lips over hers and claiming them.

Her startled gasp gives me access, and I slip my tongue between her lips to meet with hers.

Fucking hell.

My groan says it all as she reacts and gives in to the desperation of a kiss that feels like we've anticipated for seven years.

I'm still nowhere near good enough for her, but fuck if I'm not going to enjoy every goddamn second of this kiss.

It's been too long.

Too long without her taste. That soft moan in the back of her throat. The sting of her fingernails as they dig into my biceps. The feel of her body against mine.

I take without asking. Tongue and teeth and lips. Fingers tangled in her hair.

Already wanting more.

Already needing more.

"No." Bristol presses against my chest and pushes me back. "I can't. We can't."

"We did. We are. We will again." I reach for her again and she shakes her head forcefully, her eyes wide.

"No. I'll get fired."

I snort. "You're so full of shit."

"No. I'm serious." She paces the length of the room. Her hands moving just as much as her feet. "Lilah Glasnow was fired last month. She slept with a client. McMann found out."

"Like I give a fuck about Lilah what's-her-face."

"But you give a fuck about me so it should matter. I mean . . ."

Jesus. She's cute when she rambles, and I'm definitely not complaining about getting to watch the sway of her hips as she paces, her words tumbling out.

"Bristol. For the love of God, stop." I stride over to her and block her path. She tries to dodge to the right and I stop her. Then the left and she collides squarely with me. Tits against my chest. Her lips close once again. "Kissing's not sleeping so we're all good."

"This isn't a joke. I'm serious."

"I am too. Fuck McMann. How would he ever know that we kissed?" *We need to get over this hurdle, Shug, because I plan on doing a whole lot more than just kissing when it comes to you.* "Who's going to tell him?"

"He'll just know. Someone will say something and—"

"Come here," I say.

"Absolutely not. Don't order me—"

"Bristol."

She doesn't budge—she never was one to take orders—but her eyes track me as I walk over and turn the lock on the studio door. "See? Now he can't know. Easy."

"I get this is all fun and games to you, but this is my—"

"Excuse? Justification? Because from where I'm standing, you enjoyed that kiss just as much as I did. It seems every time you give in just the slightest, you put up a fight to justify why you shouldn't. We both know you want this as much as I do. First it was the truce and now it's McMann." I shrug. "If you don't want me, just say it, and I'll walk away."

I watch her lips. I wait for them to deny me. Seconds pass as our breaths remain the only sound in the room.

"I thought studio time was precious," she finally says. *I don't want you,* never falls from those lips.

I bark out a laugh. It's all I can do because I want to pin her against that wall at her back and knock those gold records off. "It is. I think I can make an exception this once."

She shakes her head. "You don't understand. You've never played by the rules so why would I expect you to do so now?"

"Fine," I finally say, pained as it is. "We can play by the rules."

Her eyes flash and her mouth shocks in an O. She wants to bend them just as much as I intend on breaking them.

Perfect.

"I forgot how hard it is for you to color outside of the lines, Shug," I murmur as I step into her and trace a fingertip over her collarbone. She sucks in a breath, and it's all I need to hear.

I've read her right.

She wants this.

She wants me.

But she doesn't know how to give in to what she wants.

Thank fucking God I know how to do it for her.

"So we'll follow the rules." I lean in, my lips right at her ear, and her perfume in my nose. "There's a whole hell of a lot we can do."

"Vince." My name is part plea, part protest, and a whole lot of gray area in between.

I love gray areas.

I lean back. "McMann says we can't sleep together. Fine. So that means sex is off the table. Care to define that term for me, though? *Sex?*"

She gives me a look—eyes wide, lips parted, cheeks flushed. That look alone is enough to get me hard.

"No touching."

"No?" I study her. "So if I were to do this, we'd be breaking the rules?" I run the back of my hand down her arm, then slide my fingers over her midsection, before gripping her hip and pulling her against the length of me. There's no mistaking what she's doing to me. My rock-hard, confined-by-my-jeans cock speaks for itself.

"Yes." She's breathless. Affected. "No touching."

"Hmm." I bite my bottom lip, the pain a handcuff on my restraint. "It wouldn't be touching if you slid your fingers between your thighs and I watched. I mean, that definitely wouldn't be sex, right? It would be me enjoying your company is all."

"We can't—"

"But we wouldn't be touching. Just like if while you were spread eagle over there—ass on that soundboard, thighs wide so I can watch those red nails of yours work over the pink of your pussy—I were to free my cock from these jeans and stroke it while I watched . . . I mean, that would still be coloring inside the lines, wouldn't it?"

She emits a sound I can't decipher, but I'd hedge my bets it's more on the side of desire than denial.

"And if I brushed my lips against yours," I say, so that with each word, our lips share just a whisper of a touch, "and then ran my tongue over your lips just like this, I wonder if you'd consider that coloring right on the lines or if it's outside."

"Vince."

"Yes, Shug?" I murmur, my fingers itching to touch and my body begging to take.

"I want . . ."

"Or is skin-on-skin contact your definition of touching? I could close my mouth over your nipple like this," I murmur around a mouthful of cloth and pebbled peak, "and technically we wouldn't be touching."

But her head dropping back and the arch of her chest pressing her more against my mouth tells me I'm oh so close to breaking that will of hers.

"I can't," she moans.

"Ah, but you just said *you want*, and I sure as fuck *want too*," I murmur as I drop to my knees in front of her and do the exact same fucking thing I did to her tit but this time to her pussy. "Hold on, Shug. My hair is there to grip if you need to."

She yelps as I hike one of her legs up over my shoulder. Immediately she fists my hair for balance at the same time I close my mouth over her.

I draw in a deep breath, drowning in everything that is Bristol Matthews . . . everything that is but the goddamn taste of her.

But I work my tongue over and against the fabric. I trace the lines of her lips as she starts to swell and her pants grow wet.

She bucks her pussy into my face—no man would ever complain about that—and a soft moan floats through the studio as I do the best I can given the restrictions.

My balls ache something fierce with a want I haven't felt in forever. If I could manage to free my cock and stroke it while holding her, I would, but I only have so many hands, and fuck if I'm going to give up any iota of concentration right now.

"Vince." My name is the sexiest goddamn music to my ears. I'll do whatever it takes to hear it again.

Her scent grows sweeter as she becomes more aroused. As I work her into a frenzy. As her fingers grip tighter and as my dick grows harder.

Fuck your coloring inside the lines, Shug.

Fuck your clothing.

Fuck your rules.

But I promised to play by them—*for her*—just this once. Next time it'll be for goddamn good.

She cries out when, without warning, I drop her leg, yank her against me, and close my mouth over hers.

"This. Just this," I murmur again before I dive back in, desperate to taste so much more than only her tongue.

I want you.

Now.

Desperately.

"Vince. We can't." She says the words but she cups my cock.

The guttural groan that fills my ears must be my own, but hell if I remember emitting it as I'm too busy touching. Her hair. Her ass. Her chest. Her—

Pounding on the studio door jerks me back to reality. I personally don't want to be anywhere near reality since it doesn't include fucking Bristol on the floor.

"Oh my God," she says as she pushes herself away from me and frantically fixes her clothing.

I watch her, chuckling. How did I forget how flustered she gets when she thinks she's going to be in trouble? It's adorable.

"Quit looking at me," she scolds in a whisper-yell. "He's going to know what we were doing. Go answer the door."

Noah can fucking wait a second while my hard-on dissipates. That, and so I can steal one more kiss from her.

"I fucking love truces," I murmur as my lips find hers.

"No." She pushes her hands on my chest, struggling against me while I chuckle against her lips.

"Relax. I'm sure there's been many worse things happen in this studio before." I take a step back and wink as I take her in one more time. "You might want to take a seat in the booth for a few seconds. Wait for that wet spot I left on your pants to dry."

She looks down and then back up, eyes wide and full of panic before scurrying into the booth to sit on the couch and cross her legs, seconds before I unlock the door.

"Hey. Sorry about that, Noah—" But when I swing open the door, it's not just Noah standing there. I cough out a laugh. "Xavier. Well, this is a surprise."

Knowing Bristol, she's probably having a fucking heart attack at the sound of his name. When I reach out to shake his hand, I get off knowing that a minute ago that same hand was all over Bristol.

"I haven't been getting any updates, so I thought I'd stop by myself to see how things were going."

"Everything okay in here?" Noah asks as he steps into the booth and nods to Bristol.

"Yes. Fuck. The locked door. It's a habit. Do it without even thinking." I smile through my lie at Xavier who is still standing in the doorway. "I had to install those keycode locks at my house because I kept locking myself outside."

"Good. Great," Xavier says, walking past me and into the booth. "The writing is going—*Matthews?* You're here."

Thank God for the dim light or Bristol's flushed cheeks, mussed hair, and nervous smile just might give us away.

"Of course, I'm here. Isn't that what you wanted? For me to report back with an update?" she asks.

He studies her for a beat. I can see her pulse pounding in the vein on her neck.

"And yet last I checked I haven't gotten one."

This fucking guy and his ego. Such a blowhard. "Yeah. Cell service in here sucks, soundproof walls and all. Besides, I needed her help," I explain before she can speak.

Be good. Don't bait the fucker. It's not your job at stake. Color inside the fucking lines.

Try to, at least.

"I have a text typed up to send to you," she says, holding her cell up with what looks like a lengthy text from our distance, "but I haven't been able to get it to send. I figured helping Vince was what was most important."

All she needs is a bat of lashes and a curtsy to help with his god complex.

"Help? How so?" Xavier asks, eyes narrowed and arms crossed.

"Recording the session for me. Stopping and starting with each take. You know, just in case something good happens so I don't forget what it is. It might not work for the current song, but that doesn't mean it won't be for the next one."

Noah busies himself, his smirk hidden from everyone but me. He knows I'm full of shit but plays along.

Xavier looks her way again. "And here I was afraid Matthews was dropping the ball and not fulfilling your needs."

I have a lot of fucking needs, Xav, and right now every single one of them has to do with that woman over there.

"No complaints here." I chuckle. "Studio time's precious, after all."

CHAPTER

fifteen

Bristol
Seven Years Ago

I'VE NEVER FELT MORE NAÏVE IN MY LIFE THAN I DO IN THIS MOMENT.

Women mill around me. Most are half-dressed in sky-high heels. Some are drunk or obnoxiously loud or *both*. All are standing near the backstage exit waiting for a brief glimpse of any of the Bent band members in the hopes they'll burst out of those doors and make the trek to their tour bus.

And in that glimpse, I have no doubt they are hoping to be seen, noticed, and then picked out of the crowd to join them for the evening.

I'm not sheltered by any means, but to say I'm not surprised by the comments being said around me is an understatement.

Getting an autograph is the last thing on these ladies' minds.

I've heard he's incredible in the sack. I plan on finding out.

If I flash them as they walk by, do you think it would help?

Panties are a no-go. I want him to see how wet I am for him through my pants.

I thought getting the concert ticket and driving the four hours to the venue was going to be the hardest part of tonight. Sure, it cost me some of my savings, but seeing Vince again was all I could think about.

The concert alone was definitely worth it. Bent was more than electric, but truth be told, I wasn't exactly paying attention. My eyes were one hundred percent fixed on Vince.

He was . . . incredible. Fantastic. Mesmerizing. All of that and then some considering I knew the boy who'd fiddle on his guitar and blush when he messed up a chord. To see him so confident and playing up the crowd was everything I'd hoped it would be.

But now I'm here. Outside the back door. One of what seems like a hundred women vying to be seen and not exactly sure how to do it.

I've tried talking to the security guards at the door. The only thing I do know is that he changed his number somewhere during the past few years. *Was it his way of making a clean break from his past?*

I'm under no pretenses how this reunion will go other than the strong urge I had telling me that I needed to be here. That I needed to see him if for no other reason than to sate my curiosity and to find a bit of closure in a wound that has long since scarred over.

The question is . . . how exactly do I do that?

The confidence I had in how I looked—my new outfit, my freshly cut and colored hair, my perfectly colored spray tan—fades as I take in all these women and their knockout bodies. I could only wish to have the confidence to wear the skimpy outfits they are wearing.

Is this what Vince likes now? Is this who he is? *Does that really matter, Bristol?* This isn't about sex. *Right?*

"Trying to get in his pants now that he's made it, huh? Don't let the lights fool you. He's still the same fucked-up loser he was back then. Maybe even more so now. Don't waste your time. He's not fucking worth it."

The slight slur to his words, the innate lethargy, the disdain for his son . . . it was horrible. The fact that I had to plead with that man . . . For whatever reason, he gave me Vince's number, and until now, I wasn't sure I'd ever use it. *But I need to try.* I can't let this moment pass me by.

I dial the number Deegan Jennings gave me and wait as it rings and rings until an electronic voice picks up. *Shit.* Then I stare at my phone wondering what to text. It takes me way too long to figure it out. There is a lot of typing and deleting, but in the end, I figure simpler is better.

Me: It's Bristol. I'm here at the arena. The backstage door. The concert was great. I know you're busy but was hoping maybe to see you for a few minutes. – Shug.

I hit send and then silently freak out. I just played the only hand I have, and it might not be enough. Vince holds all the cards now.

The minutes drag on as my hope of seeing him fades.

The door opens and everyone clambers back to the ropes as a tall man in a white shirt, ripped jeans and a hat that sits low over his brow walks out toward us. He starts pointing at different women and then hooking his thumb toward the door he just came from. "You. And you." He stands on his tiptoes and looks past the front row where I stand as those first two women squeal and all but jog in their heels toward the door. "You, you, and you," he continues, looking over me. "That's it."

Every part of me deflates as I try to get his attention. "Hey. I need to see Vince."

"So does everyone, sweetheart. Let me guess, you know him personally."

"I do. I promise. Tell him Shug is here."

A round of laughter goes off from the women blocking the view in front of me, and then there is an awed silence I can't comprehend.

"*Shug?* Is that you?"

Vince's voice rings out followed by gasps from the women around me as he comes into view.

"Vince. I'm here. It's me." My words are frantic. My heart is racing. And the next few seconds are an absolute blur as the man I later find out to be the road manager, Mick, grabs my hand and pulls me out of the crowd. I don't even have time to see or talk to Vince as the crowd squeezes in around us. Mick pushes us through the door before slamming it behind us.

"Christ, Jennings. You trying to get me fucking killed?" Mick asks as he shoves him from behind.

Vince laughs. "Too bad it didn't work."

"Fucker," Mick mumbles about the same time that Vince turns to face me.

The area we are standing in is brightly lit, has concrete floors, white walls, and Vince stands before me dressed in head-to-toe black.

He's gorgeous.

I mean, he always has been, but his boyish face has matured. His jaw is stronger, covered in more stubble, and his eyes, though lit up with surprise, are more reserved. His left arm is peppered with a few tattoos that give him more of an edge than the guy I once knew. And then there's his body. That wiry teenage boy I once loved is most definitely a man with a broad chest, square shoulders, strong thighs, and sexy as hell hands.

And in that one look, a million feelings come rushing back to me as if no time has passed.

But it has.

It most definitely has.

We stare at each other for what feels like forever but is merely seconds before a slow smile crawls onto his handsome face. "Jesus, it really is you," he says before he swoops me up in a hug, picks me up off the floor as he does so, and just holds on tight with his face buried in the curve of my shoulder.

He smells of leather and soap from the shower he must have taken after the show. His hair is wet against the side of my face, and his arms are strong as they squeeze me tight.

Processing my feelings is impossible, so I shove them away and try to memorize the moment.

"Fuck, man. If you're going to fuck her, then at least get out of the hallway," someone says as they bump past us.

"It's not like that." Vince chuckles as he sets me down.

It's now when we stare at each other that the awkwardness sets in. For the first few moments, it was like he was the guy I used to know, and now he's the famous musician I don't really know anything about.

When we finally talk, we both start at the same time.

"Sorry," we say in unison.

"You go first," I say through my laugh.

"I still can't believe you're standing in front of me." He runs a hand through his hair as he shakes his head. "What are you doing here?" he asks and motions for me to get out of the way. Distractions are everywhere around us. People moving about. Black cases being moved here and there. Voices shouting out and echoing down the corridors.

There's a harshness to it all that clearly Vince is more than used to.

"I don't know," I say and shrug as someone walks past him and hands him a beer.

"Want one?"

"No. I don't think—"

"Killer show, man," a guy says and fist-bumps him. "I love that new riff you added into *Take Me Down*. Talk about kicking it up a notch. No doubt kids'll be all over the socials trying to copy it." He laughs. "That's how you know you've made it. Hey, you heading out with us?"

Vince looks to me and then back to him. "Nah. Not right now."

The guy looks at me and his eyes widen. "Oh. Gotcha. Dude, your bus is free and clear if you need it . . ." He looks my way again and smirks. "For whatever you might need it for."

"I—I'm not—" I start to say when I realize he thinks I'm a groupie here to sleep with Vince, but the man just holds his hands up in a *no judgment* motion before taking a step backward and walking away.

"Just ignore him," Vince says with a chuckle. "He's just . . . *Jimmy.*"

I stare at Vince and suddenly feel absolutely ridiculous being here. What did I expect? That we'd see each other and things would be like they were back when we were in high school? That we'd slip back into talking about how Mr. Parker sucks as a math teacher, how my mom won't budge on my curfew . . . and I don't even know what else.

"I'm sorry." I laugh nervously and look around at this chaos he lives in and know I'm way out of my element. "I just showed up without warning. I'm sure you have other plans."

"Get your ass in here, Jennings," someone calls from an open doorway. I'm actually grateful for the interruption so I have time to calm my nerves.

"Follow me for a sec?" he asks and then moves toward the door. It's a large room—what I would think a quintessential backstage would look like. A large oriental rug, couches everywhere, and people milling about. The band members. The women from outside. Other people trying to look the part but that stand out like a sore thumb.

The music is loud and the cigarette smoke is thick as Vince introduces me to a few people. I like his bandmates immediately. Hawkin Play, the lead singer, definitely owns the room. He's charismatic and energetic even after running around on the stage for the past few hours. Rocket, their other guitarist, is definitely the class clown of the group, and Gizmo, their drummer, the more mellow one.

I'm sure the mellowness isn't hindered by the woman's throat he currently has his tongue down.

Vince is pulled in to settle a debate between Gizmo and Hawkin as I move to the edge of the room and just take it all in. This new and crazy lifestyle that he leads.

And as I stand here, it's obvious to me from the various people vying for

Vince's attention, that everybody wants something from him. His bandmates want his mediation skills. The women who keep walking up and running a hand down his arm with huge *come fuck me* eyes want in his pants. The other guests wait for a snippet of his time and seem satisfied when they get it.

How silly is it for me to still love a man as untouchable as him?

And yet, I can't bring myself to tear my eyes away from him.

Because of that inability, I see the minute he realizes I've slinked off into the shadows of the room. He stands on his toes and scans the room to find me, his smile greeting me when he does.

He's at my side in seconds. "Sorry. It's habit to unwind like this after a show."

"Don't apologize. I shouldn't have come. I—"

"What are you talking about?" Vince says, grin widening. "It's a lot. I know, but you get used to it. Come on, let's go to my dressing room. It's quieter there."

I follow him as he starts to walk, my mind still trying to process that Vince is in front of me. How very different his life is compared to mine.

And what now?

We pass open doors—one where another party is clearly going on. Another where someone shouts out his name and he just lifts his middle finger at him. A third where the smell of pot permeates the air. People stop him to compliment him or ask him questions, and after each time, he apologizes.

"It'll be quieter in here," he says and pushes open a door with his name on it. The room is medium sized. A leather couch is on one side, a table on the opposite wall with a variety of food and drinks set up on it. A rack of clothes is beside it. Jazz plays softly on a speaker in the far corner, which should surprise me most but he always did like to listen to it to unwind.

"Thank you," I murmur, still not sure what to do or say.

"Have a seat. Can I get you anything?" he asks. "Water. Beer. A Coke?"

Right about now I could use a whole bottle of something strong to battle my nerves. "A beer is fine."

He lifts his brow at me, almost as if he too is having a hard time remembering we aren't in high school anymore.

I thought this would be so much easier than it is. We've always had an effortless friendship, so I don't know how to be any other way with him.

No time like the present to figure it out.

"I didn't mean to just show up. I saw you were in town and decided to drive down. I didn't think that you might have plans with the guys . . . or other women to go out with or . . . anything. I just—"

He puts a playful hand over my mouth from behind as he hands me a beer with his other before whispering in my ear. "You always did ramble when you were nervous." He laughs. "Why you nervous, Shug?"

He lets go and circles around me to take a seat on the arm of the couch with one combat boot on the cushion beside me and the other on the floor so he can face me.

"I'm not nervous." I take a sip of beer and cringe at the taste.

He just stares at me, his head angled to the side, his hand reaching up to scratch the side of his neck. He has a couple of leather bracelets on his wrist. It's so much easier to focus on them than him, but there is one in particular that catches my eye.

It's a thin, black, faded braid of a bracelet. I remember giving him that on his eighteenth birthday, because it was all I could afford but thought he would like.

My eyes flash to his and one corner of his lips turn up, his eyes soft. "What can I say? It's my good luck charm."

"You've kept it all this time?"

"Something like that." He takes a long drink of his beer and ignores a knock on the door. A little part of me melts knowing he's kept it all these years. "What'd you think of the show?"

"I thought you guys were incredible. High energy. Good set list. The crowd was really into it."

"Thanks, but we still need work. Rocket fucked up on a song. I missed a chord on another. Hawkin forgot the lyrics and just told the crowd to sing along to cover it up."

"Didn't notice at all."

"Yeah, but there are a million other bands out there waiting to take our place." He lifts his beer again, giving me a better view of some of his tattoos. Some Japanese writing. The neck of a guitar. More that I can't make out.

"You always were hard on yourself."

"We need to be better. That's all there is to it."

"Better?" I laugh. "I'd say having the number one album in the country is pretty damn good. Can't go much higher than that."

Vince stares at me, his cheeks flushing, and his sheepish grin reminds me of a little boy before he shakes his head. "It's absolutely fucking crazy, isn't it? A total mindfuck. The guys . . . we still can't wrap our heads around it."

"I can't imagine."

"We went from couch-surfing and ramen to The Ritz and private jets all within a year."

Another knock at the door. "Gotta go. Buses are loading," a voice says through the door.

My heart sinks. This is it? That's all the time I get?

Vince looks at me and then looks at the door before jogging to it and throwing it open. "Go on ahead," he calls out. "I'll catch up." He turns to me. "I know a hole in the wall not too far from here. The food's not great, but it's dark so I won't be recognized. Want to go?"

CHAPTER
sixteen

Bristol
Seven Years Ago

"T HEN THERE WAS JAPAN. WE SOLD OUT THE STADIUM BUILT FOR fifty thousand people, before moving on to Germany. It's fucking crazy there."

I study him across a table littered with dirty plates and empty beer bottles. I have no clue what time it is because it feels like time has stood still while we've been catching up in the dimly lit dining area. The staff left long ago save for one person who Vince slipped some ridiculous amount of money to. That person is currently sitting in the back room no doubt scrolling on his phone and bored to tears.

I've enjoyed listening to him regale me with stories about his travels and crazy fans. About sold-out venues and empty dive bars. But that's the famous Vince talking.

"And then in Brazil—"

"Vince?"

He stops and looks at me. "Yeah?"

"I don't care."

"What do you mean, you don't care?" He laughs, holding his hands out.

I've had enough wine to take the edge off. I lean forward and whisper. "I. Don't. Care."

"Shug—"

"Look at you. You made it against all fucking odds. I'm so damn proud of you . . . but I hear you talking about all of this stuff and I don't care, because when I look at you, I still see the teenager standing in my window at two in the morning."

I watch my words hit him. One by one. "Bristol."

"I'm serious. No one deserves this more than you." My smile is soft and his matches as we stare at each other over the dim light.

And for the first time all night, it's there.

It being that palpable chemistry we always had. The kind we never had to work at even when we sat beside each other as I tutored him. I fought it every step of the way, wondering *how could this goody-two-shoes find a rebel so irresistible?*

I thought maybe it had gone with the years that passed us by, and there's something in the way those light green eyes of his are looking at me that says I was wrong.

The bob of his Adam's apple and glance at my lips tells me he feels it too.

"What about you?" he asks to break the silence. "We've spent all this time talking about me, I want to know about what you've been up to."

"I pale in comparison to your accomplishments."

"I want to know." He reaches out and my hand heats under his touch. "Tell me about college and how you're conquering the world."

My smile is stilted as I lie. "Just school and work. Normal things." There's no need to elaborate about how my parents' divorce threw me for a loop. How I was desperate to leave home and get some space after feeling betrayed by them. But when my dad lost his job and the economy had its downswing, money was tight, so I opted for junior college rather than put them more in debt. How I'm working nights and going to school during the day, hoping to transfer to a four-year university next year.

"Where'd you end up?"

"Cal State." I wave a hand at him, more than ready to be off this topic. "It's two in the morning. We should let this poor guy get home," I say about the employee and then realize that leaving might mean our night is over. Our time is done. And I suddenly want to take the words back.

"You're right. We should." Vince stands, takes one last pull on his beer, and throws a wad of cash on the table, admonishing me when I reach for my wallet to pitch in. He grabs my wrist. "Don't even think about it."

But when I look up to meet his eyes, my protest dies on my lips.

He's close. So close that I swear it hurts to look at him. To be this close to him, to want him and not have him. The ache in my chest is so poignant I swear he can feel it too.

My shaky inhale sounds like a scream in the silence, but Vince doesn't acknowledge it as he reaches up to cup the side of my face.

"I've missed you," he says, his eyes locked on mine as he dips down and brushes his lips against mine.

It's a soft sigh of a kiss, a reminder of what used to be. A brief touch of our tongues is more than enough to remind me how much I craved the taste of him after he left.

How much it hurt to pick up the phone and not have him there. How much I regretted not giving the part of myself to him that I could never take back.

Instinct mixed with memories and longing has me reaching up, threading my fingers through his hair, and deepening the kiss.

He puts his hand on the small of my back and pulls me into him as his other directs my head to angle the kiss. There's no urgency, just the smoldering of ashes having new oxygen breathed into them.

It lasts only seconds before he ends the kiss, but it's enough to solidify that the connection between us is still there.

When I open my eyes, his are squeezed shut and his hand is fisted at his side as if he's chastising himself.

"Vince?" Confusion weaves through my tone.

He opens his eyes, his smile tight and voice clipped. "We should go."

I grab his hand and hold him in place when he goes to walk away. He looks down at our hands and then back up to me but doesn't say a word. He doesn't have to because the steel in his eyes is harsh enough. It's almost as if he's waiting for me to give an answer he's never voiced the question to, but I don't have a chance to.

"That mistake was on me." He shrugs his hand from my grip and then turns on his heel.

I scramble behind him as his long strides eat up the sidewalk that leads to the limo. He opens the door to the car for me but won't meet my eyes and doesn't say a word as we get in.

What am I missing? Did I do something wrong? What happened?

It's like a switch was flipped, and I'm on the wrong end of it.

"Where to?" the driver asks.

"What hotel are you staying at?" He finally speaks.

"None. I wasn't planning on staying."

His sigh is heavy. "It's two in the fucking morning. Do you actually think I'm going to let you drive home right now?"

By the way he refuses to look at me, I'd think that's exactly what he wants.

"That was my plan. How was I to know we were going to go out to dinner and talk till who knows when?"

"So you figured you'd drive for four hours, say hi, shoot your shot, then turn back around again?"

Shoot my shot? "Vince. What in the hell are you—"

"The usual hotel, Brian," he says to the driver.

"I'll let them know you're coming," Brian says and then slides the partition up.

"After he drops you off, can he take me to get my car?" I ask. Vince doesn't respond, instead he just stares out the window at the city passing by. "Great. Perfect. Thanks for the response. Good to know fame went to your head and made you an asshole."

He chuckles sarcastically but finally glances my way. "I'll arrange for you to get your car in the morning. You're not driving home."

"Well, I sure as shit aren't staying with you."

"I'm not staying. The buses already have a three-hour head start on me. I've got to catch up with them. The show must go on." He clears his throat. "I'll get you up to your room, and then Brian here will get me where I need to be."

It's my turn to look out the window and let the silence eat at my thoughts. He bailed on his band, on his schedule, on his after-party, *for me*. I never expected that—hell, I was telling the truth when I said I didn't know what to expect. Guilt eats at me. Screwing up his schedule wasn't my intention.

Is that why he's irritable with me? Is he regretting his decision? Is that why our kiss—*oh shit*. Does he have a girlfriend? Did he screw up, kiss me out of nostalgia, and then when I kissed him back it made him step back?

I slide a glance his way. How weird is it to have his taste still on my tongue and feel the sensation of his guitar-roughened fingertips on my skin, and yet he suddenly seems a million miles away.

I don't know Vincent Jennings anymore.

I should have left well enough alone. Being able to see him again, see that he was happy, and to tell him I was proud of him should have been enough for me. It should have been that unattainable closure I was looking for.

Wanting Vince has always been the easy part. It was everything else that was the trouble.

I guess some things never change.

"Thank you," I whisper, fighting the warring emotions within me. Accepting that that little piece of me that held on to her high school sweetheart never should have. "I appreciate you taking the time out of your busy schedule to see me. And to find a hotel room for me."

He nods, eyes holding mine briefly before looking back out the window again. "Don't be ridiculous. Of course, I'd make time for you."

Then why do you seem so angry at me? I want to scream.

"We're here," Brian announces as we pull into what looks like a generic looking building.

"Service entrance," Vince explains as he opens the door and ushers me out. "That way you don't have paparazzi waiting for you in the morning. If someone sees us coming in the front, they'll be parked everywhere thinking I'm still in your bed. They're rabid. You definitely don't want that kind of attention."

Or is it that you don't want to be seen with me? An empty restaurant. The back door to a hotel.

He definitely has a girlfriend.

How much does it suck that my chest hurts at the thought? It's not like I haven't seen his many exploits splashed across gossip magazines and the Internet before, but having him so close, kissing him one more time, makes it all the more real.

It's not like I can lay claim to a man who was my high school sweetheart.

"You're right. I don't. Thank you," I say for what feels like the tenth time as the back door opens when we near it. A petite woman with a name tag that denotes she's the manager greets Vince with a smile and hands him a key card. Clearly, they've done this before.

They exchange quick pleasantries and within seconds we're in the service

elevator heading to the tenth floor, the awkwardness between us only growing more intense by the second.

I've never been more relieved to hear an elevator ding in my life. The
door opens to a short hallway with a lone door at the far end. I follow Vince
off the car and as much as I hate acknowledging it, I'm going to be relieved
when he leaves and I can be alone with my thoughts.

But rather than opening the door with the key card, Vince crosses his
arms and leans against the wall opposite me, eyes locked on mine. "It was
good to see you, Shug. Really good. You were a small slice of normal in this
crazy world I now live in."

"Same here. I mean, not the crazy world part but—"

"What is it you're doing here? Why are you here? Is it for money? For—"

"*What?*" His questions catch me off guard and light a match to my
temper.

"I know all about your parents. Their divorce. Your dad losing his job
and selling the house. You being at a junior college. You put it out there on
social media for all to see, and yet you sat there tonight and blatantly lied to
me. So I'll ask the question again, are you here for money?"

"Fuck you," I grit out, an acrid ball of mortification burning in my throat.
I stare at him—mouth lax, eyes wide—in utter disbelief.

"Everyone wants something from me these days. Money. Fame. A hand
up. A handout." His nonchalant shrug only fuels my anger. "*What'll it be,
Shug?*"

"You actually think that's what I'm here for?" I take a few steps away
from him and laugh because it's all I can think to do.

"One of us isn't telling the truth, and it sure as fuck isn't me. That's usually how it all starts." The way he can sling the insults so casually at me makes
them sting all the more. The way he stares at me even more so.

"There's a huge difference between lying and omitting, Jennings." I cross
my arms over my chest and stand my ground. "Just because I didn't tell you
the whole sob story, doesn't mean I want anything from you. You were my best
friend. The boy I thought I'd have forever. But I can see now what a childish
fantasy that was. I don't *need* or *want* anything from you. I sure as fuck don't
want a single dime from you." I jab my finger in his chest.

"Hmph." His smirk is as irritating as the sound.

This was such a stupid mistake.

"I just wanted to know if you were happy, Vince. That's all I needed to know." And now that I know he's become a self-entitled asshole, I'm ready to get the hell away from him.

"Everybody wants something from me, Bristol. I've got people coming out of the woodwork left and right. Family I've never met asking for money. A woman I don't know claiming to be my mom." He throws his hands up. "Christ, I even have women I've never met claiming they're having my kids to get in on the handout action. So don't give me your bullshit that you don't want anything from me. Everybody fucking does."

"*I don't,*" I scream, not caring that we're in a hotel anymore and that people will be able to hear us. "I didn't want a goddamn thing from you other than to just see you. Curiosity satisfied. Thoroughly disappointed."

I pluck the key card from his hand and stalk to the door, but his hand is on my arm yanking me back against him. We're chest to chest. "Everybody wants something from you when you've made it."

"Well, I've never wanted anything from you other than you." I try to yank my arm free of his grip but he just squeezes tighter, much like the vise tightening on my heart. "Let. Go."

The puffs of his labored pants hit my lips. The smell of his mint gum mixed with the leather scent of his cologne fills my nose.

Before I can even process my anger, the situation, his harsh words and accusations, Vince claims my mouth in a kiss laden with violent desire. It's everything I thought I wanted but am now fighting against.

I try to shake my head from side to side, try to fight the contact, but he just holds the side of my face as his scruff scrapes and his lips overwhelm.

He pulls back, eyes the clearest I've ever seen them. "I've wanted you since I was sixteen years old. Every goddamn minute of every fucking day. I've been bargaining with myself all night why this can't happen." He drags his teeth over my collarbone. My body bucks in traitorous reflex. "But fuck, Shug, you're a hard one to quit."

His words shock me. My body burns with an ache so sweet and a head so fucked up that I will myself to believe my words when I speak them. "I don't want anything from you."

"Yeah, you do," he murmurs seconds before he takes another greedy kiss that has me fisting his shirt—but I'm not sure if it's to pull him closer or to push him away.

His kiss is like a drug. A sharp hit. A wicked high. A gateway to wanting more. "You're right," I say. "I lied. I want you just as bad. Just you. Just tonight."

His eyes flash up to me, the warring emotions that have been in them ever since we left the restaurant are nowhere to be found. I only see lust. I only sense desire. "That's all I can give you. I'm in a different city every night. A different bed. I'm not worthy of—"

I press my finger to his lips to quiet his words. To prevent him from rejecting me. With our foreheads resting against each other and our bodies ready to react, I whisper, "Just give me tonight. Just give me this once. Just this."

"Shug." The word sounds pained. Like a man on the edge of control. Like a man questioning his own resolve.

"No strings. No promises we'll have to break. Just one night of sweet regret."

He leans back, a lopsided grin on his handsome face. "That's not much time to fulfill every goddamn fantasy I've had of you over the years."

"You've fantasized about me?"

His chuckle is a low rumble that I can almost feel between my thighs. "More times than I can count."

The pressure in my chest eases. The panic abates. "Then I guess we better get started."

A feral groan echoes down the hallway as Vince launches himself at me right there against the door. The worry and anger from moments ago are quickly being erased from my head with each touch. After every kiss. With each fantasy about to be fulfilled.

We kiss with a hunger I've never had before. We touch with a desperation at levels I never knew existed.

It's all so new yet familiar at the same time. The same angles, the same actions, but hell if the skill level hasn't increased exponentially.

The difference?

At seventeen, the ache lighting every part of me on fire scared me. I was curious about the burn but afraid of what and who that made me.

Now? I'm older. I'm more experienced. I know that Vince is about to turn all those things inside out, flip them upside down.

Make the fantasy become a reality I fear I'll never recover from.

CHAPTER
seventeen

Bristol

Seven Years Ago

H IS HANDS ARE EVERYWHERE AND NOT ENOUGH PLACES AT THE SAME time. Fisting the back of my shirt when I want them on my skin. On my breasts when I want them between my thighs.

More.

It's my only thought.

More.

His lips are on mine. On the slopes of my shoulders. His teeth scrape over my collarbone. His tongue wages an all-out war against my senses.

More.

Our shirts are over our heads the minute the door shuts at our backs. We don't worry about finding the light switch because we are so consumed with each other and the fire that burns so goddamn bright between us.

We bump into the wall of the suite, the bed to the side of us, and our laughs that are smothered with kisses turn to groans as we settle against it.

As the full weight of Vince's body presses against mine and hints at the dark promise of what's next.

My hands fist in his hair. My fingers scrape down his bare abdomen—long nails over corded muscles. My fingers undo his belt, then his zipper.

"I need you with less clothes on," I murmur before nipping his bottom lip and cupping the bulge pressing against the seam of his jeans.

The groan he emits is feral as he pulls my head back to expose my neck. He scrapes his teeth over my skin and murmurs in my ear. "Do you want my cock, Shug? Will you take it like the good little girl you are? Will you let me fill you up until you can't take any more of it and then let me push it in even farther? Will you scream my name when you come?"

The warmth of his breath.

His hard cock twitching in my hand.

The seduction in his words.

I arch my back to try and press my body against his, desperate for the connection with him.

His chuckle rumbles through me. "Greedy girl. Already wanting more when you haven't even gotten any yet." His hands still grip my hair as he slants his mouth over mine and takes until I can't catch my breath. "I like that. I reward greed." Another searing kiss, but this time he releases my hair and slides his hands down to my ass, pressing my body against his cock.

Teasing me.

Taunting me.

Warning me.

His lips are a whisper from mine, our eyes locked on each other's through the dim light. Anticipation builds as my breathing labors. Desire overwhelms as he grows harder, and I become wetter.

And just as I think he's going to kiss me again, he steps back, his gaze daring me. "Take off the rest of your clothes. I want to look at you."

I swallow over a nervous lump in my throat but do exactly as he says. My insecurities hide in the darkness of the room. The fear of not feeling like I'm enough for him dissipates.

It's his groan that I hear. The flare of heat in his eyes that I see. The, "Christ, you are gorgeous," that has me standing taller under his praise. That has me feeling beautiful and fearless and desired.

Just like Vince always has.

"It's your turn to watch, Shug. Don't take your eyes off me. I love knowing how desperate you are to touch me. To taste me. To feel this inside you." He sheds his pants on those last words and his cock springs free. The sight of it—thick and hard with a glisten of precome on its tip—has me swallowing forcibly.

He stands there in the same swath of moonlight I'm in, but for him it looks like he's onstage and the spotlight is highlighting his beauty. The dark ink of his tattoos. The lick of his tongue to wet his lips. The bob of his cock in response to my stare.

"Is your pussy wet? Do your nipples ache for me to touch them? Is your clit swollen and ready to be played with?"

"Vince." His name is a plea.

"Don't worry, Shug, we've got all the time in the world." He takes a step closer. "Time for us to use each other. The first round where we can finally pleasure each other." Another step. "One where you can tell me what you want." He reaches out and pats the V between my legs, causing shock waves to ricochet through me. "One where I can get mine." This time he takes his hand, fists it around his cock so that we both watch as he pumps it slowly. "And then who knows what'll come next."

"Yes. Please." The words are panted.

His chuckle is low and suggestive. "I don't think you have any idea how much I like hearing those words come from your mouth." He leans in and licks over the seam of my lips. My heart races. My nipples harden. The ache for him grows. "Get on the bed like a good girl and spread your legs so I can see what I want to fuck."

Jesus.

I mean, my thoughts are as scrambled as my insides as I do exactly what Vince commands. This is a whole different side to him and I'm not complaining . . . nor did I ever think words like *good girl* would turn me on, but hell if arousal isn't coating my inner thighs as I scoot back on the bed. Vince stands at the foot, his shoulders broad, the muscle in his jaw pulsing, and his fingers rolling a condom over his dick as he watches me open my thighs for him.

"Mmm. You listen so well," he murmurs. "I bet your pussy tastes as good as it looks."

I don't even have time to squirm before he grabs my ankles, pulls me toward him, and he takes a long, wandering swipe of his tongue through my slit and closes his mouth over my clit and sucks.

My yelp turns into a mewl as my hips buck and my hands fly to tangle in his hair as sensations swamp me. This whole foreplay dance has made me more ready than I've ever been, and all I want is him in me. On me. Working me over.

"You *are* a greedy girl, aren't you?" He presses a kiss to my abdomen while he tucks three fingers into me. "Knowing that makes me so fucking hard." He closes his lips around my nipple and sucks. His fingers move in. Out. "Makes me want you so fucking bad." He licks a line up my chest that connects with every nerve within. "Makes me want to show you how you taste for me." He slants his lips over mine, his tongue slipping between, so I can taste the sweet tang of my own arousal.

This man is doing things to me—physically, emotionally—and he hasn't even pushed into me yet.

"We'll taste more of that later," he murmurs against my lips and stands despite my hands trying to keep him against me.

"Quit teasing me and just fuck me already," I demand.

He pats my clit with a bit more force this time. A reprimand I want to be punished for again. Anything for his touch. Anything to sate the sweet ache he keeps feeding.

"I've waited a long damn time to fuck you, Shug. Years and years. I've thought about what it would be like. What it would feel like. What you would look like lying beneath me. Don't mind me, but I think I'll admire this pretty pussy of yours for a second more before I punish it to pleasure."

He runs the head of his cock up and down, spreading my wetness around. My muscles tense with anticipation and need and greed and a whole lot of want. With his tip resting just at my entrance, he runs his hand up and down the length of my inner thighs causing goosebumps to chase in their wake. His thumbs brush over my clit as every nerve ending begs for more friction. For more of him.

He gives it to me. At a leisurely pace when I want fast. A press here followed by his chuckle. A rub there complemented by praise.

Pressure builds, my body riding the high of the moment.

He sinks his teeth into his bottom lip and pushes his way into me ever so slowly. I swear his groan rattles the walls, but I can't be sure because I'm too blinded by the pleasure washing over me.

He goes slow. Inch by inch. The sweet burn of my muscles adjusting and accepting him.

"You're a strong girl. I know you can take me all in," he coaxes when I reach my hands out to press on him to give me a second. And he gives me that time, but then he takes my hand pressed against his hip and moves it to where we're now joined. "Wrap your fingers around the base of me. I want you to feel me. To feel us. To guide me in until you can't take any more of my cock."

I encircle him. The hardened base. Note how I feel stretched around him. How wet I am. It's a major turn-on. Even more so is the look in his eyes as he stares at me. As he watches when he bottoms himself out in me.

I tense my muscles around him. A silent demand to give me what we both want. What we both need. What we've both waited years for.

The tendons in his neck grow taut as his hands tighten on my thighs. His restraint's being visibly tested, and I love that I'm the one doing it.

I squeeze him again and watch his eyes roll back in his head.

"Look at you." His chuckle is strained, his breath becoming labored.

"Mm-hmm. Look at me," I murmur as his eyes meet mine. "I've been a good girl, Vince, now make me yours."

Restraint snapped. Desire unleashed. Feral groan emitted.

When he begins to move, we both know there is no turning back. He drives us toward the edge, calling out my name over and over like an oath he'll forever keep.

I know there's no way in hell one night with Vince will ever be enough. I lied. To him. To me.

I lied, and I know never having him again will be the price I'll pay for it. But it's a price worth paying.

CHAPTER
eighteen

Vince

Seven Years Ago

GRAB MY JEANS OFF THE FLOOR AND PULL THEM ON. EACH BUTTON ON the fly harder than the last one to fasten. Every button done means another second closer to walking away from her again.

She deserves better.

She deserves more.

A man who can be there every night for her. A man who is worthy of her love. A man who won't disappoint her.

I pull my shirt over my head and then touch the bracelet I still wear. The piece of her I've kept with me all these years.

Four years is a long fucking time to wonder if what we had was real.

Now I know.

It was.

And as I stand here and stare at her, every reason I ran before comes back with a vengeance and then some.

I have to go.

It's for the best.

I lean over and press a kiss to her temple. It's her lips I really want—one last taste of the only real thing I've ever had in my life—but I can't risk waking her. If I do, the next steps I have to make will be even harder.

"Goodbye, Shug," I murmur against her skin and breathe her in one last time.

My throat feels like it's collapsing as I walk the few feet to the door. One last look over my shoulder at my teenage fantasy and my adult downfall.

It's her.

Hasn't it always been her?

I left before because I loved her and thought I wasn't enough for her.

I leave now because I know I love her, and I'm still not good enough for her.

"I love you. I always have."

The pain hits the second I shut the door at my back.

CHAPTER
nineteen

Vince

THE BEAT COURSES THROUGH MY VEINS. MY FINGERS MANIPULATE THE frets as I close my eyes and get lost in the only thing I've ever been able to control—music.

My fingers fly. Fast and furious. Full tones emphasized with a touch of treble. The house band switches it up, and I welcome the challenge to adjust, to improvise, and to contribute to the fucking killer music they're making.

The Viper Room is packed. It always is. But I don't feel any pressure from the audience's stares. I don't feel the heat of the stage lights beating down on me. I don't feel the burden of having to produce an album that will succeed.

It's just me. It's just my guitar. It's just an off-the-cuff invite to jump on-stage and play a little with the house band.

To remember how hungry I used to be for this feeling. For this freedom. For the lack of expectation from anonymity and the adrenaline hit when you know you're absolutely fucking killing it.

No vocals required.

No front man shit expected.

Just me and my instrument and a fuck ton of inspiration.

I open my eyes and almost expect to see Hawkin at the mic, Rocket beside me, and Giz behind me on the drums like the old days.

Like how I want them to be.

I pour my anger into my playing. I add the hurt onto it. It's the only way I know how to cope.

The only way I know how to sort through my confusion.

The only way I know how to survive.

"That was fucking awesome, man." The lead singer of the house band fist-bumps me and then pats my back. "Honor of my life to get to share the stage with you."

"I appreciate the invite."

"Normally I'd play it cool, but, dude, it's fucking you. I mean, me and the guys saw you walk in. We wanted to ask you to play with us but were so fucking nervous we had to play Rock, Paper, Scissors over who was going to do the asking." He chuckles and gives a flick of his cigarette.

"I'm glad you did. It felt good to just jam without expectations."

"Isn't that the fucking best?"

I lift my bottle of beer to my lips and peer into the crowd around us. Women are everywhere—tight tops, short skirts—making *come fuck me* eyes each time I connect with them. Then again, they are always everywhere when you live my life.

Typically, I'd pick one for the night. Use them to help chase the high performing onstage gave me. But no one piques my interest tonight.

The one I'm looking for isn't here.

"It is." Let's see how fast word spreads on the Internet. I give it twenty minutes until Xavier calls.

He won't be pissed that I did it. He'll be pissed that it wasn't his idea. That he wasn't in control of it.

And I need to leave while I can before word spreads and people flock here.

"I'm out." I shake his hand again.

"Come back any time."

I jostle my way through the crowd. In an attempt to not be a complete asshole, I stop every few feet and give a half-assed smile for someone's selfie or picture. I'm ushered to the backstage area and out the back door.

The paps are there. Fucking knew they would be. Flashes go off like fireworks in the dark alley. My sunglasses help save my eyes.

But with the flashes come the barrage of rapid-fire questions. One after another as I try to push through the crowd to get to my car.

"Vince. Over here."

"Is it true you broke up Bent?"

"When does the next single drop?"

"Did you sleep with Hawke's wife? Is that why they kicked you out of the band?"

My hands fist as I use every ounce of restraint to be on my best behavior.

"Get the fuck out of the way," I say and wave my hands at them as I struggle to get my door open against the rush.

I use my forearm to shield against more flashes as I start the car and begin to pull away.

When my cell rings, I just laugh.

"Keeping tabs on me, McMann?" I laugh out the question.

"Yeah, but I ain't McMann."

My fingers grip the steering wheel harder at the sound of my dad's voice. "Dad."

"Son," he mocks me. "Haven't heard from you in a while."

No shit. That's the plan. "Didn't know you needed to."

"Ah, I'm always up for a little one-on-one time. Me. My boy."

Throw in some insults, some demeaning comments, and it's a downright Jennings party like only he can throw.

"It's a little late for you to be up, isn't it?"

"Cancer knows no hours."

I bite back the smart-ass remark the asshole in me would love to say. "Why are you calling me?"

"Ah, did little Vinnie get his feelings hurt the last time we talked? Don't blame your old man for telling the truth. A spade is a spade."

"What'd you need, Dad?" *Don't ruin my good night. Don't start with your bullshit.*

"I was getting a little light on cash. Needed some CBD for the nausea and you know that medical grade shit is expensive."

I snort. "I pay for your insurance. I pay for your out-of-pocket expenses for treatment. I pay to keep a roof over your head. That's about the equivalent of what you did for me growing up. I don't owe you any more than that." He's not getting another dime out of me.

"Does it make you feel good to say that? To try and stick it to me?" His chuckle makes me clench my jaw. "It's no wonder your mother left you, you talentless fraud."

"I'm fulfilling my obligation to you. Nothing more. Nothing less."

"You think those people who came poking around here, the ones who are doing that story on you, would want to know what a worthless piece of shit you are for how you treat your dying dad?"

"Be my guest. I stopped fucking caring about what you thought of me a long time ago," I lie.

"Ooooh, your balls finally dropped. Took them long enough. Congratulations. Finally something I can be proud of you for."

Fuck you, Dad.

Fuck. You.

CHAPTER
twenty

Bristol

"There's my Stolie." My dad's voice booms through the phone. The nickname he's called me forever, two drawn-out syllables. "How are you? How's school? How's your asshole of a boss?"

"Good. Dad—"

"Those new pictures you sent me of Jagger? I've been showing them to everyone. Phyllis, my tennis friend, can't believe how big he's gotten. Josie. You know Josie. You met her a few years back at that barbecue we went to where the sauce wasn't sweet enough and they ran out of dessert. That was her house. Anyway, I ran into her at the store—in the produce aisle to be exact—and she thinks he's starting to look more and more like you."

It's not exactly hard for someone to think when they don't have any knowledge of who his father is to make a true comparison.

"And then I showed Randy. He caught a ten-pound rainbow trout, so he's convinced Jagger is good luck. He wants you to bring him back here sometime soon so he can go fishing with us."

I love the man to death but he's exhausting in every sense of the word. And I need him not to be right now.

"Dad. I—"

"Oh. Speaking of—"

"Dad," I bark out even louder. "I need your help."

"What's wrong?" Concern oozes through the line.

The same concern I feel as I look around the mostly empty parking lot outside of work. "It's my car." My chuckle is one of disbelief as I pinch the bridge of my nose. "I'm trying to start it and it's not turning over."

"Where are you?" he asks as if he's right down the street and not several hours away.

"Outside my apartment," I lie. The last thing he needs to know and worry about is me being alone in a parking lot at ten o'clock at night. "I know you can't do anything, but I thought maybe I could try to start it so you could listen to it. That way when I get it to the repair shop, they don't try to take advantage of me."

"Sure. Of course."

We go through the routine of me attempting to start the car so he can listen several times. "My guess is a bad alternator or starter but pop the hood. Take a picture of the battery cables to see if they're corroded. If that's the case, it's a simple fix."

"K. One sec." I go to pop the hood but it takes me a moment to find the release and even longer to find where to put the little thing that safely props the hood up. The flash of the first picture I take blinds me temporarily.

"Hey?"

I yelp at the voice at my back and turn around, instantly on the defensive. But then I see Vince the minute I register that it's his voice.

"Stolie? Are you okay? What's wrong?" my dad's voice barks.

"Yeah. Sorry. I'm fine." I turn my back on Vince and lower my voice. "AAA showed up."

"Make him show you his ID so you know he is who he says he is."

"He already did," I lie.

"Okay. Call me later and let me know the estimate. If it's too much, I can always drive down and change it for you."

My smile softens. "Thanks. Love you."

When I turn back around to face Vince, he's already leaning under the hood of my car. He's holding up the flashlight on his cell with one hand and tugging on the battery cables and tightening things I don't know the name of with the other.

"I assume it won't start? Cables look good. Maybe the alternator or starter," he mutters as he inspects everything.

"Make yourself at home," I say, with a quick glance up to the office building at his back.

"You don't write. You don't call. You ignore me at all costs." He glances my way, the grin on his face enough to stop anyone's heart, let alone mine. "And then you pretend your car is broken down in the parking lot because you're so desperate to see me, but you're not quite sure how to go about admitting it without looking weak." He winks. "It's okay, Shug. I'll play along."

Why does he have to be so charming? So amiable when it would be so much easier if he were the asshole to me that he is to many other people.

"You can't be here."

"Little too late for that," he says and turns to face me. Without pretense, he grabs his shirt by the back of the neck, pulls it off, and wipes his hands off on it.

But I'm not looking at his hands or the grease on them. Not when Vince is standing there shirtless in the moonlight. It's one thing to feel the hard lines beneath his shirt, it's another to see them.

And oh, can I see them.

The grin on his face tells me he knows exactly what he's doing.

"I'm serious. McMann is watching me like a hawk. There are cameras in this parking lot he's probably studying for all I know. Ever since the studio the other day, he knows something is up—"

"Something was most definitely *up*," he murmurs as his eyes scrape down my body.

"See that? That right there can't happen." I take a step back and scrunch my nose.

"So you don't want me to figure out what's wrong with your car?"

"No. I don't want you to stand there like that, half-naked in my work parking lot."

"I'll gladly be half-naked elsewhere. Like my hotel. Like your place." He hooks a thumb over his shoulder. "The back of my SUV over there could work too but might be a little cramped." He chuckles. "It wouldn't be the first time we made out in a car, though."

"Will you stop? Please?" The man is exasperating. And sexy. And . . ."I told you we can't do this, and I meant it."

"Shug, you can tell yourself that till you're blue in the face but give me some credit. We both know differently. Good, bad, indifferent, this thing we have doesn't seem to want to go away."

"Put your shirt on," I order, completely ignoring him.

"You weren't at the meetings today. Earlier tonight. Is this part of the *we can't do this so I'm going to ignore you* thing again?" he asks as he takes a step closer.

Keep your eyes on his.

Not his body.

Not the dark tattoo snaking up his biceps and part of his torso.

Not the happy trail that disappears just beneath the band of his jeans.

"I had my reasons," I finally say.

"Which were?"

I couldn't stop thinking about you or the way your hands felt on me. The way your lips tasted. The thought that I don't think I could ever get enough of you.

But that's just lust, Bristol. Pure, unadulterated lust fueled by one Vince Jennings, the hottest man I've ever seen.

That, and it doesn't help that it's been some time—*a very long some time*—since I've had sex. Being a single mom means Jagger comes first. It means my needs aren't always met, and while I've completely accepted that, it doesn't make them go away.

But me being horny and in a dry spell doesn't mean I have to give in to the man making my body ache with need.

Because Vince is still Vince. He'll leave. I'll be left behind. And risking my job to satisfy this itch he's created isn't worth it.

And the other day in the studio came way too close for comfort. It was a moment of weakness that I have no intention of repeating regardless of how incredibly hot he looks standing there shirtless.

I'm not just living for me anymore. Isn't that what it all comes down to?

That kind of selflessness is something Vince has no clue about.

But those are all things I can't exactly explain to him, so I settle on, "I was busy." His expression tells me he knows I'm full of shit. "I figured you'd be at the studio."

He snorts. "I'm stuck. Writer's block or whatever you want to call it. It's becoming a thing and I'm not particularly thrilled with it."

"So why are you here?"

"Had a last-minute meeting with Will and Jasmine. Needed to discuss a few things that have come up that I want and don't want to cover before we head back to Fairfield next week."

The statement intrigues me. The mention of having to go out of town next week, not so much.

"You must have a crap ton of work to do if you're still here at ten at night," he says.

"I was enjoying the silence. The incredibly fast Internet. The lack of interruptions." I shrug and know with my next statement that I'm letting him in more than I think I had previously intended to. "It's the best place to study."

"Study?" Even in the moonlight, I can see the surprise in his eyes.

"LSATs. Better late than never, right?"

"Bristol." He stares at me with a subtle shake to his head. "That's great. Congrats—well, congrats on a high score because I know you'll get one, but . . . why didn't you say anything before?"

"You don't need to know everything about me."

His chuckle rumbles through the night. "You let me stick my face between your thighs, but get offended as if I'm invading your privacy when I ask about going to law school?" He reaches out and tucks a strand of hair behind my ear. "Are we back to being *Stand-offish Bristol* again?"

I huff and he laughs. "I didn't think it mattered. In a few weeks, you'll be back to your world, and I'll stay here in mine. You knowing I'm taking the LSATs doesn't really matter in the scheme of things."

He angles his head to the side. "Why can't you study at home?"

"Why can't you call Hawkin and try to fix things with your best friend?"

"That was a subtle change of topic." His laugh is quick and his sigh is heavy.

"Nothing gets by you."

"Like you said, in a couple of weeks I'll be back to my life and you to yours and my reconciliation or lack thereof with Hawke won't matter."

"True, but you miss him. You miss them."

"That's neither here nor there." He clears his throat, cups the side of my face, and runs his thumb over my jaw. I should step back, need to, because for all I know, Xavier scans the cameras every minute, and yet for once, I give myself the grace to tilt my head into his palm. "You're exhausted. Burning the candle at both ends, huh?"

"I'm fine," I say and, as if on cue, my yawn comes.

"Let's get you home."

"I have to call AAA. My car—"

"Will be fine here for the night. I'll get it taken care of for you."

"I can handle it myself. I don't want anything from you."

Vince's eyes flash up to meet mine, the words from our past still as poignant now as they were back then. "I know you don't. But sue me for wanting to take care of it for you."

CHAPTER
twenty-one

Vince

S HE'S HOLDING SOMETHING BACK FROM ME.

Something that's happened to her. Something that has derailed her. I don't know what it is, but Bristol isn't telling me the whole truth.

And I hate it but also at the same time, I have no right to know what she isn't telling me either.

Just like you haven't said shit about your dad to anyone.

I scrub my hand through my hair and glance over to her where she's dozed off in the passenger seat.

Her head is resting on the window, her eyes are closed, and her breathing is even. The lights and shadows play across her face as I make my way to the address she typed into my phone.

There's something so right about her being here, beside me, letting me take care of her. It shouldn't be, but it *just is.*

It's her. She always felt so right. Her trust isn't something I deserve—especially after how I left things last time—but it's what I desperately want.

Should I be flirting with her? No.

Do I hope she loses her job? Fuck no.

But she's like a drug, and all I can think about is the next taste of it. *Deserved or not.*

I navigate through an older neighborhood. Apartments line the streets and the sidewalks are cracked. Trees compete with streetlights for space.

It feels generic.

Just like Bristol's car.

And not that there is anything wrong with that, because isn't that where I came from? The norm where everyone is like everyone else, all struggling to survive the day to day, all fighting to get a leg up in the world?

A place I should still be, in all honesty.

But most definitely not where she should be, though.

Guilt eats at me. It's raw and real and unfounded as I pull up to the curb, but it's there nonetheless.

What if I hadn't left last time?

What if I knew how to fix the fucked-up inside me so I could be what she deserves?

What if. What if. What if.

I shift the SUV into park, strangely hoping to have a few more moments with her, but the motion startles her awake. Her hands flail, knocking her purse off her lap so some of the contents fall onto the floor mat.

Flustered, she clambers to gather everything and shove it back in her purse. "I'm sorry. I fell asleep. I didn't mean to—"

"Bristol." She shoves another thing into her purse. "It's okay. Relax." I place my hand on her forearm to calm her down. Funny thing is, I didn't know how much I needed the connection too. Her eyes meet mine and when she smiles, the only thought I can manage is, *why is this so easy when it simply can't be?* "You're burning the candle at both ends. Don't apologize."

I climb out of the car and open her door for her. "Let me walk you up."

"No. I'm fine. Really. It's just up the stairs." She smiles and I write off her jitters for just having been startled awake.

Every part of me wants to kiss her goodnight. Wants to follow her up those stairs. Wants to feel the warmth of her body against mine. Wants to wake up next to her.

Turn it off. Shut it down. Walk away.

It's not about what's best for you when it comes to her, Jennings. It's always been about what's best for her.

Why change now?

I lean forward and brush a kiss to her cheek. "Good night, Shug. Get some sleep. Text me in the morning, and I'll make sure you get to work on time."

I expect a refusal but am greeted with a sleepy ghost of a smile and a quick nod. "Thank you. Night."

Bristol walks away with a quick look over her shoulder before she disappears between two apartments in a trove of darkness.

Conflicted over things I'm not even sure of, I stare where I last saw her for way longer than I should. It's only when I climb back in my SUV that I notice her driver's license on the passenger seat. It must have fallen out of her purse.

She looks back at me in the photo. Her hair is a little darker and her smile crooked. I'm brought back to picture days in high school and waiting to see which one of our student ID cards was worse. How she'd carry mine around in her purse and keep them long after the school year ended.

But there's something else that catches my eye. The address. It's different than where I'm parked. A quick glance at the issue date of her license says it's only a few months old. That means the address should be correct.

Curiosity has me punching the address into my GPS and heading there.

The little cottage-like apartment is two blocks over and one block down from where I dropped Bristol off. The driveway in front is empty, and the front porch has some potted flowers that spill over their edges.

Just as I pull to the curb on the opposite side of the street, a light flicks on in the front room, and Bristol moves to the windows and closes three sets of blinds.

I'm not sure if I'm hurt or impressed by her deceit. Hurt that she doesn't want me to know where she lives and impressed that she had the balls to deceive me.

The question is, as her silhouette moves about the room, why doesn't she?

It seems someone else is keeping her guard up too.

So why does that make me even more determined to tear it down?

I sit there and stare at her place long past the time the lights turn out. It's either sit here or stare at my ceiling. Insomnia is a bitch to say the least.

Those fucking what ifs come back to haunt me in the silence of my car.

My fingers begin to tap out a riff on the steering wheel.

Chords start repeating over and over in my head.

Those fucking lyrics that have eluded me week after week materialize out of nowhere.

One night. Love shined.
The taste of you stuck in my mind.
Sunrise. Goodbyes.
The words we said were total lies.

Long roads. Dead ends.
Being fine alone was all pretend.
On the road. On the stage.
To live without you I had to disengage.

You were the one, right from the start.
Because of that, I broke your heart.

I've always loved you,
But could never keep you.
You won't forgive.
And I can't forget.
You've always been my sweet regret.

I look down at the words I scribbled on the back of a receipt I had in my wallet. I read them over and over, the music to accompany them all but composing itself in my head.

I guess my muse is talking again.

Too bad I can't tell her the words she deserves to hear.

CHAPTER
twenty-two

Vince

A TRIP BACK TO FAIRFIELD WASN'T EXACTLY ON MY BUCKET LIST. ON the outskirts of the Bay Area, it's known for being close to vineyards but not having any, hot summer weather, lack of jobs, and home of one Deegan Jennings.

I'd much rather not have it claim that last fucking part.

When I left here, the only thing that ever tempted me to come back was Bristol. It's not lost on me that she was here today too as I strolled down memory lane. A lane where the only good ones were with her.

A visit to the only high school. A reunion with the school music teacher who taught me how to read music. Another to the first underground club I played in where I lied about my age so I could take the stage. A sit-down interview that ate up the rest of the fucking day.

Word got out I was there. Fucking small town. By the way people showed up, I'm sure texts were flying over where the camera crews were as the day wore on.

I didn't mind it. It's not like I'm not used to it yet. McMann fucking loved it, but attention is his thing.

The fuck all of it was that it had me looking in every single crowd, worried my dad would be there. Concerned he was going to show up drunk, make a scene, and reveal me for the imposter he says I am.

Just because he didn't show didn't mean he was immune to the rumors. The texts came. Oh how they fucking came. One after another.

Dad: Ah how cute, you're pretending to be a real rock star today.

Dad: Where can we meet up?

Dad: You know where to drop off a check.

Dad: I'm sitting here waiting.

Dad: Last. Fucking. Chance. Make it right.

Same shit. Different day.

I scrub a hand over my face, grateful to be rid of all the goddamn makeup they put on me today so I wouldn't look washed out during filming.

And more than grateful for the hour-long car ride away from that shithole town and relieved to be sitting amid the bright lights of San Francisco. The skyscraper-peppered skyline. The red of the Golden Gate Bridge lost in a haze of fog. The haunting shadow of Alcatraz in its midst.

My beer is empty.

My mind is wandering.

My body is tired.

And my sigh weighs a fucking ton when my cell rings. But when I look at the screen, I'm surprised because it's not who I think it is.

"Hawkin?"

"Hey."

Awkwardness permeates the silence.

How are you?

I fucked up.

I miss the fuck out of you.

"What can I do for you?" I ask, voice gruff, head spinning, and pride refusing to let me say the things I need to say. *Should say.*

"You good?"

"Great. Perfect. Why?"

"No reason." He clears his throat. "I was at the studio today."

"Yeah?" *Why is he telling me this?*

"Yeah. Noah played me the last track you laid down," he says, and I wince. "It's good, man. Really good."

"It's shit and you know it."

"You always were hard on yourself."

"Some things never change, huh?"

"Yeah. Guess so."

Why is it so hard to talk to the man who used to be my closest friend?

"How's Quinlan?"

Go back to your pretentious fucking wife.

My own words echo back to me, and I deserve the hesitation he gives in response. "Things are good all around."

"Good. Glad to hear." I pinch the bridge of my nose, uncertain how to swallow my pride and take that step forward.

Just fucking do it, Jennings.

I go to open my mouth, but before I can get anything out, Hawke speaks. "I've gotta get going."

"Yeah. Sure. No prob."

"Maybe I'll talk to you sometime."

"Maybe," I murmur, the silence stretching. "Hey, Hawke?"

"Yeah?"

"Thanks for the call."

"No problem."

When the connection ends, I stare at the screen for longer than I should, uncertain how I feel about the conversation other than feeling fucking reckless.

The last thing I want to do is have dinner with Xavier. The fucker is so far up my ass he can see out my belly button. I'm used to freedom, to not being managed with kid gloves, so maybe that's why I'm feeling confined.

And it's all the worse knowing he's on one side of my room and Bristol is on the other.

Fuck it.

Bristol's eyes are wide with surprise when she opens her door and finds me there.

"You're back."

She took a separate car back to the city than we did so she could stay behind and visit with her dad.

"I have been. Why, what's up?"

Over her shoulder I can see a laptop and textbooks scattered all over the bed. Her hair is pulled up in a messy bun that only serves to highlight her long neck in the off-the-shoulder sweatshirt she's wearing.

"We're going out."

"No, we're not." She steps forward and looks back and forth down the hall, no doubt for Xavier.

"Where's your sense of adventure?"

"Rooted firmly with keeping my job." She offers me a saccharine-sweet smile before trying to close the door.

I stop it with my hand and walk in after her. "You want to be a lawyer, right? Become an agent and manage talent someday?" I move in front of her so she can't avoid me. "You can study all you want, Shug, but the most valuable lessons you're going to learn will be hands-on."

"No doubt you think those hands should be on you." She rolls her eyes.

"See? You're already getting smarter." She swats at me but laughs as I catch her hand, hold on to her wrist, and start pulling her to the door.

"No. I can't."

"I'm taking you to the kind of school only I can teach."

"What are you—"

"Shh." I put my finger up to her lips and wink. "I'm about to tell your boss I'm not feeling well and am skipping dinner tonight. The last thing you want him to do is hear you kidnapping me." Her eyes widen as I lead her by the hand down the hall, passing in front of his room, to the elevator.

"Vincent Jennings," she whisper-yells . . . but only halfheartedly.

"Help!" I play as the doors shut on us. "I'm being manhandled and abducted."

"That's not even funny." She shakes her head and looks at me, cheeks flushed but smile wide. "I need my purse. I need—"

"No, you don't."

I slide a glance over to her and pat myself on the back. We're going to paint the fucking town while I spoil her rotten.

And I'm going to enjoy every fucking second of it.

I motion my finger for Bristol to do a twirl. She just gives me *the look*—every man knows what *the look* is—but when the overly attentive salesclerk leaves the dressing area to remove the discarded clothes, Bristol does just that.

Her skirt is short but classy. Her top is tight with killer cleavage and long sleeves. Her black boots are so high that all I can think about is what a hard time I'd have unzipping them since my hands would want to keep running up her thigh to her pussy.

I may have paid for the boutique to stay open and cater to Bristol, but I'm pretty damn sure that price didn't include the right to fuck her against the wall like my dick is begging me to do right now.

It doesn't mean I haven't thought about it, though. But that would require quick and quiet—me getting mine only—and after waiting seven years to have Bristol Matthews again, you best be sure I want to take my time.

But a man can dream.

Fuck, can he dream.

"That's the one," I say. Visions of peeling it off her later are already concrete fantasies in my mind.

"I don't know." She grimaces as she studies herself in the mirror. "I think it's too tight and shows too much—"

"And you look incredible in it," I say as I walk up behind her and press a kiss to the back of her exposed neck.

When I meet her eyes in the mirror, she's looking at me with an expression I'm not sure I can read but don't think I'll forget any time soon.

She gives a quick shake of her head, almost as if she's clearing whatever thoughts she's thinking, and then refocuses on her reflection. She smooths her hands down her hips and narrows her eyes in indecision.

"I'm telling you, that's my favorite."

"In case you haven't noticed, I'm not as skinny as I used to be."

Fucking society and its bullshit standards.

"I hadn't noticed."

She snorts and rolls her eyes. "Yeah, right."

My silence pulls her eyes back to meet mine. "You think I'm lying?"

"Vince . . ."

I put my hands on her shoulders and turn her to face me. She does so reluctantly, her dubious expression reminding me so much of when we were in high school. It's hard not to smile.

"When I look at you, all I see is you. Don't you get that? This body that has turned me on since I was sixteen years old. I assure you—"

"This body has changed some, though."

"So has mine. More scars. More tattoos. More—"

"*Abs.*" Another roll of her eyes that has me smiling.

I reach out and frame her face so she's forced to meet my eyes. "Your different is your beautiful, Shug. It always has been for me. It always will be for me. Don't you see that?" For the first time since I've come back, when I brush my lips over hers, she doesn't fight me and she sure as shit doesn't hide the tears welling in her eyes.

"Decided yet?" the salesperson says as she walks in the room, her heels stopping abruptly when she sees us. "I'm sorry. My apologies—"

"We'll take all of them."

"Vince—"

"She'll keep this one on. The rest can be sent to our hotel."

CHAPTER
twenty-three

Bristol

YOUR DIFFERENT IS YOUR BEAUTIFUL.

I haven't been able to get that damn comment out of my head. Not after the boutique when he took me to a salon to get my hair and makeup done. Not after dinner on a rooftop with the view of the Golden Gate Bridge. And yet, it paled in comparison to the man across from me.

"What about you, Vince? You're here now, but where will you go next? After you finish the album. Back to New York? To London?" I take a bite of food, needing to have these answers to cement the many reasons these feelings—that keep growing through all the cracks of my heart like invasive weeds in a sidewalk—need to be ignored. "Do you ever plan on settling down? Settling in?"

Vince tilts his head and stares at me. The same stare he gave me when he kissed the back of my neck earlier in a rare show of true affection. "I don't know if I'll ever settle. I'm a selfish bastard, you know that," he says with a ghost of a smile to cover up the self-deprecation. "The word home always had a bad connotation for me. A place to stay away from, so . . . who knows." He chuckles, the emotion in his eyes cleared, the wall partially back up. "Maybe in my forties. This industry moves at a lightning pace. People come and go, are forgotten and buried when the next big thing comes. I just want to take the ride as long as I can, as far as I can. Every road takes me farther away from him and the life I never plan to have."

I think it's the most honest thing he's said to me since that night he left my bedroom. And it hurts at the same time.

"What about Bent? About plans for—"

"I don't make plans for the future. It's better for me if I just don't." He reaches across the table and squeezes my hand. "Enough about me. Tonight's all about you. Too much of the world revolves around me—it seems like everyone fucking already knows everything and if they don't, the documentary will help that along." He lifts a glass of wine to his lips but stares at me over the rim. "So tell me more . . ."

"There's not much more to tell," I say, hurting, because the biggest thing in my life, the thing I talk and brag to everyone about, I can't tell him. If I did, he'd ask for a picture and he'd know immediately.

Jagger was my decision. He is my responsibility. And if there's one thing I'm learning about Vince today—and the man I had sex with seven years ago—is that he doesn't want to be trapped by anyone. He's sick of people wanting things from him. The last thing I want is for him to think I had Jagger to bind him to me. To us. To contain him and prevent him from reaching his goal—conquering the world.

So I won't burden him with this truth. He's made it clear a child is the last thing he wants. And I'm okay with that. I've more than come to terms with that.

By the same token, I don't want Jagger to believe he's not wanted. It's better to have no father at all than to know you have a father who doesn't want you.

"I'm sure there's plenty to tell about your life, Bristol. I want to hear it all."

Dinner led to selfies on the Golden Gate Bridge. Laughter and antics. So much laughter. Sundaes at Ghirardelli. And to me standing backstage at Bottom of the Hill, with a huge crowd waiting, and Vince about to take the stage unannounced.

I look at myself in the mirror across from me, my hand on my stomach, and wonder who this person is whose reflection is staring back at me.

I definitely don't look like the mom of a six-year-old . . . and dare I say it feels kind of awesome to be a little of my old self again.

And while I say that now, it's been less than twenty-four hours, and I miss Jagger ridiculously.

It doesn't help that my head's buzzing from the whirlwind of tonight, and every time I look at Vince my heart races a little faster.

"What are we doing here?" I glance up at the neon blue sign that says Bottom of the Hill and back to Vince.

"Giving you your lesson for tonight." He grins and it makes my pulse jump. He takes me by the hand and pulls me into what looks like a club once we're inside. He ushers me to a back area and then pushes me forward at the small of my back.

"This is why you brought your guitar with you." The realization dawns on me that Vince intends to play here tonight. I was curious why it was in the car when we left the hotel.

"Have guitar. Will travel." He holds it up and flashes me a smile. "I'd planned to play here all along. It was the before playing stuff we did tonight that was impromptu."

"So then what do you need me to ask—"

"Tim's the owner. He drives a hard bargain and is a stickler when it comes to his schedule and not messing with it. Ask for him and then–"

"I don't want to be a promoter, Vince. I want to be an agent."

"And being an agent is advocating for your client. I'm your client. I want to try out my new stuff tonight. I'm so unpredictable and such an asshole that if you don't give me what I want, I'm going to trash some shit up and give you even more to worry about." His shit-eating grin tells me he's joking, but the point is made. "Now what demands has your unpredictable client required you to fulfill?"

I meet his eyes and sigh, secretly excited by the rush of adrenaline racing through my veins. "Say you want to play but be announced only as a special guest and not by name. That you need to have a quick sound check."

"Yep." He looks at the time on his phone. "And they open their doors at ten so we've got to get moving."

"Okay."

He lifts his chin toward the back of the room. "He's the one with the dark blue shirt on."

I start to walk away and am yanked back without warning, met with the slow, seductive warmth of Vince's lips on mine. The butterflies in my belly flutter to life.

"I wouldn't be kissing my client," I say when he steps back and winks.

"I know but I figured we could both use some luck."

I glance over to Vince. He's standing alone on one side of the room. His head is hanging down, his hands that have been fiddling with his guitar are now idle at his sides, and one could either think he has the weight of the world on his shoulders or he's about to take on the world.

Both give him a vulnerability I haven't seen before.

My chest constricts. Instinct has me wanting to walk up to him, slide my arms around his waist, and offer him moral support. But circumstances—*our circumstances in particular*—tell me I'm not sure that would be welcome. This isn't high school. He's a grown man.

Tonight has been . . . incredible. Amazing. Once in a lifetime. The last thing I want to do is ruin it.

"Hey," I murmur, needing to do or say something.

Vince lifts his head and meets my eyes. His gaze is strong, resolute, and the soft smile and subtle nod he gives me says even more. Tonight has meant something to him too.

His hand goes to his opposing wrist, the one with the bracelet I gave him so many years ago, and he smiles. His smile lights up the room despite the sudden sense of gravity I feel from him. But the moment is fleeting as the staff swoops in and tells him it's showtime.

I'm nervous for him. The crowd is small compared to the sold-out arenas he's used to, and yet I still can't imagine willingly standing onstage and opening myself up to everyone's criticism, judgment, and let's face it, adoration.

He's announced as only a "special guest." I watch from stage right as the lights go up on him standing center stage, his head down with the hood of his sweatshirt casting shadows over his face, and his hands positioned on his acoustic guitar.

He doesn't speak. He doesn't look up. He simply starts playing.

It's slow and haunting at first. Just Vince and the acoustics. Just bated breath from the audience and chills chasing over my skin. Just his fingers and his talent and a microphone to share it.

It's one thing to watch him from the nosebleed seats in an arena. You can hear the music there and sense that he's enjoying himself.

It's another to stand a few feet from him and watch the music take over him. Own him. Soothe and possess him. Become a part of him from the posture of his body and the tendons taut in his neck.

He finishes the guitar solo, lets the note die until the silence eats the room. And with timing that has clearly been perfected, before the crowd begins to clap, Vince flings his head back, so the hoodie falls off, and kicks into Bent's most popular song.

The crowd recognizes both him and the song and goes absolutely batshit crazy. Even from where I stand behind the speakers, the roar is insane.

Vince soaks it all in, his presence dominating and a cocky smirk on his lips. He plays the chords without thought before stepping forward and singing the opening bars of the song.

The words Hawkin usually sings.

Play me. Beg me. Take me. Make me.
Be the one to make me fall.
Be the one to take it all.

It doesn't matter to the crowd, though. They're still in shock over their luck to be here tonight. Phones are out recording, live-streaming, sharing everything that is Vince Jennings.

I catch the quick glances over his shoulder as if he's looking for his band—something from years of habit. I notice the stutter of his expression on his face when he realizes his bandmate brothers aren't there. But it's slight and it's quick.

But it's there.

"How're you all doing tonight?" he asks after a few songs. He's breathless, sweaty, and by the grin on his face, loving every minute.

The crowd roars in response. He hangs his head sheepishly and laughs before looking back up at them and taking a seat on the stool that a stagehand has run out to him.

"So, I was in town for a few things and got the itch to play. My people contacted their people and asked if I could play a few songs for you tonight." He runs a hand through his hair that's already damp. "I hope you don't mind that I crashed your evening."

He doesn't even finish. The audience drowns out his words with their appreciation.

"I guess that means I'm forgiven." More cheering. "Smaller is sometimes better. *Venues.* I'm talking venues, people. Fuck, man. Get your minds out of the gutter." He laughs. It's the purest sound to me.

And it sounds just like Jagger.

The thought staggers me when it shouldn't. The guilt that I'm keeping this incredibly perfect human being from Vince even more so.

But standing here, watching him, knowing him . . . loving him, I know this is where Vince is meant to be.

This was why he left all those years ago.

He belongs to them.

Not to me.

And I was right all those years ago not to try harder to make him something he didn't want to be, no matter how much I'd love him to be.

"So, I've written some stuff for the new album."

"I love Hawkin!" a woman screams from the darkness.

Vince's smile is bittersweet, his voice a reflection of it. "I do too, sweetheart, but I have a feeling your type of love might involve knee pads and handcuffs." He holds his hands up. "To each your own."

The crowd laughs and the heckler shouts, "Damn right."

"As I was saying," he says through a chuckle. "I've written some new stuff. I wanted to try a bit of it out. See if you guys like it so I know if I'm on the right track. Do you think if I played it for you, that you could let me know if you like it?"

More riotous applause.

"Okay. Sounds good." He clears his throat as he grabs his guitar pick and then adjusts the mic. "This one uh . . . it means a lot to me. You see . . . it's about a girl . . ." Vince looks over at me. His smile softens. His eyes swim with so much emotion I don't know which to settle on. "A girl whose different is her beautiful. The song's called *Sweet Regret*."

Mistakes. Headaches.
My heart is here, it's yours to take.
Drowned out. Holding on.
Is your love for me still going strong?

Drawn lines. Mixed signs.
I walked away without a word.
Blocked calls. Punched walls.
Your silent tears I never heard.

You were the one, right from the start.
Because of that, I broke your heart.

I've always loved you,
But could never keep you.
You won't forgive.
And I can't forget.
You've always been my sweet regret.

CHAPTER
twenty-four

Bristol

SOMETHING HAS SHIFTED BETWEEN US.

I don't know if it's the song or the look he gave me afterwards or the tears I pretended not to cry, but something has shifted.

Almost a resignation of our fate.

Didn't he say as much in the song he wrote? In the lyrics he sang? In the way he came offstage, pulled me against him, and just held on as if he were saying goodbye?

It's almost as if in his lyrics, Vince put all his cards on the table and yet we both realize he still can't win the hand. There's a small victory in making the play and a quiet defeat in knowing it still isn't enough.

We don't speak on the car ride back to the hotel. Our fingers are linked and glances are shared, but no words are exchanged.

Just absent thank-yous and you're welcomes as doors are opened, as the elevator button is pushed, as we walk toward my hotel room door.

I open it without inviting him in. I don't need to. He just walks in behind me and closes the door at his back.

He knows just like I do. No matter how much either of us was going to fight this, *this undeniable draw we have toward each other*, that in the end, it's stronger than us.

I give myself the grace to stare out the window at the city beyond. I'm not going to convince myself that being with Vince is for closure, that I'll be able to walk away on my terms.

Haven't the years taught me that there are no terms when it comes to Vince? There is just the here and now. The moment to revel in. The tomorrows to forget about. The sensations to lose myself in. The feelings that I need to rein in and not let go of.

"Shug." His voice is quiet, so very different than the larger-than-life persona onstage a couple hours ago.

With my heart in my throat, I turn to face the man I've loved most of my life with the knowledge that love alone is not enough.

He reaches out and cups my face, making me feel like I'm the only one he sees. He moves closer, his eyes searching, for what I don't know.

Our faces are inches apart.

Our bodies already heated.

Our heads already imagining what the other will feel like again.

Our hearts already knowing this might break us, but we can't change what's written in the stars.

"I've thought about being with you again so many times," he whispers and brushes my lips with his. "On lonely nights." He unzips the back of my skirt. "When something reminds me of you." He pushes it down over my hips as he kisses the curve of my neck. "When I allow myself the right to miss you."

Nerves rattle through me, stealing the moment away. My insecurities have me reaching to tug my shirt down to cover the stretchmarks on my hips. To distract from the sag of my breasts. To hide the thickness of my thighs. The battle scars I attribute to motherhood.

"Shug. Look at me."

I plaster a smile on my face, but he doesn't buy it for one second. "What? I'm fine. Just nervous. I'm not the same as I used to be."

He nods almost as if admitting that he's nervous too. Almost as if he's acknowledging that there is so much riding on this moment, so much anticipation built up toward it, that he's afraid to mess it up too.

He kisses me again. Our tongues dance and lips talk through actions. And as we do, he reaches down and takes my hem from my hands before slowly lifting my shirt over my head. My bra comes next.

When I stiffen, he just shakes his head, slides his hands down my body, and lowers himself as he goes.

"You're beautiful, Bristol." He kisses my stomach. "You always have been." Another kiss to each of my hips. "You always will be." He runs his hands down to the top of the boots I'm still wearing before going back up to cup my ass. "I'd offer to turn the lights off for you." A kiss to the underside of my breast. "To make you feel more comfortable." A kiss to the other. "But I'm a selfish man." He's back at eye level with me and there is no mistaking the desire in his eyes. "I don't want to miss a single thing tonight and that includes getting to see you." He kisses me tenderly. "I bared myself to you tonight. I laid it all out there for the world to hear. For you to know. Please don't hide from me."

"Vince—"

"Let me love you, Bristol. Let me show you the only other way I know how."

I initiate the kiss this time. My hands thread through the hair at the base of his neck as the soft cotton of his shirt tickles my bare skin. We kiss like we've never kissed before. Slow and timid. Soft and searching. Like we never want it to end.

There's intimacy to it. In reveling in the calm before the storm. In enjoying the now and forgetting about tomorrow. In trying to memorize every groan and gasp and the way he tastes and how his touch feels.

I was too young to think about that last time. To try and burn the moment in my mind knowing it would be the only time. Not this time. Not now.

It's his shirt I take off.

It's his pants I unbuckle and push down now.

It's his body I admire in its incredible entirety.

I kiss my way down his torso. Lips on his chest. Down the line of his abdomen. His happy trail. The dent of his hips. And then as I lower myself to my knees, I look up at him.

His eyes grow dark, his breathing shallow, as I grab hold of his cock and slowly suck it into my mouth.

His head rolls back on his shoulders and his thighs tense, but his hand finds its way under my chin and holds it there. I look up at him with his cock still in my mouth and my entire body begs for me to go faster so I can have his touch.

"Keep going." His dick twitches in my mouth. "I want to watch you. Your lips. Your cheeks. Your hand. Your eyes. I want to memorize this moment."

I begin to work him slowly. The softest scrape of my teeth earns a hiss of pleasure. The suction of my lips garners a firmer grip on my chin so he can fuck my mouth. The lick and hum over his length gets me murmured praise.

"That's it."

"Just like that."

"Let that fucking gorgeous mouth of yours work me over."

But woven in that praise is gentleness this time. A solemnity about the moment. An unspoken understanding that just like last time, we're only getting one night.

To make amends.

To make up for lost time.

To love each other knowing there are no tomorrows.

"I need to be inside you," he whispers before helping me to my feet. He takes a moment to protect himself before sitting on the bed where I then straddle him.

I lean forward and kiss him with an edged desperation as he positions his cock, and I sink ever so slowly down onto him. Our kisses smother his moan and my gasp as I seat himself fully within me.

There's a moment when we're completely connected, when our eyes meet, and I swear to God he can see every single truth I'm hiding. That I love him. That I've only ever loved him. That I fear I'll never be able to love another like him. That I'm the mother of his child.

Time suspends.

Emotion wells in our eyes.

Then I begin to rock over him. Gentle. Slowly. Without any urgency.

Our lips meet. Our hands roam. Our skin warms. Our bodies heat with desire and longing fulfilled.

My fingers fist in his hair as my body starts to build. Layer upon layer. Brick upon brick. Emotion upon emotion.

My breaths are shallow.

My heart races.

His name is a hum on my lips as his hands help me with each rise up and grind back down over him.

"Look at me," Vince murmurs.

But I don't.

Can't.

There are tears in my eyes that I don't understand. That confuse me, but only make the pleasure more intense and the moment more poignant.

I love him with all that I am. With all that I have.

"Dammit, Shug. Look at me. I want to remember you like this. I *need* to."

The break in his voice has me meeting his eyes as our bodies move together. As my fingernails begin to dig into his biceps, and my muscles tighten around his cock. I struggle to keep them open and locked on his because the sensations are too raw, too intense, too real. Every nerve feels touched. Every ounce of blood feels invigorated. Every suck in of breath feels intoxicating.

"Eyes on me," he murmurs as his face begins to pull tight and his muscles tense against mine.

The orgasm hits me like a surging tidal wave instead of a bolt of lightning. It's a slow swell of sensation that builds and builds and builds until it hits with a ferocity that's deceptive.

I rock my hips over Vince's, wanting more friction to prolong the pleasure. To make the moment last.

"Vince." It's a breathless plea and within a beat, he has his hand on the back of my neck and is bringing his lips to mine in a hungry kiss. One packed with the same violent desire that's pulsing through me.

"I've got you, Shug. *I've got you*," he says as he holds me in place and begins to do the work for me with his own hips.

He sets a bruising pace that is just what I need to set off the ripple effect again. To prolong the downfall. To keep us in this moment for as long as possible.

And just as I begin to surge up again, just as I fall off that waterfall, Vince cries out my name in two broken syllables.

His hands are on me, pulling me against him, squeezing around me as his lips find mine again. There is no space between us. No breath of air that isn't shared. No heartbeat that isn't reciprocated against our chests.

It's just Vince.

It's just me.

It's just one last sweet regret.

CHAPTER
twenty-five

Bristol

I REACH OUT AND REST MY HAND OVER VINCE'S HEART. ITS BEAT IS STRONG and steady. Much like his presence in my life, even when he's nowhere near me.

He's on his side, arm under his head, elbow bent so the dark ink of his tattoos is stark against the crisp white of the pillowcase. His eyes are closed. A dusting of stubble is on his jaw. His expression is one of peace.

It's weird how I still see the boy in the man before me. Or maybe it's the other way around. But they're both still there. The one who ruined my heart, who filled it up with a love he doesn't know about, who it will always love.

I prop myself up on my elbow and study the dizzying array of tattoos on his arm and chest. Music notes, a guitar pick, the logo for Bent among others, but there is one in particular that I didn't notice before that has me leaning closer. It's on his left flank, written sideways, and completely out of character with the rest of them. $C_{12}H_{22}O_{11}$.

Tears burn in my eyes, the memories coming faster than I can process them, as I reach out to touch the molecular formula for *sugar* scarred into Vince.

"You're not concentrating."

"Because chemistry is boring." Vince sighs in frustration. He immediately starts tapping his fingers on the desk to that beat that only he can hear in his head.

I reach over and grab his wrist to stop him. *"Maybe so, but you need it to graduate, Vincenzo."* I draw the nickname out I've given him. The one I've taken to using because not only does it annoy him, but because it makes me feel special. Like I have an inside joke with the cute boy at school. No one else is allowed to call him that.

He rolls his eyes when I say it, but his cheeks flush pink.

"Let's face it. The minute I graduate I'm out of here. The last thing I'm ever going to need to know is molecular structures and the difference between neurons and protons."

"Neutrons."

"Same thing."

I laugh and slide another glance his way as he lowers his head to read the textbook once again. His teeth are sunk into his bottom lip, and that dark brown hair of his falls over his forehead covering the cut there that he said was from hitting an open cabinet door.

I've heard the rumors about him before I agreed to tutor him last week. A loner who doesn't care what people think. A bad boy who's quick with his tongue and his fists. The guy your mom warns you about and that a girl like me should stay away from.

We've only had two sessions, but I don't see any of that. I think he's just misunderstood. Smart but doesn't like to apply himself. Motivated but only to learn music. Here because he has to be or else his dad will lose his shit. Moody but with a crooked smile that flusters me when he graces me with it.

And hot. In that mysterious, sexy, aloof way that has me stealing glances every now and again.

He shakes his head and sighs. *"It doesn't matter how many times I read them, I'm never going to remember these. Mr. Johnson's going to fail me. I'll drop out. You'll never see me again. End of story."*

"You're not going to fail. You're not going to drop out. And if you didn't come back, I'd come looking for you."

"You would?" There's something about the way he says it that has me setting my pencil down and studying him.

"Of course, I would," I say when he just nods and averts his eyes. "Now, come on. Let's concentrate so we can get this done. The first compound you need to know is for sugar. $C_{12}H_{22}O_{11}$."

"Like that's easy." He rolls his eyes.

"Then let's try and associate it with something. Something you'll remember that—"

"Like you."

"Like me?" I laugh.

He nods and angles his head to the side as he stares at me. "You're sweet. Like sugar."

"Thanks. I think." Heat creeps up my cheeks. "The question is how exactly is me being sweet going to make you remember the compound?"

"I don't know, Shug, but I guess we better figure it out."

He tattooed my nickname on him. He wears something I gave him years ago. He carries me with him everywhere he goes. Every country he travels to. The different beds he sleeps in every night. Even with the other women he sleeps with.

He loves me in his own way but won't allow the love to be returned.

I thought I could do this. Sleep with him again. Be with him again. Enjoy him without needing closure or tomorrows or everything in between, but truth be told, I love him. I love him and it only seems to end up hurting me.

There's a reason we can't be together. Why that is, I have no clue . . . but it just is and it's time for me to accept it.

I've been chasing the impossible for eleven years. Maybe it's time to stop chasing. Maybe it's time to start figuring out how to live without him.

I lean forward and press the slightest of kisses to his lips.

I get dressed.

I gather my things.

I stand and stare at him lying in the bed, and for the first time ever, I understand why Vince left me how he did that last time. Without a word. Without a goodbye. Without closure.

It's probably best if I'm not here when he wakes up. Call me a chicken. Call my actions chickenshit. But it will save us from pretending that there might be more to this than meets the eye. From making promises we don't intend to keep. From holding each other back from the people we were meant to be.

At least I know the truth. He does love me. *But not enough.*

"I don't know if I'll ever settle. I'm a selfish bastard, you know that. People come and go, are forgotten and buried when the next big thing comes. I just want to take the ride as long as I can, as far as I can."

If only Vince realized that he's already the next big thing.

He can love me all he wants, but he said it himself.

I've always loved you,
But could never keep you.
You won't forgive.
And I can't forget.
You've always been my sweet regret.

CHAPTER
twenty-six

Vince

KNOW SHE'S GONE BEFORE I EVEN OPEN MY EYES TO LOOK.

The only trace of her is her perfume that rubbed off on me last night and her lipstick left on the wine glass next to the bed.

"Fuck." It's a groan. It's resignation. It's resistance.

I'm not sure which one I want it to be more. Nor how I feel about them as a whole.

I reach for my phone, not expecting a text from her to be there but looking anyway.

Nothing.

As if on cue, my cell rings, but it's the last person I want to talk to.

"Yep," I answer.

"Have you seen social media?" Xavier asks.

"I was busy seeing the backs of my eyelids."

"I thought you weren't feeling good last night."

Shit. I scrub a hand over my face. Screwed that lie up. "I felt better. Got a little restless and ended up at Bottom of the Hill." I yawn. "What's up?"

"That song you sang. That new material? It's going viral. Fucking apeshit. You need to lay that track down and get it released ASAP."

"Yeah. Sure. I'll talk with Sony."

"I don't think you understand, Vince. It's all over the place. I've got my people online pushing it too. It's like it's all coming together at the right time. It's fucking gold."

I sit up, the foil of a condom wrapper from last night floating off the bed. I can't drum up any more excitement than this. "Gold is good. Platinum is better."

"That might be in the cards. Look, man, you wrote that song. You spoke your words. The public is hearing them loud and clear."

"Humph," I say. By the empty bed beside me, I guess someone else heard the words loud and clear too. "Great."

I need a fucking drink already.

"You should have had Jasmine and Will there last night. Would've been great for the documentary."

Fuck the documentary.

"Apparently there's enough footage on social media already. I'm sure they'll find a way to use that."

"Agreed." He clears his throat. "So we're still on for an eleven o'clock lunch, and then we'll hop on the jet and get back. We'll discuss strategy on how to keep this momentum going during the flight."

"Sure." I'm still in a fog. "Will Bristol be at the meeting today?"

"She left about an hour ago. Commercial flight back. Something about an emergency at home. Don't worry though. We'll get her up to speed once we figure everything out. Good?"

"Good."

I end the call and toss my cell on the floor where I can't reach it.

This is what I've been working for, right? Solo success? Charting my own territory? I should be ecstatic. I should be surfing the Internet and soaking it all in.

Then why does it feel so goddamn fucking empty?

An emergency, my ass.

Walking away is something I've seemed to have mastered and mastered well.

Seems you have too, Bristol.

Tou-fucking-ché.

CHAPTER
twenty-seven

Bristol

Seven Years Ago

"YOU TRIED TO CALL HIM AGAIN?" MY MOM STARES AT ME, ARMS OVER her chest, concern etched in every damn line of her face.

She looks old. No doubt these past two weeks are the culprit enhancing that.

"I have. A ton of times. I've left messages. I've sent texts."

"He hasn't responded?"

"Kind of hard when he blocked my number."

"How do you know that?" she asks, her cup of tea growing cold in front of her.

"Because now when I text, they don't go through. When I call, it says the number isn't available." Coming to that realization didn't hurt at all or anything.

"Huh," she says. "What about his dad? You called him before—"

"No. Absolutely not. The man is a prick, and he's only going to give me the same number that's now blocked me."

"What if we called your dad to—"

"No. *Please.*" I pinch the bridge of my nose and sigh. "Dad can't know who the father is. I hate saying that because he's Dad, and I love him, but he's also Dad. The man who can't keep a secret to save his life. If I do this—"

"Then no one can know," she says quietly.

"For the baby's sake. Yes. He or she needs to know they come from a place of love, not from one of abandonment."

"This doesn't sit right with me, Bristol."

I reach across the table and grab her hands. Tears well and I blink them away. My emotions are all over the fucking place with these hormones. "I know, but this is my decision, and I need you to respect it. I confided in you because I value your opinion. I told you because I can't do this alone. I know you think I'm jumping the gun and don't know the half of it when it comes to parenting. And you're right. I don't. But neither does anyone else. Isn't that the beauty and the pain in it? All I know is that this baby was made out of a love that I've never felt with anyone else."

"You're young. You have a life ahead of you to find a love that's even better. That's even sweeter."

She doesn't understand. I saw the love between her and my father. It was subtle and understated. I know the love I felt with Vince, even at a young age. It was unrelenting and unique.

"I can't explain it. You just have to respect it."

"Vince has a right to know."

"He does." I blink away more tears and ignore the burning in my chest. The same burning that I felt when I imagined a life together with him and our child. The same damn burning that turned to utter heartbreak when he refused to call me back. When he refused to take my calls. "He's the one who has blocked my number. He's the one who gave that interview I just played for you saying he has no desire to have kids ever."

"Saying it and meaning it are two different things."

"You weren't the one the road manager humiliated when he offered to give me a thousand dollars to use as I please—okayed by Vince himself."

"You don't have to keep the baby. There's no shame in admitting you're not ready. In making a choice for you and your own future."

I close my eyes and quiet the tears. "I'm not being naïve in this. I know it'll be tough. I know it'll derail my plans for a while, but this is my decision. I'm keeping it."

CHAPTER
twenty-eight

Vince

Seven Years Ago

"DOES IT HURT BEING SO POPULAR?"

"What the fuck are you talking about?" I ask Mick, our road manager.

"Chicks calling me to get to you. To get with you. To—"

"Tell them he's a lousy fuck and that the drummer is better," Gizmo says.

I raise a middle finger at the same time I empty the rest of my beer. "You're just jealous, man."

"That girl you were with in . . . Jesus, what city was that?" Mick asks.

"Which fucking girl?" Hawke asks and chuckles.

"Shit, I think she said her name was . . . *Crystal.*"

We all burst out laughing. "The fucker calls everyone Crystal," Rocket says and then downs the rest of his beer.

"Yeah, well. *Crystal* called," Mick says, grabbing the bottle of Jack and pouring himself some.

"What fucking city was it again?" Hawkin asks. "Vince has been on a doozy of a pussy bender since . . ." He leans back and looks at me. "Since what city was it, Vin?"

Since Los Angeles. *Since Shug.* I've been trying to fuck her out of my system, so that all the women blur together, and I can try to forget her.

Call me the asshole. Call me a hell of a lot worse. Especially when I made Hawkin take my cell, block her number so it'd get lost in the fray of the hundreds I've already blocked, before erasing every goddamn trace of her from my contacts so I can't call her back.

That's what Bristol fucking Matthews does to me.

I scrub a hand over my face. "City? Fuck if I remember."

"Perfectly said, my brother," Rocket says and fist-bumps me with a laugh. "*Fuck* if you remember."

"So what did *Crystal* want?" Gizmo asks.

"For you to be her baby daddy," Mick says followed by a collective groan from all of us.

"What number is that this month?" I ask. It's becoming a fucking weekly occurrence. And since I have a *no glove, no love* policy, I'm not worried in the least.

"Five. Is that five?" Gizmo asks.

"I think it's five," Rocket answers. "Collectively. Not just for Vin. We don't want to give him a big head or anything."

"Fuck off," I say.

"That sounds like a 'please take care of it for us' if ever I've heard one," Mick says.

"Perfect." I rest my head back on the couch as the dressing room begins to spin.

"Maybe we leave all the *Crystals* alone for a few days," Hawkin says.

"Only if you leave all your *Cherrys* alone for a while," I say, referring to the name he uses collectively.

"Welcome to fame, gentlemen," Mick says, holding up his glass. "Now you know you've officially made it."

CHAPTER
twenty-nine

Bristol

"DINO NUGGETS FOR THE WIN," I MUTTER TO MYSELF, TAKING ANY victory I can while Jagger goes through his picky eater phase—and a clean plate left behind is definitely a win.

I wash the plate, put it in the drying rack, and contemplate what I want to do with my night now that Jagg is asleep and the house has been tidied up.

I *should* finish going through the rest of my current LSAT study guide.

I *should* answer all the emails I haven't gotten to yet.

I *should* text Vince . . . and say *what*? It's not like he's tried to reach out to me since I left.

But my open bottle of wine and a true crime documentary I've been wanting to see are winning out over everything.

A glass is poured and the remote is in hand when a knock comes at the door. It's not unusual to have someone knocking at the door—the cottages in my complex look the same so people often get them confused—but not at this time of night.

I tiptoe to the door and look through the peephole only to jump back. *Vince.* What the hell is he doing here? How does he know where I live? JAGGER.

My heart leaps in my throat, and I freeze momentarily as my body takes a second to catch up with my brain's thoughts of simply pretending not to be home.

Knock. Knock. Knock.

"I know you're in there, Shug. You were just standing in the window. I'm more than ready to stand here and knock all night until you answer the door."

Knock. Knock. Knock.

Ignoring him is a more than valid option, but that means he'll knock and knocking will wake Jagger, and then Vince will hear him and who knows what will happen . . .

I grab my phone that has the room monitor on it just in case he wakes, open the door, self-preservation my only thought, and step outside, closing it *and* my secret life behind me. "What are you doing here?"

I don't ask how he knows where I live. I'm truly afraid of how much digging he can do.

"Hi." His smile doesn't reach his eyes as he holds up a twelve-pack of beer, two of them already missing.

"Hi. Is everything okay?"

"That's subjective." He helps himself to a seat on the concrete like a little kid with his back against the wall and his face to the sky. "Join me?"

Our eyes hold for a beat before I take up a similar position beside him. We sit like this in silence, the crickets around us and half a moon above us.

"Your car running okay?" He finally breaks the silence.

"It is. Thank you again for helping. I wish you'd let me repay you."

"You haven't been at work," he finally says. "Everything okay?"

I nod, a motion I'm sure he can see in his periphery. "Had a few projects to do offsite. Ones I was on before you came on, that I had to finish." I take a beer he hands me and take a sip simply for something to do. "I hear congratulations are in order. The song is huge, and it hasn't even been released yet."

He shrugs and gives a noncommittal sound. "It's all relative."

A car drives by. A few dogs bark somewhere down the street. A stink bug crawls oh so slowly up the side of the stucco.

"You want to tell me why you're outside of my place at ten o'clock on a Tuesday night?"

He brings a beer to his lips and takes a long pull on it before placing the empty back in the box and grabbing another one. The pop of the cap has the stink bug freezing. "For a lot of reasons, I guess."

"Like?"

"Like why you told me you lived a few blocks away when you really live here."

My sigh is heavy. My heart even more so because something about this whole situation feels so final. Somber.

"Truth?"

"Always."

I take a sip for courage. "Because I'm embarrassed that you're you and I'm me, and this is all I have to show for it."

"Christ, Bristol. Do you think that really fucking matters to me?"

"You wanted the truth."

"I did. Doesn't mean I have to like it. But why is the question. What happened to set you back? That's what you're not telling me."

The beautiful part of you who's asleep inside, fifteen feet away. The little boy who tilts his head the same as you. The one who got his first guitar from his grandpa yesterday and spent hours pretending to play it.

"Vince . . ." *Tell him. Say it.* The words are there but the finality in his tone, the regret woven in it, have me hesitating.

"It's okay. You don't owe it to me. I understand that."

I close my eyes momentarily, uncertain if I'm relieved or upset when he doesn't press. Probably a little of both. "Thank you."

His head still against the wall, he turns to meet my eyes. "We all have secrets we don't want to tell, Shug. It's okay."

Emotion lumps in my throat. "Is one of yours why you're here?"

He shrugs and then starts playing with the label on his bottle. He looks like he has the weight of the world on his shoulders. "I've fucked up in so many ways that I don't know how to see my way out of it."

I try to piece things together, try to understand what he's talking about. "I doubt that." His chuckle is a low rumble that has my heart hurting for him. "Is this about Bent? About—"

"For one."

"You miss them."

He snorts. "Next question."

"Why not go back? If you're so miserable being alone, why not—"

"Because I fucked up. See? Told you. Story of my life, right? I can't hack it at home so I leave. I have this good gig that millions would kill to have where I get to hang with my best friends every day and do what I love with them, and I leave."

"I don't think you're being fair to yourself."

"It's like when everything is at its best for me, he comes back and I have to leave."

"Who are we talking about, Vince?"

He opens another beer and downs the entire thing in one long drink. "He's dying of cancer."

"Who?" I demand, freaked out and confused.

"*My dad.*"

"Oh." It's all I can think to say as I consider how to react. I don't know how to feel about a man I've vilified for almost fifteen years. "I'm sorry," I murmur.

"I'm not." His words scream in the silence. His chuckle that follows mocks it. "That makes me a heartless bastard, doesn't it? The fucker's dying, and I feel absolutely nothing inside over it."

I reach out and link my fingers with his, wanting to show support. "It makes you human, Vince."

"It makes me weak. He always had a way of doing that to me. Making me weak. Tearing me down just when I thought I'd made something of myself or figured my shit out. Letting me know how little he thought of me. How little the world thought of me."

"I understand why you might think it looks that way, but—"

"No wonder I need to stand on a stage and have thousands scream at me to feel a thing." He runs a hand through his hair and sets his head back again to look at the sky. "He broke me in a way that I don't think can ever be fixed. I've tried. Over and over, but it's just no use."

"You're not broken, Vince."

"Humph."

His words eat at me. They weave into my soul. They explain things I've only ever assumed and never knew for certain.

"You never talked about him. I never knew or I would have . . . helped. I don't know." I shake my head. "I don't know what I could have done. But from what I could see, I don't think you owe your dad much at all. I'm sorry he's dying of cancer—no one, regardless of the life they lived, deserves that—but

I'm mostly sorry he hasn't loved you like a father should. Dads are supposed to love and support their kids. They're supposed to pick them up and dust them off when they're hurt. They're supposed to be a pillar of strength, not a barbed wire fence holding you back."

"That night? The window? That's why I had to leave. I couldn't do it anymore. I feared what he had turned me into. That I'd snap and either become him or do something I could never take back."

"Vince."

"The irony is now I've spent years doing things I can't take back. Fucking up. Proving him right." He flexes and unflexes his hand.

"I disagree. You've—"

"And now I'm desperate to prove him fucking wrong before he dies so I can give him the ultimate fuck you. So I can win. How sick is that? What kind of person does that make me?"

"A real one." *A broken one.*

I rest my head on his shoulder and try to process all these things he's throwing at me, that he's been holding in, and I still don't know how to help him. I don't know if I can.

He presses a kiss to the top of my head and just leaves his mouth there, his thoughts so heavy I can practically feel them. "Do you ever wonder what could have been?" he murmurs.

"In regard to?" I ask when I already know the answer. The same question I've asked myself a million times, not just for myself but for the little boy tucked in his bed inside.

"Us."

My exhale is even, my thoughts measured. "I did. For a long time. Then I didn't."

"Why'd you stop?"

Because I had to. Because you didn't give me a choice. "Because we're two different people now. We live vastly different lives."

"But despite that, there's still something there. There's still something between us that we keep coming back to somehow."

"The chemistry sure. But when the lust fades, when it's not years in between that we'd see each other, but rather minute to minute or hour to hour, I'm not sure that there'd be much left of us." I have to believe that. If I don't then I'm left with hope for something that will never be.

"Is that why you left me in San Francisco?"

It's my turn to look at the sky. To try and find any star that hasn't been drowned out by the city lights. "It seems we're better at walking away from each other than we are at actually being together."

"Well, at least I can claim to be good at something, huh?" His laugh falls flat though.

"Still doesn't make it hurt any less."

He nods, his lips pursed. "Then why did you let it happen at all? You could have shut your hotel room door, stuck to your guns about McMann, and I would've had to suffice with my hand and my fucking misery."

I smile at the image he paints, and it softens at the memory of us together. Giving and taking. Loving and letting go.

"I didn't let it happen," I finally say.

"Uh. I was there. I'm pretty sure it wasn't just me."

"That's not what I meant. It was inevitable, right? *It was us.*"

"You say that like it's a bad thing."

"We're like a match, Vince. We start out hot, almost violent in our need for each other, before burning completely out. The other night, *we struck the match.*"

"And now?"

"Now, there's just smoke." I shrug.

"But where there's smoke, there's fire."

"And where there is fire, things get destroyed. Devastated. Become unrecognizable of what their former self was."

"Hey."

I turn to look at him, really look at him for the first time in this conversation. "Hmm?"

He reaches out and runs the back of his hand down my cheek. Rubs his thumb over my bottom lip. Settles his hand on the curve of my neck so his thumb can idly move back and forth over my collarbone.

"What are you saying, Shug?"

You wear a bracelet I gave you, but you wouldn't take my calls.

You permanently marked yourself with a tattoo of my nickname, but you never thought it was enough to tell me.

You look at me with love in your eyes, but it's been over ten years since you spoke the words.

You love me from afar, but don't think you can love me in person.

I reach up and cup the side of his face. Feel the coarseness of his stubble under my palm. Take in the heat of his breath on my skin. "I love you, Vince, but we can't keep doing this. I deserve more than a piece of you every couple of years. No one's to blame. Not you. Not me. It's just the way we were probably meant to be."

I lean forward and kiss him. I pour all the love I have for him into this simple connection as tears slide down my cheeks.

We rest our foreheads against each other's almost as if we're trying to let this "new reality of us" settle in. Almost as if it's something we knew all along but now have to face.

And when I lean back to look at him one last time, the lone tear that escapes and slides down his cheek devastates me.

"I lied," he murmurs.

Jagger flashes through my mind. *So have I.* "About?"

"About needing the stage to make me feel." He clears his throat. "You make me feel complete too." He drops his eyes for a beat before looking back at me. "But it's not enough, is it?"

"No." It hurts to get the single syllable out. He nods subtly as I stand, our fingers still linked. "Your different is your beautiful too, Vince. It always has been. It always will be."

With that, I turn and go into the house.

I shut the door.

I lock it.

I let the dust particles settle back down in the darkness.

And then I slide down it, crumple on the floor, and cry until I can't cry anymore.

I'm not sure what time it is when I go to bed, but when I peek out the window, Vince is still sitting there. Still staring at the stars. Still looking as broken as ever.

CHAPTER
thirty

Vince

THE HOLDING CELL IS BRIGHT AND THE CONSTANT CLANG OF THINGS and chatter of people is enough to make a drunk man sober.

Oh.

Wait.

Never fucking mind.

I've been here forever the fuck long and the room is still moving.

Maybe because it's easier to stay drunk. Simpler to live in the haze than to feel like my chest has been pried open and my heart ripped out for shits and giggles.

"That bad, huh, man?" my cellmate says from where he's rolling around on his cot, unable to sit still.

"Fuck off," I mutter.

"Ha. Sounds like a woman to me."

"Sounds like mind your own fucking business to me."

"Chill, man. I was just making small talk."

I grunt and roll onto my back, my forearm over my eyes, replaying the events of tonight. Morning. Who the hell knows what it is because I lost track of time.

Bristol. Her porch. Her words. Her kiss goodbye.

A bar. O'Hallahan's, I think was the name. I don't remember. Minding my own business. An asshole. Then another asshole who wouldn't leave me alone. Then that fucking prick who shoved me because I didn't want to take a goddamn picture with him.

Bad fucking idea.

Or maybe not. At least in here, I can't hurt anybody else.

The damage is done.

Done and fucking over with.

I should have tried harder years ago. I should have never listened to Cathy. And as I sit in this hellhole, all I can do is replay the fucking conversation from six years ago over and over again. The conversation that convinced me to forget about Bristol for good.

"Hello?"

"Shug?"

"I'm sorry you have the wrong number." Something sounds off with her voice.

"Bristol. It's me."

The woman laughs. *"Hi, it's me. This is Bristol's mom, Cathy."*

"Cathy. It's Vince. How are you? It's been years."

There's a long, measured pause. *"It has."*

"I was looking for Bristol."

"I figured since you called her phone." She chuckles but there's something in the sound of it that has me sitting a little straighter. *"How'd you get her number?"*

I snort and run a hand through my hair. *"It's a long story."* Like how I spent hours scrolling through all my blocked numbers trying to find it to no avail. Then breaking down and calling Fairfield High School alumni committee to track down someone who might know it. *"Is she there? Is it possible for me to talk to her?"*

"She's sleeping right now. Pulling double duty at the moment."

Double duty? *"Everything all right?"*

"Mm-hmm."

"Then what is it?"

"Vince." A sigh that doesn't sound good. *"You know I think the world of you, but I think it's for the best if you forget this number."*

"I don't understand—"

"I think you do." She pauses and the silence eats up the distance. *"Waiting a lifetime for someone to love you back is not a happy and healthy way to live."*

"Cathy . . ."

"Yes, I know. You love her. In your own special way. But your love is looking backward to the past instead of looking forward to the future. She deserves the forward, Vince."

"I don't know what to say."

You're right.

You're wrong.

I wish I could, but I can't.

"You're a good man, but at some point, you have to get off the roller coaster." She sniffles, and I swear to God the sound hurts just as much as her words do because she's right. All of it.

She's fucking right.

I can't love Bristol the way she deserves to be loved. Isn't that why I walked away in the first place? Isn't that why I'm not putting up a fight right now?

"Why are you telling me this?"

"I'm the one who has to help her pick up the pieces. After she sees you. After she catches you on the TV. After she hears you on the radio. After . . . after this last time."

Can't blame her. You blocked her fucking number. You cut her off because you couldn't deal with wanting a woman you couldn't have. For loving a woman who deserved more. For doing exactly what her mom is saying you're doing.

"If you love her, the way I think you do, then you need to let her go."

"Jennings? You're sprung."

"Fuck," I groan as I sit up. My head feels like Gizmo is using it for a kick-drum. It should be a crime for them to take your sunglasses in here.

"Lucky you," my cellmate says.

"Eat shit."

"You first, you grumpy fuck."

I shuffle out of the hallway, take the bag of my belongings they hold out to me, and do a double take when I walk into the waiting room and see Hawkin standing there.

What the fuck?

My expression must say as much because he says, "Were you that drunk that you don't remember calling me to bail your sorry ass out?"

I scrunch up my nose and give a shake to my head. *I did?*

"I take that as a yes." He chuckles. "Even you can't talk your way out of those guys pressing charges."

"I don't remember much."

"You did a number on them." He points to my hands and sure enough, they're bruised and bloody.

A chair breaking comes back to me. The crunch of my fist connecting with a nose.

"The fuckers were asking for—"

"Save it for outside. You don't want whatever it is you're going to say posted all over the fucking place." He puts a hand on my back and pushes me forward. "Bail's paid. Let's go."

"Wait." I scrub a hand over my face. "There's something I need to do first."

"Like what? Kiss your cellmate goodbye?" he jokes.

"More like post the fucker's bail."

"Fine. Go ahead. I'll wait. But just a warning. You're going to want to put those sunglasses on and pull that hat down or be prepared to say cheese when we walk out the doors. Word's already out."

CHAPTER
thirty-one

Vince

I CROSS MY ANKLES IN THE BED OF THE TRUCK AND LEAN AGAINST THE cab at our backs. It's that time of morning before the sun rises when the sky and the ocean are the same damn color, and you don't know where one ends and the other begins. The seagulls' squawking is ridiculously loud. Errant cars come in the lot every couple of minutes. They park and surfers get out, coffees in hand, wetsuits on the ready, and shoot the shit like they belong to some club I sure as fuck don't want to be a part of.

"Do you want to talk about it?" Hawkin finally asks. He picks up the bottle cap from his beer and tosses it into the case beyond our feet.

"Nah. Not really."

"Classic Jennings response. Good to see that hasn't changed."

"You're the one who kidnapped me and is refusing to take me back to my place."

"*Kidnapped?*" He shakes his head. "How about *saved your ass* when I shouldn't have?"

"Semantics."

"There are videos, Vin. From the bar. From your arrest. Leaving the station. That fancy new PR company you hired is going to need to do a lot of cleanup."

"Or not. I'm an asshole. Isn't that common knowledge by now?"

"I'm not taking the bait. Last time I did, I lost my best friend." He pauses, his words hitting me as hard as that fucker did at the bar. "If you want to talk, then I'll listen. If you want to tell me to shut the fuck up . . . then say it."

I blow out a sigh. "I don't know what I want anymore."

"Fair enough." He pops the top off a beer and hands it to me. "Hair of the dog and all that."

After a long, hard stare, I shake my head. "Nah. I'm pretty sure I consumed my fair share last night."

"Point taken."

Another car pulls into the lot a few spaces down. Their music is loud and their engine sounds like shit. I watch the guy driving lean over and kiss the girl in the passenger seat.

My stomach twists.

Last night—the part of it before the bar—replays in my head. Her tears. The break in her voice. The hurt in her eyes.

You did that to her.

Forgiving myself isn't an option.

"Talk to me about Bristol."

I whip my head in his direction, but he just stares at the ocean beyond like this is an everyday conversation we have.

"What about her?"

"You mentioned her when you called me last night."

"And what did I say?"

He chuckles and it feels like sandpaper in my eardrums. "You tell me."

"Jesus, Hawke. Really?"

He turns his head and studies me. "Why are you trying so hard to fuck shit up for yourself?"

A smart-ass quip is on my tongue, but I let it die. It seems I've done enough damage to the people I love in my life. The problem is, I'm sitting at the bottom of a well and have no goddamn clue how to climb out of it. I don't know how to do life solo. I don't know how to go through life feeling so untethered. I've taken her with me everywhere for over a decade, but I'm not sure I can do that anymore.

And Bristol's words keep coming back to me.

"I love you, Vince, but we can't keep doing this. I deserve more than a piece of you every couple of years. No one's to blame. Not you. Not me. It's just the way we were probably meant to be. Your different is your beautiful too, Vince. It always has been. It always will be."

And then her mom's, which is strange considering I haven't thought about that conversation in years.

"I'm the one who has to help her pick up the pieces. After she sees you . . . if you love her, the way I think you do, then you need to let her go."

Why I try so hard to fuck shit up is what Hawke wants to know, though. So, I answer him with honesty.

"Seems I'm good at it."

"Or it's a convenient excuse. Beats having to face what you're most scared of—people caring about you." When I go to refute him, he just holds up his hand to stop me. "I don't want to hear it. You pushed me away. You've always pushed her away. The question is why."

"I'm dealing with a lot of shit."

"Alone. When you don't have to."

I nod. My bruised hands are easier to look at than my best friend. *I'm lucky I didn't break any fucking bones. If I had, that would've royally screwed up my ability to play guitar for some time.* "There are just some things I need to do. Need to prove to myself that I can do."

"I can respect that. But then what, Vin? What'll you have to come back to if you set fire and burn the world around you?"

I'm not pushing you away.

I'm protecting everyone from me.

"No response needed." He pounds a fist on the side of the truck. "This conversation is way too touchy-feely for this goddamn early in the morning. Before I've had my coffee." He points to my cell that keeps buzzing against the truck bed, text after text from McMann. "You better call that prick back or he's going to blow a gasket."

"Might be more entertaining to watch if he does."

CHAPTER
thirty-two

Bristol

"SEE?" SIMONE POINTS TO THE YOUTUBE LIVE FEED ON HER COMPUTER screen. "You give that hot stud no action, and he goes and gets himself in a bar fight and arrested because of all his sexual frustration from pining after you."

I roll my eyes, hoping that I'm able to pull it off enough for her to believe me. I'd give anything to be able to tell her the truth. To have someone else to confide in and get advice from. But telling Simone is hitting too close to home when it comes to work and my security there.

"Your lack of response is telling me I'm right."

"Yes, you're a mind reader. Vince got in a fight because of me." I roll my eyes and then glance again at her computer screen. The live feed on her screen shows the press room at McMann Media. The camera faces a table at the front of the room and from the angle, you can see the heads of reporters as they wait patiently for the press conference to start.

"You know McMann is creaming his pants right now. He can marry

Vince's heartfelt apology and work it in so that while the world is watching, announce when the single will be released. There's nothing he loves more than a crisis so he can step in and use his big-dick energy to pretend he saved the day."

"Hmm."

"There's a reason he sent you to Burbank with me today. With you off-site and Kevin on vacation, no one can steal any credit away from him."

It's sad that she's one hundred percent right, but I'm more than happy to have trekked across town today. The last thing I needed today was to face Vince.

Not after last night.

Not after second-guessing and then knowing I did the right thing. *No matter how much it hurts.*

Not after the guilt I feel knowing our conversation was most likely the catalyst behind it.

I've seen the images circling the Internet. The crazed look on his face. The unfettered anger. The utter despair.

I did that to him.

I pushed him to act out.

I hurt the man I love.

I attempt to focus back on our work at hand, but to be honest, concentration is hard to come by with how little sleep I had. Especially with the constant reliving of everything we said to each other. It's not like I had time to get it off my chest and tell my mom any of it in our hi-bye exchange when she showed up and I ran out the door. Besides, it's not like I can tell her with Jagger standing there.

"Do you think with Vince leaving, that McMann will keep your status in no-man's land between a junior associate and an associate? Or will he pull you fully into one role or the other?"

"I'm sorry—what do you mean *Vince leaving?*"

"Clearly you haven't read your emails yet today."

"No. I was running late. Then the traffic was brutal." I shake my head. And I've possibly been avoiding any and all things that deal with him. "What did it say?"

"Short version? Vince told McMann he was heading back to New York. Something about wanting to work with a producer there. It was all last minute. Decided this morning. Maybe some jail time gave him an epiphany."

She laughs. "But there was a big scramble to coordinate appearances and a press junket so they could launch the single as soon as Sony Music okays it. I mean—"

"Ladies and gentlemen," Xavier says as he steps up to the table with Vince. They both take a seat.

Vince looks rough. Tired. His smile is there for the cameras, but it rings empty to someone like me who knows him.

"I'd climb that man like a tree and ride him so hard all his fruit would shake off. Damn," she murmurs.

"Thanks for the visual," I say, unable to take my eyes off Vince. It's hard to watch the person you hurt, hurting.

Brutal, really.

"Any time."

"Thanks for coming today," Xavier says. "As per McMann Media's policy, whenever an issue arises with one of our clients, we like to address the situation immediately to stop a torrent of misinformation from spreading like wildfire across the Internet. We have so many exciting things on the horizon for Vince, and we don't want any of this nonsense to distract from them." He looks at Vince beside him, and Vince smiles and nods as if he's in agreement.

But he looks about as happy to be there as someone who is getting their wisdom teeth pulled. *Without Novocain.*

"With that said, I'd like to introduce you to Ms. Paula Gladstone."

A woman in a burgundy pantsuit takes a seat beside them and smiles at the press in front of her. "Good afternoon. I'm Paula Gladstone with Gladstone and Associates, the firm representing Mr. Jennings in what we hope will be a matter settled sooner rather than later. Last night, Mr. Jennings was trying to enjoy some peace and quiet in a local establishment when several patrons began badgering him. For conversation. For autographs. For photos. He obliged their requests for a few moments, but then, when he asked them to respect his space and privacy, things were blown out of proportion and taken offense to, as sometimes happens when alcohol is involved. The actions of all involved resulted in Mr. Jennings having to defend himself against three other men. All participants were charged with disorderly conduct and disorderly intoxication. In hopes to capitalize on the situation, the other participants have brought assault charges against Mr. Jennings. Seeing as Vince was merely defending himself, we are anticipating these charges to be dropped in the coming days." Paula looks toward McMann and nods before stepping down without taking any questions.

McMann takes the moment to smile and make sure he's front and center to the camera. A small murmur begins to ripple among the press corps. It's slight but you can hear shuffling and see heads moving as they all look down at what one could assume is their phones.

Simone looks at me. She notices it too.

"As is natural these days, when someone steps into the spotlight, they attract attention—good and bad. And with that spotlight shining bright on Vince with the viral explosion of his soon-to-be released new single, *Sweet Regret*, that is exactly what this is." Xavier gives a curt nod as more muted noise comes from the media. "We'll open the floor up to a few questions, but time is limited as we're expected on a flight to New York shortly."

There is jostling of reporters as Vince's name is called out. One voice rings loud and clear over the others and catches McMann's attention. He points to the reporter standing.

"Vince. Gil Litman with TMZ here." Vince smiles. "Bar fights. Acting out. Getting drunk and taking whatever it is out on unsuspecting patrons . . . what kind of message does that give to those who look up to you? To the little kids who want to be like you?"

Vince's eyes lower for a beat, and he gives a slight nod in resignation. "There's no excuse for what I did," he says, toeing the company line all of us at McMann have heard time and again and could repeat by heart. Clearly Vince got the same lesson we all have. "Fighting's never the option. It's—"

"But what about what you're going to tell your own kid?" Gil persists.

Vince's laugh is low and condescending. Flippant. "I don't have a kid so the question is irrelevant."

There is another murmur of restlessness along the press that has me sitting a little straighter. They all shout for attention again, their questions getting lost in the noise.

"Let me have a follow up on that then," Gil says, stepping forward to try and win whatever points he's trying to make. "Per the article that just broke in *US Weekly*, you do in fact have a child. Would you like to comment on that?"

Vince's laugh is sarcastic and drowned out by the pounding of my pulse in my ears and Simone's dramatic whistle.

"Anything to fabricate a story." Vince rises from his seat. "We're done here."

"Your father gave an exclusive. About you. About your son you've been hiding from the world that you refuse to claim as your own. Would you like to be the first to comment?"

I'm a mix of emotions, and the one riding shotgun is confusion. What in the hell is going on?

"You're fucking crazy," Vince mutters and begins to move off the stage riser.

"Or you're bullshitting us, which is exactly what your dad said you'd do."

"The man's a money-grubbing asshole who probably got paid for his lies, so don't put too much faith in his claims."

"That's enough, Vince," McMann says, losing control of the narrative and the spectacle that this is becoming. I battle between wanting to search on my phone and not wanting to miss a single minute of what's transpiring on the computer screen.

"Read for yourself." Gil holds out his phone as Vince's feet stop. "His name's Jagger."

The world drops out from under my feet.

No.

I struggle to breathe.

No.

To think.

God, no.

To force myself to look at Vince and his cocky, disbelieving smile at the reporter like he's going to prove him wrong with the same punch he threw last night. "Jagger, huh?"

Gil doesn't miss a beat. But my heart does. It misses every single one as the reporter looks Vince straight in the eyes and says, "Yes, Jagger Matthews."

CHAPTER
thirty-three

Vince

ALL THE AIR IS SUCKED OUT OF THE ROOM.

My lungs feel like they're collapsing.

My heart feels like it stops.

My head feels like it implodes.

"You're lying," I say, the whisper on my lips but a scream in my head.

Jagger Matthews.

I struggle to process. To think straight. To refute what a part of me feels to be undeniably true.

The urge to knock the phone from Gil's hand is strong. The impulse to grab it and read every goddamn lie that my fucking father said just as strong.

McMann grabs me before I can do either and ushers me out of the room as the reporters go apeshit at my back.

It's just white noise.

It's just white lights ahead.

It's just an unbelievable pressure in my chest that increases with each and every second.

"Vince."

"No. Don't touch me." I throw my arms up to push Xavier's off me. "I just . . . I need to go. I've got to go . . ."

See if I have a son?

See if Bristol has been lying to me?

See if my father is right?

"I just have to go."

CHAPTER
thirty-four

Bristol

TEARS THREATEN BUT DON'T COME.

My chest burns but is forced to breathe, each inhale hurting more than the one before.

My hands grip the steering wheel as traffic closes me in much like the claustrophobia I feel right now.

The phone rings over my Bluetooth. Again and again. The electronic voice Vince uses for a message speaks. "Vince. I need you to call me. Please. We need to talk."

I dial the next person I need to speak with. The phone rings. Over and over as my knuckles turn white. "Pick up the phone, Mom. Pick up. Pick up. Pick up."

"This is Cathy. Please leave a message."

"Mom. Please call me. It's urgent. He knows about Jagger. *He. Knows.*" My voice breaks.

And it feels like everything else within me does too.

I dial Vince again.

CHAPTER
thirty-five

Vince

THE WRONG ADDRESS.

Not inviting me in.

The setbacks in going to law school.

Minutes. Moments. Seconds. Each one I've spent with her need to be dissected and reconsidered and mind-fucked to death, but the only things my mind can focus on right now is getting to her house.

Is finding out the truth for myself.

Is knowing if Jagger is real or not.

Is plowing a fist through my old man's face.

I pull up to the curb, yank my SUV into park, and then realize the kid might not even be here. Her work. His school. A babysitter. Who the fuck knows.

But I jog up the sidewalk anyway, knowing that if I have a son, he's here.

But how is it even possible? We used a condom each and every time that night. There's no way this is possible.

Can't be.

I pound on the door. One fist after another.

"What is the prob . . . *lem*," Cathy says when she opens the door to find me there.

Her eyes are wide. Her lips are lax. And the last conversation we ever had comes zooming back in a way that makes more sense than ever before.

She knows that I know.

"Vince." My name is a whisper that I don't hear as I shove past her and into the small apartment.

But all my gusto, all my reasons why this isn't real, how he cannot be mine, goes to shit when I see the little boy sitting on the couch. *He's so little.* His head is down, a mop of dark hair falling over his forehead as he focuses on a small acoustic guitar braced across his lap. He makes out-of-tune noises as his small fingers try to operate the fret and strings on the face of it.

He angles his head to the side and purses his lips in concentration, much like I've seen in hundreds of photographs taken of myself.

Words escape me.

My head shakes back and forth as I'm frozen in place staring at something I told myself I'd never allow to happen.

Everything else disappears when that little face looks up and sees me there. I'm met with my own eyes looking back at me. With a crooked smile that's the mirror image of mine smiling in return.

The wind is knocked out of me.

Every image I've seen of myself as a kid is sitting across from me, staring at me with a curiosity in his expression and an innocence in his eyes.

"Hey. Who are you?" he asks in a raspy voice.

"I . . ." I glance over to where Cathy stands, tears welling in her eyes, before she smiles as if to tell me it's okay to talk. "I—I'm a friend of your mom's."

"Huh." He angles his head to the side and takes me in, his eyes lingering on my tattoos, making me feel self-conscious about them when I never have been before. "How do you know her?"

"From a long time ago. We've known each other longer than we haven't."

"What's that mean?"

"Nothing. Just that . . . we've known each other a long time." I smooth my palms down my jeans, needing something, anything to do with my hands. It doesn't stop them from trembling. "Do you mind if I sit down?"

He gives the subtlest of nods, his eyes never leaving mine. "You kind of look like that singer we see on TV, doesn't he, Nana?" He looks at Cathy. "The one that makes Momma sometimes get tears in her eyes."

"Kind of," Cathy murmurs, her hand resting over her heart, her smile concerned yet hopeful.

"Are you him?" he asks.

"Maybe," I whisper and finally find the courage to move farther into the room so I can sit across from him.

"Then does that mean you know how to play this?" He lifts the guitar. "My papa bought it for me. It has some scratches but he says scratches give it character. Momma's saving up for lessons for me but I'm trying anyway."

My throat burns with emotion. "I do know how to, yes. Maybe I could teach you sometime if your mom and dad don't mind."

His smile falls. "Just Momma."

"Oh?" The sound gets caught in my throat.

"My dadda loves me more than the world, but he wasn't ready to handle all this awesomeness," Jagger says, with a sheepish but bittersweet smile on his face. "Maybe someday."

I open my mouth, but words don't come. I'm still overwhelmed with such violent contrasts of emotions. Disbelief married with shock. Hurt with anger. Awe warring against skepticism.

"A huge amount of awesomeness," I say, my voice breaking. "How old are you?"

I ask but already know the answer. *He's six.* The empty restaurant. The limo ride. The hotel. The walking away without looking back. Her voice-mails that I erased because it was too hard to listen to them, and her calls I then blocked.

"Six. It's a good age, don't you think?"

I laugh, and for the first time I feel like when I inhale, oxygen reaches my lungs. "It is definitely a good age."

"How old are you?"

"Thirty."

"That's old." His eyes grow wide as he catches himself. "Sorry, Nan. It's not old."

She laughs, and it's like the sound eases some of the tension in the room. But the barbed wire that's wrapped around every goddamn sensation inside me remains.

"I think someone really wants to get ahold of you," he says, pointing to my pocket where my phone buzzes incessantly.

"Oh well. I don't want to talk to them." I toss my phone, and it lands with a thud on the floor.

He giggles, and I'm not sure if it's the best or the worst thing I've ever heard. Best because . . . *Jesus*. Worst because he's six, and it's the first time I'm hearing it.

"I'm Jagger," he says and holds out his hand. "It's nice to meet you."

I reach out and take his hand. It's tiny and mine engulfs it . . . but his touch. It's knowing he's really real that has me choking over my own name. "Vince." I offer a smile but am not sure if I manage to pull one off. "So nice to finally meet you too."

I hold on to that little hand, the weight of the moment crushing, as I stare at this little human and struggle with comprehending what and who I'm looking at.

My son.

The son I've never known about . . . *because Bristol believes I'm unworthy of knowing.*

"Maybe someday." No, she never would have told me.

I'm just the fuck-up.

The useless piece of shit.

A worthless, talentless hack.

His words ring true, don't they?

Over and over again, they run laps through my head.

And now I know that all along, Bristol has felt the same way.

I may have blocked her before, prevented her from reaching me, but she's had weeks to tell me now.

But why tell me about a son when she wants nothing from me?

The panic attack hits me out of nowhere.

Head dizzy. Mouth dry. Heart beating a million miles a minute.

"Mom? Jagger?" Bristol's shouts are heard seconds before the front door bangs open. A choked sob comes from her throat, and then she sees me. Tears stain her cheeks and her eyes beg me, for what? I'm not certain. "Vince." Measured. Apologetic. Terrified.

I rise from my seat as I struggle to breathe, and my vision begins to tunnel. The awe of Jagger diminished by Bristol's betrayal. By the panic clawing its way up my throat.

I should say goodbye to him.

I should promise to teach him how to play the guitar.

I should hold on tight to him and not let go.

Instead, I offer him a smile, even though it wars with the chaos inside me.

I pick up my phone and walk the short distance to the front door, every part of me rioting against the other.

"Vince." This time it's a strangled, desperate cry of my name as Bristol reaches out and grabs my arm.

"Don't." I grit the warning out, but it's enough that when I meet her eyes, she gives the subtlest of nods before releasing it and stepping back.

I stare at her. At the only person I've ever truly loved and, for the first time in my life, I know what true heartbreak feels like.

Because she just shattered my heart.

CHAPTER
thirty-six

Bristol

J AGGER SITS CURLED UP IN A BALL, HIS HEAD ON A PILLOW IN MY LAP, fast asleep. I play absently with his hair, unable to take my eyes off him, and wonder when he's older if he's going to hate me for the decisions I've made.

"You can go, Mom. I'm fine," I murmur for what feels like the hundredth time. A part of me needs her to go so I can process everything while the other part of me is terrified to face all of this on my own.

"I'm not going anywhere. Besides, even if I wanted to, I don't think I'd be able to leave. It's a parking lot out there with all those damn camera people camped out front." She looks over her shoulder as if she can see them through all the closed blinds. "It's amazing how fast they found out where you live."

"Welcome to the Internet, Mom."

"But how? They were here within an hour."

"Everyone's willing to be paid for information these days. Case in point, Deegan fucking Jennings." I lean my head back and close my eyes. I've reread the article, his exclusive interview, so many times I can see it in my mind. It was a desperate attempt by a mentally sick and terminally ill man to land one last blow on a son who finally told him to fuck off. A son who should have done as much years and years ago.

"I always hated that man."

"Agreed, but I have no one to be mad at but myself."

"Your father never should have—"

"Shouldn't have what? Showed off pictures of his grandson for bragging rights? How was he to know Deegan was standing behind him at the bar or that when Deegan caught a glimpse of Jagger's picture, he immediately saw Vince as a kid in him? There's no way Dad could have known that Deegan remembered the year I called him, desperate for Vince's cell, only because it was the night of his thirtieth high school reunion. That he heard Dad say Jagger's age and then calculated backward to how long it had been since then to see if the numbers lined up? That's a lot of dots to connect that Dad could never have known would happen. That Dad could never have thought someone would use to hurt me or Jagger. Dad may not be your favorite person, but you and I both know, he'd never purposely try to hurt us."

She nods, firmly put in her place, even though that wasn't my intention. I'm just frustrated and desperate to talk to Vince, to try and explain to him, but when I call him, it goes straight to voicemail.

"What if he won't talk to me?" I finally murmur, my biggest fear coming to light.

Scratch that, I think my biggest fear would be Vince meeting Jagg and never wanting to see him again.

I can say I'd understand if he did, but that would be a lie.

"You need to give him time to digest everything."

"Digest? I broke up with him for good, told him I loved him but still needed to end things, and then the next day he finds out I've been lying to him all along about the biggest thing in our lives. I'm thinking there needs to be a stronger word than digest here."

She nods but there is something bugging her that she's not telling me.

"What is it, Mom?"

"I told him not to call you." She stares at her hands rather than meeting my eyes.

"What are you talking about?"

She forces a swallow. "He called you. You had just had Jagger. You were exhausted and heartbroken and had finally fallen asleep, so I grabbed the phone and answered it so it wouldn't wake you. It was him."

My heart lodges like a ball of hurt in my throat. "Mom . . . look at me."

"I was sick of seeing you hurt." Tears well in her eyes as her fingers fidget and shoulders shrug. "Please forgive me, but I couldn't handle him getting your hopes up again just to crush you again." She hiccups over a sob. "I told him that if he couldn't love you the way you deserved to be loved, then he needed to let you go so that you'd stop living just to wait for him." I hang my head as her words hit me like a one-two punch. "I'm sorry, baby."

I stare at Jagger through blurred tears. At my sweet boy. At my whole damn world. Will I have to ask him for the same forgiveness someday? Will I want him to accept my apologies for the mistakes I made with his best interest in mind?

Perspectives change when you have a child.

I understand that now.

"It's okay, Mom." I'm going to sit on this one for a long time, but in the end, it changes nothing.

I pick up the phone to call Vince again.

I need to.

I have to.

It's the only connection I have to him right now besides the little boy in my lap.

His voicemail picks up. I rehearse all the things I need to say to him in my head and hope I get the chance to.

How I'm sorry his father sold him out to the highest bidder.

How I'm sorry I betrayed him, but felt it was done with the right reasons.

How I'm just so sorry . . .

CHAPTER
thirty-seven

Vince

DRIVE.

Hour after hour.

Mile after mile.

I drive to clear my head. To process my thoughts. To wrap my head around what Bristol did and around Jagger as a whole.

I have a son.

I've sworn up and down that I would never have a child and then, when I saw him for the first time, something felt like it broke in me.

My resolve?

The choke hold on my anger?

Everything I've held on to for so long that's held me back?

Fuck if I know.

I have a son.

I can't get him out of my head. His little fingers trying to hold the guitar.

His huge green eyes looking at me. His smile. His laugh. The truths he told about his dad.

Are you ready to handle all his awesomeness, Vin? Are you man enough to?

My eyes blur as I sit in my car with a scalding cup of coffee and debate my fucking life. My fucking choices. And I finally turn on my phone.

It dings instantly. Constantly. Missed calls. Missed texts. I'm not exactly sure I'm ready to deal with any of them yet.

As if on cue, it rings in my hand, and it's probably the only person in the world I can talk to right now.

"Hey."

"You doing okay?" Hawkin asks. "And don't come back with your *what do you think* crap. I'm serious. You just had a shitload land in your lap. Talk to me, brother."

I sigh and appreciate that he lets it sit there without pushing me. "Did you read the article?"

"I did. You?"

"I've been a little busy processing the fallout of it all to get a chance to read more than the headlines and quotes people were texting me."

"You want to know?"

If I trust anyone to give it to me straight, it's Hawkin. The man I pushed away. The friend I refused to let see me hurting. The brother who is still on the other end of the line anyway. "Yeah."

"It's a desperate attempt by a piece of shit to have control over you one last time before he dies. And I'm assuming that last part—the dying part—you already knew about."

"Yeah. For about a year."

"So about the time you walked away from us."

"I told you I've fucked up a lot of shit. I don't need a lecture—"

"No lecture, Vin, I'm just trying to put the pieces together so I can help you the best way possible."

"Thanks." The word is barely audible.

"He tries to paint you in a bad light—the famous son who has cut off his dying father—but his slimy greed comes through. Hell, the writer even says cashed checks proved that you've paid for all his treatment—which for the record, is more than I'd do for that fucker—but I digress."

"I know."

"He slams you for not being successful on your own. Sounds like a real fucking douchebag, to be honest. Clearly the asshole hasn't checked social media lately because you can't watch anything without hearing that fucking bridge from *Sweet Regret* on it . . . so *fuck him*."

"*Fuck him.*"

"The gist is, it was a total fluke that he learned about your son. Reading between the lines says that he figured if you weren't going to give him the cash he wanted, then he'd sell you out to the tabloid to get it himself. What does he care about the fallout? He's dying, right? So yeah, *fuck him*."

"Fuck him."

"Nothing's changed about him, Vin. It never has. And because small men hurt others to feel bigger, he's making one last charge to turn your world upside down simply because his rotted soul can. He's going to be gone and in hell and you're going to be hurt . . . so my question is this. Is your world still spinning, or are you already trying to steady your feet?"

"I'm all over the fucking place, man."

He's quiet for a few seconds. "Jagger, huh?"

The name alone has me closing my eyes and seeing him sitting there. "Yeah," I all but whisper, this territory completely uncharted.

"Cool name. It's almost like someone knew you were a Stones fan," he says with a knowing tone.

The notion that Bristol gave him a piece of me, the singer's name from the first music I ever learned to play on my guitar, even without telling me isn't lost on me.

"I met him yesterday." I can barely get the words out. Not because I fight them but because it's still so overwhelming.

"You want to talk about it?"

"I'm still trying to wrap my head around it."

"That's typical when blindsided."

I grunt.

"Want my two cents?"

"Yeah. I do." I can practically see the shock on his face from me saying that.

"You've got to stop running, man. I can name three reasons why right off the top of my head."

"Of course, you can."

"The band. Bristol. Jagger. And not in that particular order."

I laugh. It's the first time I've cracked a smile in a while. "Fuck, man."

"I can't make you fight, hell, I can't even make you *want* to fight, but I can tell you that those three things just might make you a better man than the kick-ass one I already know you to be."

This, coming from the man I used as a verbal punching bag months ago. Who I left high and dry mid-recording on an album. Who I walked away from because of my own fucked-up head. "Point taken."

"Hey, Vin?"

"Yeah?"

"One last thing. Wouldn't the ultimate fuck you to your dad be you becoming the exact opposite type of father he was to you? To prove you're nothing like that piece of shit?"

CHAPTER
thirty-eight

Vince

"I KNOW I'M THE LAST ONE YOU WANT TO HEAR FROM RIGHT NOW. I get it," Cathy says, "but I don't know who else to call with experience who can tell me how to handle this."

"Handle what?" I ask, my own feelings like a tornado spinning inside of me.

"They're everywhere."

"Who's everywhere?"

"Photographers. Paparazzi. Whatever you call them. They're camped out on the lawn. Sitting in the trees across the street. Trying to peek through the blinds. Even going through our trash for Christ's sake. Anything to try and get that first picture of Jagg and cash in. I know he's not your responsibility, but he's terrified. How do I make them go away?"

He's terrified.

Those two damn words replay in my head as I haul ass to Bristol's place. I have no plan in place. Hell, I haven't even sorted out my feelings and sure as shit don't feel like talking to her yet, but I have eight years of experience dealing with this kind of chaos. It's nothing a six-year-old should have to deal with.

I'll get them out of there.

I'll protect them from it somehow.

Then I'll figure out what the fuck I'm going to do about . . . *everything*.

Her street is chaos when I drive down it. Cars are parked on every free inch of curb and occupy every space in the apartment lots. Photographers, some I recognize by sight now since I've been in LA so long, mill around in what are considered the public places. The ones who have taken up residence on lawns have paid the residents for access no doubt. Their lenses are long and monstrous. Their appetites for invading and disrupting people's lives is shameless. Their drive for the first exclusive shot, tenacious.

I pull up to the front of her place and park in the only spot I can find—the middle of the street. By the time the paparazzi register who I am and scramble to run after me with their shouts and flashes, I'm already pounding on the front door, shoulders rounded, head down.

The minute I hear the door unlock, I open the door, step inside, and shut it at my back. But the noise is still there, muted, but riotous.

Cathy stands in the center of the family room, her eyes solemn, her expression somber. "I begged her to call you," she whispers. "She didn't think she had any right to ask for help, but I told her maybe you could tell her how to sneak out of here. How to avoid them. I didn't mean for you to have to come here. To face her and . . . *him* again before you were ready to."

I nod as I notice things this time. The half-built Lego set in the corner. Jagger's artwork framed on the wall behind the small dining room table—a display of a proud parent. A stack of books on the end table. Framed photos of Bristol and Jagger over the years scattered on surfaces around the place.

I'm drawn to them. To memories I don't have a right to but want to see anyway. Jagger a few months old with a dark shock of hair and a gummy smile. Bristol holding Jagger at the beach as he tries to shove a handful of sand into his mouth. The two of them on a dock together where it's clear Bristol is trying to teach him how to fish. One after another. Bits and pieces of a life being lived.

When I look up, Cathy is gone and Bristol is standing there. "Hi." She clears her throat while I just stare at her, seeing her in a different light.

As the woman I loved.

As the woman who kept secrets from me.

As the mother of my son.

And I wonder how that last one comes into play now. Will it be the thing to bring us together or will the hurt her decision caused be what tears us apart?

That's what I'm struggling to comprehend.

"Is he okay?" I ask.

She gives me a halfhearted smile but doesn't answer the question. Protecting her son from the outside world and *from me.*

Fuck, man. I don't know how that makes me feel.

"You didn't have to come," she says quietly. "You could have told me what you thought was best over the phone."

I nod and take a few steps toward her. "He didn't ask for this. He doesn't deserve this. The least I can do is help him with the mess I made for him."

Tears well in her eyes. "Thank you."

I clear my throat and resist the urge to go to her. To find comfort in the only woman I've ever looked to for it.

"We need to talk about ... *everything,*" she says.

Another nod because it's easier than talking. "Not now. Not yet. I'm struggling with what to say ... and how to feel about you."

I think punching her in the stomach would have hurt less than the words I just said, but she takes it on the chin. "I know."

"Pack a bag for a few days," I say as a plan forms in my head. One triggered by the pictures I just looked at. "Till everything dies down some at least. Call McMann. Ask for some time off—"

"No need to. He fired me this morning for fraternizing with a client," she says quietly.

"Christ." I feel helpless. The fucker fired her because of me. Fired her because of something she didn't do. "I'm sorry. I'll talk to him. I'll leave the agency so there's no conflict of interest. I'll—"

"Right now, all I care about is getting Jagger out of here. He's my only priority."

"Okay." That word feels so utterly inadequate.

"I'll go pack." She turns and goes down the short hallway. A part of me wants to follow her, to see where Jagger sleeps, to run a hand over his things, while another part of me questions how I can even think that.

I turn back to the photos, reaching out instinctively to touch them as if I want to insert myself into the memory.

"It wasn't an easy decision for her. You need to know that."

"I'm sure it wasn't," I say to Cathy but don't turn to face her.

"She tried for months to get ahold of you. Your road manager tried to pay her off after you blocked her. She was certain of two things. That she was keeping the baby and that he was made out of love."

Tears burn and threaten. I clear my throat. "That was the past, Cathy. I can't change that. But I've been here for weeks now. Weeks where Bristol and I've spent time together and she still opted not to tell me. I had a right to know."

"You did. I told her as much. And then she showed me a few interviews you gave. *Rolling Stone* was the one I remember the most. You talked about—"

"Fatherhood." *Fuck.* "I said something about how I'd rather be sterile than ever take a chance at being a father."

That's on you, Jennings. One hundred percent on you.

When I face Cathy, lines of concern and worry are etched in her expression. *Did my mom ever care enough about me to have that look on her face?*

"Has it been hard for her?" I ask the question, needing to hear the answer I already know. Needing to be punished for being who I am. For saying the things I said. For being such a chickenshit about how I felt about her that I blocked her number. That I caused this.

She nods. "She put her dreams on hold for a new dream she never expected to have happen yet. She refuses monetary help. She . . . you know how stubborn she can be."

"You worry about her."

"Every day." She smiles softly. "She burns the candle at both ends all the time. She doesn't want to give up on her dream so she can prove to Jagger that it doesn't matter how old you are, you can still accomplish it. At the same time, she feels guilty for missing so much time with him because of work, that she tries to be super mom in all other aspects. I wouldn't be a good momma if I didn't worry."

"I'm going to take them away for a couple of days. Then what? I don't know. You're welcome to come. I know if you stay here that you'll be harassed too."

"I'll be fine. You three need this time to . . . do whatever it is that you decide to do." She looks down at my hands where I'm holding a picture of Jagger. I didn't even realize I picked it up. "You're a good man, Vincent. Your parents don't make you who you are, but sometimes they can make you think you are who you aren't."

Shuffling down the hall has my complete attention, and when I look, I swear to fucking God, my heart balls up in my chest.

"Excuse the boots," Bristol says as Jagger clomps his way down the hall in a pair of oversized cowboy boots. "We're going through this is my favorite phase."

"Hi," Jagger says, waving the hand of his that's not holding his mom's. "Cool boots, dude."

He looks down at them and then back at me from where he's hiding partially behind Bristol's hip. "Momma says we're going on a little trip with you."

"Just for a few days." I squat so I'm down on his level.

"She said I can't bring my guitar. It's too big."

"There are guitars where we're going. Maybe I can give you that lesson you wanted."

He nods, his teeth in his bottom lip, and steps out a little farther. "Mmkay."

"How are we going to get through all of that?" Bristol asks and lifts her chin, meaning the paparazzi.

"I bet you like to play hide and seek, don't you?" I ask Jagger and get a nod in response. He smiles and it takes me a second to find my voice. "I bet you're good at it."

"Momma can never find me."

"So that means you're really good. So here's what's going to happen. We have to go outside to the car, but all of those people are out there."

"They're scary."

"They are. That's why we're going to play hide and seek." I look around the room and spot a blanket on the couch. "I'm going to carry you out to the car while you hide under this blanket so no one can see you."

"Do you think it will work?" he asks.

"I know it will. But while you're under there, I want you to plug your ears because it's going to get really loud for a few seconds. Can you do that for me?"

He nods as Cathy grabs the blanket for us.

"You ready?" I ask as I pick him up without thinking. But the minute he's in my arms, legs wrapped around my waist, hands clasped together at the back of my neck, I freeze. The enormity of who I am holding hits me. He looks at me, fluttered lashes and rosy cheeks, and I struggle to breathe.

My son.

"Blanket?" I ask, my voice breaking on the syllables, as I turn my face from his so he doesn't see the tears in my eyes. But Bristol does. She just holds my gaze, a well of emotion in her eyes that I don't have time to unravel.

But I know one thing—I'll never forget the look in her eyes or the expression on her face for as long as I live.

Jagger giggles as Cathy puts the blanket over his head, and he rests his head on my shoulder, his arms holding tighter.

"Cover your ears, buddy," Cathy says as she rubs a hand over his blanket clad back.

"Ready?" I ask Bristol. When I see her nod, I open the door and step out into the chaotic abyss. Shouts, requests, and flashes rain down on us as I push through them to get to the SUV. Instinct has me reaching back for Bristol's hand to make sure she's okay.

We fight our way to the SUV. To open the door. To get both Jagger and Bristol in the back seat before I make my way to the driver's side.

I know once I start driving that some will give chase. I know others have already called coworkers to tell them we're on the move.

All questions are ignored. I just keep my head down until I have the car started and am pulling out of the neighborhood.

"Good job, Jenzo," Bristol says, ruffling his hair after she makes sure his seatbelt is fastened.

"Jenzo?" I ask.

Her eyes meet mine in the rearview mirror. "Jagger Enzo Matthews."

Vincent.

Vincenzo.

Enzo.

Jagger Enzo.

Another piece of me she gave our son. *Something else I may have never known.*

CHAPTER
thirty-nine

Bristol

THE REFLECTION OF THE SUN OFF THE LAKE CAUSES PRISMS TO DANCE all over the kitchen.

Sun kisses.

Isn't that what Jagger called them yesterday when he sat here and tried to count them before erupting into a fit of giggles when I shifted and one landed squarely on my face?

Memories.

We're making memories here. The kind of memories that come when you're removed from your everyday norm and have the chance to be mindful of every minute of your time. Memories that Jagger is no worse for wear from but that feel so very bittersweet to me since I'm on the outside looking in.

It's been three days since we left my house, hopped on a private plane, and arrived here at Lake Chelan in Washington.

Vince's house here is overwhelming in size. A huge great room is the main focal point and from it, halls branch out on either side with every room a wall of windows so as not to miss the lake's crystal-blue water. It's a mixture of modern and minimalist that somehow fits together.

Then there's the property itself with its massive lawn, a sizeable pool, and a deck out over the water.

Add to that it's completely private with a gated entrance and state-of-the-art security system . . . and so far, no paparazzi sitting in trees with telephoto lenses.

The privacy and space have given me nothing but time to think. It doesn't help that Simone's texts are still coming fast and furious. About me holding out on her when it came to Vince. About what utter bullshit it is that McMann fired me. About everything I kept secret from her.

But at least I can now confide in her, even if it's just to know that someone else is there for me in this time of absolute chaos.

I'm out of a job. Isn't that what I feared happening all along? And now that it really has, there's not much I can do from where I'm sitting, hiding out in the Washington wilderness.

So I've had to put my job hunt on the backburner—the worry, the anger, the confusion—because all that matters right now is making sure that Jagger is okay. That he thinks this little vacation is simply that—a trip with Mommy's new friend, instead of an escape from all the crazy people who were at our house.

And I've yet to even be able to explain that to him. But I need to figure it out because no doubt the question will come again.

In the meantime, Jagger is having the time of his life. He's never had a yard this large to roam free around, to stage imaginary battles on, and a pool to swim in whenever he wants.

For him this is heaven. He gets me without work or school. He gets the outdoors and some freedom. And he gets to play with his newfound friend.

And that newfound friend of Jagger's, Vince, has caused nothing but complete and utter misery for me.

Not because of what he has done, but more because of what he hasn't—which is essentially disregard me unless he *has* to interact with me.

Three days is a long time to live with the silent treatment. To try and act like everything is normal for your six-year-old, while hoping your next interaction with Vince will be the catalyst to finally open the lines of communication.

Because we do need to talk. Correction, *I need* to talk. To explain. To justify my reasons and everything else in between. This waiting is killing me, and the few times I've caught Vince looking at me, hurt radiates like an aura around him.

The studio on the second floor is where he goes when he's not spending time with Jagger. When he's there, avoiding me, a mixture of sounds will escape the open windows and float down to us where we sit in the yard. But it's the lyrics I can't make out, and they are what I want to hear the most. I have a feeling they might be my only window into what Vince is feeling inside.

A *sun kiss* hits my face again, much like yesterday, and snaps me from my thoughts and back to the matter at hand—getting the snacks Jagger requested for our picnic.

With hands full, I head back outside to where he's building a Lego set at an outdoor table. But when I turn the corner, my feet stop working and my heart flips in my chest. Vince and Jagger are sitting side by side on the outdoor wicker couch with matching acoustic guitars resting across their laps.

Vince is patiently explaining hand positioning and helping put Jagger's little hands in the right place.

"Like this," Vince says and plays a few chords. Jagger looks down and tries the same, then makes a sound when he can't get it right. "Don't get frustrated. There are a lot of moving parts. I'm here to help you."

Jagger looks up at Vince, at his dad, and the absolute trust in his eyes, his unjaded innocence, has tears welling in my eyes.

"Come here. Let me show you." Vince sets down his guitar, and then picks up Jagger and moves him onto his lap. From there, he wraps his arms around Jagger's arms and hands so he can help him.

Even from here, I can see that Vince is doing all the work as a few chords are played, but the gasped shock and grin of pride on Jagger's face owns every part of my soul.

And if that didn't get me in the feels, after they're done, when Vince sets Jagger back beside him and asks him to play with him—and they both hold their heads at the same angle and purse their lips in the same way— that would have.

What I'd do to have a photo of this. To be able to capture this moment and put it in a frame to place among all the others I have at home.

But I don't want to move and chance ruining the moment. Nor do I think I'd be able to walk away and risk seeing it with my own eyes.

As they play, as Jagger looks down, concentrating like I've never seen him concentrate before, Vince happens to look up and meet my stare.

There are a host of emotions in his eyes—all of which would be conjecture for me to guess. But one thing is clear, my decisions have robbed much from both the men in my life that I love.

Time.

Memories.

Moments.

Mentorship.

Love.

The question is, if I had to do it all over again, would I have done it differently knowing what I know now?

I don't know.

I just don't know.

CHAPTER
forty

Bristol

I HEAD TOWARD JAGGER'S ROOM, UNCERTAIN WHAT THE SOUND I JUST heard was. Did he have a bad dream? Did he have to go potty but is scared of the boogeyman under the bed who might grab his feet when he jumps down?

He's in this big, unfamiliar house with different shadows and creaks than he's used to. It's normal for any kid to be a little skittish at that.

But when I reach his room, see his door ajar, and peek in, I find Vince there. He's sitting on the edge of the bed, hand on Jagger's back and eyes fixed there.

How many times had I dreamt to have a moment like this? To see Vince with our son? To watch them interact? To realize what mirror images they are of each other and be a little jealous of it at the same time?

To see the love he has for our son even if he can't or won't acknowledge it himself?

Oh, Vince. What are you thinking? What are you feeling? Please talk to

me. Please yell at me. Please do whatever you have to do—write a song telling
me what a piece of shit I am—just to get it all out so we can start somewhere and
figure out the next foot forward.

I take a step backward to leave him be, but my movement must catch
his attention. He looks up to me before rising and heading out of the room.
I stand there, hoping maybe this will be the time to talk to him. The time
for healing to start somehow.

But he closes the door softly and says, "I'm going to work in the studio."

"Vince . . ." His name is a plea, but it's met with a dead stare before he
turns on his heels and heads down the hall to his studio without another
word.

I scramble after him and follow him into the studio, blocking the door
with my hand when he shuts it as if I'm not there. "You have to talk to me at
some point. You have to—"

"I don't have to do shit," he says as he starts messing with the small
soundboard he has in there, his back to me, his ability to ignore me frustrating as fucking hell.

"Yes. You do," I say and glance over my shoulder to the open door, worried about Jagger hearing this. "At some point, we need to get it all out."

"You want to fight?" he shouts and then stalks over to the door and shuts
it soundly. "*Let's fucking fight.* You're in a soundproof studio, Bristol. Jagger
can't hear us, so let's get it all out. Maybe it'll make you feel better, but I think
it'll take a long fucking time for me to get there."

"We *have* to talk. We have a son together—"

"You're goddamn right we do," he thunders as he turns on me and gets
in my face. "*We* have a son." The words are gritted out. The tendons in his
neck taut. The hurt he feels almost palpable. "A son you neglected to tell me
about, so don't you tell me what we do or don't have to do because you lost
every right the minute you fucking lied to me."

"I didn't lie to you."

"Uh-huh. Not telling me is the same in my book."

"But I tried. I fucking tried. I called you. I texted you. And I called you
again and again. You're the one who blocked me. You're the one who checked
out—"

"Because it hurt too goddamn much, Bristol. Don't you get that?" He
hangs his head and shakes it. The pain in those words rips into me. "It hurt

so fucking much to see you, to get a fucking taste of what could have been, and to know I couldn't have it."

"That's on you, Vincent. Not on me. You're the one who walked away every fucking time. *Not me.*"

"So it's my fault?" He throws his arms out and chuckles. "You want to blame me? Blame me. You want to hate me? Hate me. But don't throw stones in fucking glass houses if you don't like picking up shattered pieces of glass that you helped break. You made decisions that had everything to do with me, so don't act like you fucking didn't."

"You're right. I did." I step into him, my finger jabbing him in the chest. "And I'd do the same damn fucking thing again if I had to. I'd pick Jagger over you every day of every week because he's there. *He's mine.* And no one can ever take him from me." I turn my back to him and walk to the window. I meet his eyes through the reflection, my own courage not strong enough to say these next words to him face-to-face. "He was the only part of you I had left, Vince. The only part of the only man I've ever loved who didn't think he was enough to love me himself." My voice breaks and the first tears fall, but I don't care. All I care about is the years of hurt and worry and second-guessing finally being over.

"And in doing so you took decisions away from me. Instead, you gave my son the same fucking fate as my mom handed me. You left him to feel like he wasn't worthy enough to be loved. Like I'd abandoned him. Like his—"

"Don't you fucking dare," I shout, turning in a flash. His accusation staggers me and stuns me. How did I not think of this? How did I not look through Vince's eyes and see the correlation he would make? "That little boy has been loved every second of every minute of every day. He deserves nothing less, so I tried to give him everything I could to make up for the decisions I made. Don't you dare accuse me of not giving him enough love."

I say the words, but the images of the past few days flash back and gut me. Jagger and Vince on their guitars. Jagger wrestling with Vince on the grass. Jagger falling asleep on Vince's chest as they watch action movies together.

Guilt. It fucking owns every part of me and makes me fight even harder to prove that I was enough for Jagg. That I didn't deprive him of his needs because of my fear and selfishness.

"You asked me what derailed my dreams? My plans? It was that love for him. I never left his side. I tried to be both parents and then some, so stop breaking the glass too unless you want to bring the whole goddamn house down."

I can't breathe. I can't think. My chest hurts as I mentally own my mistakes and shortcomings. As I acknowledge the things I deprived them both of.

Vince just stares at me with hollow eyes. All I want to do is hug him. To fight him. To rebel against this history of ours that has done this to us.

"I asked you what set you back, Bristol. I opened the fucking door so wide for you to tell me that it broke off its hinges. Christ, at your house, on the porch, I told you I knew you were holding something back. Why couldn't you have trusted me then?"

"I nearly did. I was this fucking close," I say and hold my thumb and forefinger an inch apart. "But you know what you said to me?"

He shakes his head. Still so angry. "Nothing that justifies your excuses."

"You said, 'It's okay. You don't owe it to me. I understand that.'" I close my eyes momentarily but not before I see his shoulders fall and his jaw clench.

"So that's why you didn't tell me? Because I gave you fucking permission not to? You're impossible to fucking love, you know that?" he says.

"Me?" I startle. "You're the selfish prick who can't acknowledge—"

"Selfish?" He lets out a growl that echoes off the walls of the studio. "You're so full of shit. So wrapped up in excuses you can't see straight."

"Excuse me for being just like you then . . ."

He stands a foot away from me, with that muscle pulsing in his jaw, his hair a fucking mess, his eyes glaring at me, and everything I've ever wanted just within reach.

One second stretches to five.

And on the sixth one, we strike the match and willingly welcome the flames.

CHAPTER
forty-one

Vince

MY LIPS CRASH OVER HERS.

Taking what *I* want.

Taking what *we* need. The time since we last touched feels like years rather than weeks. Weeks of wanting a woman, knowing no other will satisfy me. Hours of thinking what it would feel like to have her again.

Our kiss is hungry. Desperate. Winner takes all. And fuck if it's not exactly like I feel right now. I'm so sick of wanting her but hating her. Of loving her but resenting her. Of missing her but being confused by everything that comes with *us*.

Just fucking us.

I let my needs take over. I allow the anger to drown out my head. I permit my body to use the feel of her to get lost in the moment.

And Jesus, does she feel good.

The taste of her tongue. The smell of her skin. The heat of her body. I'm desperate for more of her. Of this. Of not thinking.

Everything about her makes me feel out of control. My emotions. My reactions. What happens next.

It feels so damn good to fist my hand in her hair and gently tug her head back. Her lips are swollen. Her chest is heaving. Her cheeks are pink. "You think you can come into my studio? Fight with me? And then fuck me?"

Defiance is in her smile and desire owns her eyes. "Isn't that the best kind?"

My balls ache at her words. At her challenge. At getting the chance to fucking do this again. Do her again. "This doesn't solve anything."

"No?"

"No," I murmur with the shake of my head and a lick of my tongue up the side of her neck. She tastes like salt and sex, and I'm fucking here for it. "Fucking you. Pleasuring you," I whisper into her ear. "Doesn't fix a goddamn thing except for fucking up my head more than it already is."

Except for only making me want you even more.

Her throat bobs with her swallow, but the ghost of a smile remains on her lips. I take my free hand and slide it beneath her waistband. The absence of panties is a welcome surprise, but it's the strip of tight curls that tickle my fingers and the slickness just below it that has me emitting a tortured groan. She widens her legs without me having to ask and grants me access to the heaven between.

"I want you, Vince," she murmurs, her lips inches from mine. "I never stop wanting you. Even when we're fighting, even when we're apart, even when you hate me, I never stop wanting you."

Her words do things to my insides. Overwhelm me. Fuel me.

I crash my mouth back to hers as my finger tucks inside her warm, wet heat. My tongue slides in and out of her mouth much like my fingers do in her pussy. I take and take and take from her until we can't breathe and her hips are bucking forward into my hand.

Enough fucking foreplay.

Enough fucking waiting.

I break off the damn kiss and hold her eyes. "We're going to get undressed, Shug, and then you're going to get on your hands and knees like the good girl you are so that I can admire your ass."

I release her hair and with our eyes still on one another's, we both undress. Shirts overhead. Pants shoved down. And then she lowers herself to her knees and looks over her shoulder at me, as she props herself up on her hands.

Jesus fucking Christ.

The sight of her here like this. Ass up. Thighs glistening from her arousal. Pussy just waiting for me to pound.

I don't think I've ever been this hard in my life. Or this desperate.

"That's my girl," I murmur as I drop to my own knees, grab the globes of her ass with both hands, and then dip down to stick my tongue in her pussy. Her yelp fills the room and her taste owns my senses.

I bury my nose between her thighs and lap up everything she gives me. With the guidance of my hand, I press her hips back and forth so she's fucking my face. Her scent. Her taste. The feel of her. It's a goddamn high like no other.

Well, except for one.

And I'm about to take that right now.

"You like that?" I murmur as I bite her ass playfully. "You like knowing you can own me like that with your taste? That you can drive me fucking crazy?"

"I was so close to coming." Her words are breathless, strained, and fuck if they don't all but undo me.

"Mmm." I run my hand from her neck down her spine and then pat her pussy hard enough that she quivers in response.

Talk about a beautiful sight. All that slick, pink flesh reacting like that.

"I want to be inside of you when you come, Shug. I want to feel you. I want to see you. I want to own you."

She moans as I trace my fingers ever so gently around her opening. And with lips and chin and nose wet and smelling like her addictive scent, I rear back up, jacket myself with a condom, and push my way into her.

Fucking hell.

This woman.

She's going to be my goddamn downfall and my only fucking salvation.

I hold her still by her hips as I revel in the feel of her. In her wetness coating my balls. In the sensations slowly beginning to build when I haven't even started yet.

I look down. At her ass. At the inch or so of my cock unable to fit inside her. At the stretch of her skin around me, accepting me, and then fighting to keep me in as I slide out for the first time.

Bristol pushes back onto me, little pulses back and forth of her body so my head can hit whatever spot within she needs.

It feels like heaven.

She feels like heaven.

"God, you're beautiful like this. I love the way you do that." She moans as I grind into her slowly. "It's never felt like this before. Never," I say and then lean forward to press my lips to her shoulder. The motion pushes me even farther into her and earns a panted plea of my name. I chuckle against her shoulder as I close my hand around the front of her throat like a necklace. "You take my dick so goddamn well, you know that? So fucking well." I nip then suck on the curve of her neck.

And when I raise back up, lightheaded and body burning with need, I know I can't hold back anymore. I've stalled long enough that the pleasure has now turned into pain. That my need has now become greed.

"Hey, Shug?"

"Hmm?"

"Brace yourself because it's my name I want on your lips when you scream."

This time I pull out and then slam back into her with enough force that her ass jiggles from it. Between the sight of that and the feel of her and the sound of her soft, begging mewl, the restraint snaps.

I fuck her. Hard. Fast. Unrelenting. With a savage passion I can't control.

Our bodies slap. Her pussy soaks me and flexes around me as my cock swells so much it hurts.

"C'mon. C'mon. C'mon," I beg, because I'm doing everything I can to stop myself before she can go. My fingers bruise her hips. My thighs burn with restraint. My goddamn balls ache for release.

And the minute she calls out, "Vince," I'm a goddamn goner.

My vision goes black and my breath falls short, as I pump everything I have into her until my thoughts are gone and my heart is full.

Until I know that no one will ever be able to make me feel the way she does. Never.

And that only confuses matters even more.

CHAPTER
forty-two

Vince

"**H**OW COME EVERY TIME WE GET TOGETHER, I END UP ON MY BACK?" Bristol asks through a panted breath.

I shift up on my elbow so I can look at her. Her hair is a mess, her cheeks are flushed, and her smiling lips are swollen from mine. I could never get tired of looking at her like this—gorgeous, sated, looking back at me with something in her eyes that makes my heart feel like it's going to beat out of my chest. I lean forward and brush a kiss to her lips before leaning my forehead on hers and reaching out to rest a hand on her stomach. When she tries to shift away, I tighten my fingers on her side, forcing her to let me leave my hand there.

What was it like when she was pregnant? Did she have morning sickness? What weird foods did she crave? What did Jagger's heartbeat sound like? What did it feel like when he kicked against her swollen belly? What did his first cries sound like?

And where the fuck did those thoughts even come from? *For a guy who never wanted kids, Jennings, you sure as fuck are thinking too much.*

And yet . . . the questions I'll never have answers to still linger.

"I played him your music all the time," Bristol murmurs almost as if she can hear my thoughts. "Interviews that you'd given. Songs that you'd sung. I rested the phone on my belly and played them over and over. I wanted him to know your voice."

Processing all of this has been a mental and emotional overload. To go from zero to one hundred eighty in what feels like two seconds is overwhelming and discombobulating.

To think I've been content with not wanting one thing my whole life to now having it and trying to understand why I'm not fighting against it harder.

To look at Bristol and resent her for what she did. Sure, I could look at myself—at Mick putting her off, at having Hawke block her in my phone, at not returning her calls—but rehashing the past doesn't justify her silence over the past weeks. It doesn't give her a free pass.

To look at Jagger, I see myself in every fiber of him, and then in the few places I'm not, I see Bristol there.

I offer a slight nod in response and then lie back on the rug and stare at the ceiling. What am I supposed to say, *thank you?* Because while I am glad she tried to keep me present in his life—*I wasn't in his life in the most important way possible.*

"Vince . . . I'm sorry. That's all I can say to you, and I hope you really hear it. I'm sorry. I did what I thought was right. It never crossed my mind what you said about your mom and Jagger being left to feel the same way about you." She sounds as conflicted as I feel. "Please know I did call. I did try, but when you blocked me, when your road manager offered me a check to take care of it in whichever way I pleased, I—"

"*Christ.*" The memory comes back with a vengeance. Even after all these years, the conversation stuck out in my head then and now, again. *The joke about Crystal.*

Crystal.

Bristol.

He could have easily heard one name when she said the other.

I run a hand through my hair and sigh with a heaviness Bristol will never understand. Talk about making subconscious choices.

I was so far down a rabbit hole trying to convince myself that I didn't love Bristol, would hearing she was pregnant make any difference? I'd like to think I'm a better man than that, but back then . . . hell, there's a huge difference from age twenty-three to thirty.

I'd like to think the man I am today is better than that . . . but I guess that remains to be seen.

"What's wrong?" she asks.

"Nothing. It's just . . ." *It's just you can't go back, Vin. You made as many mistakes as she did, just in different ways. If you can forgive yourself, does that mean you should forgive her?* "That explains why you were so angry with me at the video shoot. So bitter with me," I say, dots connecting the more I replay all the time we've spent together.

"Yeah." It's barely audible. "I was shocked to see you there. It was like part of me wanted to jump into your arms and hold on, while the other needed to keep you at arm's length, terrified you'd find out about Jagg before I could figure out the right thing to do. A lot of good all that did me, huh?"

"Humph." But it makes sense of something I couldn't put my finger on before. Why I felt her pushing so hard against me when her eyes said the exact opposite.

"The *no fraternizing with clients* thing was real, though . . . as my current state of non-employment shows."

"I'll take care of that for you."

"I don't want you to take care of anything for me. I've caused enough turmoil for now. I can figure out my own life."

And even though I clearly know she will since she's done all this on her own thus far, I still want to take care of it for her. In fact, I know that I will.

But thoughts of McMann and her job are easy targets for me to focus on, distractions, instead of what we really need to talk about.

I close my eyes and see him sleeping. The rise and fall of his chest. The hair mussed by the pillow. His skin that smells like lotion.

"I stare at him sometimes. It's impossible to look away."

"I still feel that way," she whispers.

"He's incredible, Shug. You . . . you've done such an amazing job with him."

She doesn't say thank you. She doesn't reach out and grab my hand despite the sex we just had. It's almost as if that specific contact after everything we've been through would be more intimate. Would mean we're fine with the things we've done to each other when neither of us are anywhere near being so. Rather, she just sits in silence beside me, trying to judge where and how I feel, because I'm still trying to figure that out myself.

"Why are you so scared of him?" she finally asks.

She can still read me like a fucking book. And my response is the most honest answer I've ever given in my life. "I don't want to ruin his *perfect.*"

The admission costs me more than I thought it would. Emotion burns in my throat and tears well in my eyes, as regret rivals resentment inside me.

"Vince. You're not going to—"

"I ruin everything that matters."

She presses a kiss to my shoulder and just leaves her lips there as she speaks. "For the record, he's far from perfect. He's been on his best behavior while we've been here. His perfect falls from grace every once in a while, and we're left with tantrums and obstinance and a refusal to eat anything that's the color *vegetable* as he calls it."

I should know that. I should know what he likes and doesn't like. How he gets cranky when he's tired. How he pitches a fit when you tell him no.

But would I have wanted to if I'd had the decision before he was born to know that? Is it easier because I can't refute it since he's in living color in front of me?

My thoughts keep fucking with me. Keep playing devil's advocate against me. Keep rioting against accepting what I feel so easily.

"I know, Vince. I can hear you thinking. I robbed you of knowing any and all of that. Of experiencing it firsthand. There is nothing I can say other than I'm sorry."

When she reaches out to place her hand over mine, my whole body tenses. She can feel it. I know she can feel it. But she doesn't move it. She doesn't walk away like I've done to her. She leaves it there almost as proof that no matter how much I feel like running, she's staying still.

"Shug?"

"Hmm?"

"I'm struggling with how I feel about . . . everything."

"I understand."

"No. I don't think you do."

"Then tell me. Talk to me." She shifts so she can see my face. "Do the one thing you've never done before—explain it to me."

Explain it to me. Sounds so damn simple to say, but it's something I've never explained to anyone. *How do I even fucking start?*

"Do you know what it's like to live a lifetime telling yourself you can't have something? Then when you unexpectedly have it at your fingertips— when you touch it, when you experience it, when you realize you were completely wrong—you struggle with refuting every reason you've ever used to convince yourself otherwise?"

Our tear-blurred eyes meet each other's, and when she nods, a tear slips down her cheek. "I do," she whispers. "I've felt that way almost every day since you left my window that night."

You started this decade of hurt, Vin. It's up to you to finish it, one way or another.

I clear my throat. "I had my reasons." Reasons that feel so meaningless now.

"I know you did."

"I've tried to let you go more times than I can count, Bristol. I've tried desperately. The first time I walked away because I had no choice. The second time, the night we made Jagger, I realized that cutting you out of my life was the only way I could survive. I couldn't bear the thought of tarnishing *your perfect* with my shit. I couldn't give you anything. I could only give you love but never keep you."

Those words.

"I think maybe I was doing the same, in my own way, on my end." She shakes her head ever so slightly. "Like you told me, I'm impossible to love."

"No, that's not true. I said those words, but that's more because of me, *about me*, than you. I'm impossible to love. I think . . . I need time. This is all too much. Too fast. I'm trying to figure out how to move forward without dragging all those reasons with me." I draw in a deep breath. "To make amends with my demons, and there are a lot of fucking demons."

"There is no pressure on our end. He doesn't know that you're his dad. I don't want your money. I don't want anything from you. You're under no obligation to be in our lives." She clears her throat and sets her jaw. "When things calm down, Jagger and I can leave, go back to our lives. I'll find a new job. I'll get into law school. We'll move on, and you can do the same. We can put out a press release about your dad being wrong. Say we did a paternity test that agrees and call it a day."

Good in theory, but that would never fly. The paparazzi are ruthless. It only takes one of them to dig up a picture of me as a kid and compare it to Jagger's school picture they're no doubt paying some classmate's parent for right now and they'd know we were lying.

Her words press on a deep wound, though. They hurt in a way I never thought words could—and that's saying a shit ton considering Deegan Jennings is my father.

"How can you say that? Do you really think that's who I am? That that's the type of man I am?"

"No, but I also know you have a life that has nothing to do with this. With me. With him. You have a career that you want to go back to. A public who adores you." She shrugs but can't meet my eyes. "I heard you on the phone earlier. The single is releasing next week, and I'm sure you're itching to go promote it. To get on a stage in front of people. To travel without strings. I don't . . . *I won't* fault you for choosing those things over this. Just because I chose *this* for you, doesn't mean you have to do the same. I won't think less of you for it."

But I would.

"Bristol—"

She reaches out and puts her hand to my lips and shushes me. "Don't make decisions now. We've unpacked a lot of shit and still have more to go . . . but it's a start, and that's further than we've ever gotten before." She rises, her beautiful body tempting me as she stands over me. "Don't give me that look." She smiles for the first time all night. "We've never had a problem with the physical. But we've used it to ignore everything else. This time we can't."

She's right, but it still doesn't stop me from staring and wanting.

"I know," I murmur.

"The ball is in your court. I won't push. I won't question. I'll stay out of the way so you can spend time with Jagg. We'll go from there, if and when you want to." She grabs her clothes then stops at the door. We stare at each other for a few seconds. You'd have to be blind not to see the love in her eyes. The same love I pretended not to see in the past. The same love I've always felt for her. "Good night, Vince."

I lie there on the rug, staring at the ceiling till the early morning hours, replaying the conversation in my head.

We'll go from there, if and when you want to.

Has there ever really been a choice when it comes to her?

Never.

It's always been her, even when I didn't want it to be.

Even more so now when I hold our son and see the best of us in him.

Now I need to convince myself I'm worthy of it. *Now I need to try my damnedest to be the man they deserve me to be . . .*

CHAPTER
forty-three

Bristol

"**A**ND?"

"*And what, Mom?*"

"I've heard all about the fun things that Jagger is getting to do—swimming and kayaking and learning to play the guitar—but you're not telling me about you. About Vince. About how it's going in general . . . if it's going at all."

I sigh and then smile as Jagger's and Vince's mutual laughter carries over to me from where they're huddled in the fort they built. It's a tent with a cardboard box set as a tunnel entrance to fight off space invaders—meaning *girls*—since only boys can enter. "He's really good with him, Mom. Like I wonder how this is something he didn't want when he is so completely natural with him."

"He was scared of repeating the cycle. Maybe he's seeing that it's something you choose, not something you're ordained to be."

"It hurts in the best way possible to watch them together. To realize how much Jagg needed a male figure in his life. I tried to be that for him, but there is no substitute for the real thing."

"Do you think Jagger has any clue who Vince is?"

"On some subconscious level, maybe, but otherwise, no."

"But he likes him?"

"Who *doesn't* like Vince?" I ask. McMann had one thing right—they wanted him everywhere—and right now, thanks to that viral video from San Francisco, he's freaking everywhere. And instead of being out promoting his new single, he's here, with us. With Jagger.

Actions speak louder than words and right now those actions are unmistakable. He loves Jagger. He might not be able to recognize it, but it's clear as day for those of us watching from afar.

I'm just trying not to get my hopes up about what the future holds.

"True." She clears her throat. "But . . ."

"But what?"

"Where does everything stand?"

"The ball is in his court. How can it not be given the situation?"

"But you've talked about everything?"

"Yes and no." I know that answer is going to frustrate her so I elaborate. "I blindsided him, Mom. I ripped the rug out from underneath him, so I have no choice but to stand back and let him find his footing."

"But how are you?"

I sniffle. "I don't have a right to be anything. You told me when I made the decision that Vince had a right to know. In hindsight, yes, he did, but I can't live looking backward. All I can hope is that he feels the same way. For Jagger's sake."

"And for yours."

I nod but she can't see it. "Jagger is who matters right now. What's best for him is what I am focused on."

"You're worried he's going to walk away, aren't you?"

"I'm worried because that's always what Vince does when things get too tough. But then I see them together—their smiles, their laughter, their bond after only two weeks—and I can't help but hold out hope. I can't help but see a future."

"Maybe in some skewed way, Jagger will prove to Vince that he is enough. Maybe that will be all he needs to stop running."

"Is that enough to overcome years of thinking otherwise?" I sigh. I'm so sick of thinking about this, worrying about this, obsessing about this. I would say I just want my life back to the way it was, but then I stop and take stock and realize this has been a taste of what it could be. I don't know what's worse though. Having a taste of it and then it being yanked away or never knowing what it's like at all.

"He'll forgive you," she murmurs.

But I want more than forgiveness. Every minute that we're here, that I watch him with our son, I fall more in love with him. More than I already was.

Forgiveness is just a small part of the whole that I want. That we deserve.

But I can't tell him that. I can't add that pressure when I've already created enough.

All I can do is stand by with my heart in my hands and wait to see if he still wants it. *If he still wants us.*

"I can hope."

"He's a good man, Bristol. He just needs to see it. Once he does, he'll be everything you need and more."

And if he doesn't?

That's the question I'm afraid to put words to.

"Momma?"

I startle and look to my right where Jagger is getting a piggyback ride from Vince. "I have to go," I say to my mom. "What's up, buddy?" I make sure to focus on Jagger instead of Vince.

"We're going to go out on the boat."

"Oh, okay." I smile. The boat ride has become their daily adventure together. They explore inlets. They stop, dock, and get ice cream cones at the store on the other side of the lake. They jump off in the middle of it and pretend they are pirates. They sing music at the top of their lungs. Funny enough, the songs that Jagger asks to be repeated over and over are Bent songs. Songs he's told Vince he knows from watching them on television with me. "Do you need me to get you some snacks for the trip? Some sunscreen?"

"No, I want you to go with us," he says.

"Oh." My smile falters as I figure out how to extricate myself from their time together. I've managed pretty well thus far, having excuses on the ready so that Jagger doesn't feel like I don't want to go with them, but rather that I simply can't for one reason or another. The last thing Jagger needs is to sense tension between us or for Vince to feel like I'm forcing his hand. "Thanks, buddy, but I've got some studying to do. My old professor offered to help—"

"Studying can wait, can't it?" Vince asks. "*We* want you to come with us."

"Vince?" I meet his eyes.

"*I* want you to come with us." He nods, almost as if telling me this is the start of whatever might be next for whatever this is.

At least I think that's what he's telling me.

"You sure?" I ask.

"I'm sure."

His words hit me in the best way. They weave into my soul and wrap around my heart. They tell me this just might be the beginning I had hoped for instead of the ending I've worried about.

"Okay."

"Yay! Momma's coming with us."

The ride is everything I thought it would be from my observations on the shore. A lot of Jagger pointing at Vince and telling him where to go. Even more of Vince ruffling Jagger's hair and explaining things to him. There is even Vince putting Jagger on his lap and letting him drive the boat. The look on Jagger's face—pride edged with worry—as he glanced my way every few seconds now that one of their secrets was out.

But more than anything were the few times I'd catch Vince looking at me. Our eyes would meet and a soft smile would curl up the corners of his lips.

I was content with that. In fact, I was thrilled with the baby steps it felt like we'd taken forward. It was more than enough for me . . . or so I thought.

Then Vince goes and steals more than my heart. He offers me hope too, when he looks at me and says, "This feels right, Shug," followed by the softest smile I've ever seen on his face.

Yes, Vince. This really is real.

I want to tell him that and so much more. Like how each day he grows closer with Jagger, he's proving his father wrong. That he's not a worthless human being. That he's a good man, a talented man, and that more than anything else, he deserves this. Love. A family to call his own. A future with us.

I want him to be a part of our lives. *Always.* I just don't know whether he'll ever want the same thing.

I'm hoping this moment is an indication. A glimpse of what could be.

An amended, hope-filled verse to his sweet regret.

CHAPTER
forty-four

Vince

THE BEER IS COLD. THE SKY IS MUTED IN PINKS AND ORANGES FROM
where the sun has set over the mountains, and the sound of Jagger's and
Bristol's laughter floats up to me from the grass down below.

They're playing some benign game of tag. He runs. She pretends to
chase. Then she lets him sneak up on her and tackle her down. Tickling en-
sues. Then laughter. And the scenario repeats itself over and over.

"It's company policy, Vince."

*"What is? To be your errand girl and be at the talent's beck and call? To use
her for a past connection she had with the talent—me—but then fire her for having that past? We knew each other before I became your client. C'mon, Xavier.
You're grasping at fucking straws here. If Bristol wanted to, she could sue you
seven ways from Sunday for unlawful termination."* Fucking McMann.

"It's not that cut and dried."

"Then make it cut and dried." I take a pull on my beer, knowing Bristol

would be livid with me for this conversation but needing to have it, nonetheless. "Your reputation is preceding you and not in a good way."

"Are you threatening me, Jennings?"

"I don't have to resort to threats for you to make things right. Her work speaks for itself. She doesn't need someone like me going to bat for her."

"And yet you are."

I nod, even though he can't see it. I most definitely am.

I'm just hoping that maybe when Xavier calls Bristol and offers her her job back, that she tells him to shove it where the sun doesn't shine.

It's about time someone does.

More giggles pull me from the conversation replaying through my head. They make me lean forward a little more and look out the second-story window from my recording studio.

It's still a shock to see him. Still a jolt to my head and heart to realize he's part mine, made from me, and that he's incredibly perfect.

It's impossible to hear that belly laugh and not smile myself. Is that normal? Is it just because this is still all so new?

This feels right.

Isn't that what I told Bristol? And it fucking does. I can't explain it, but it's almost like we've spent all these years apart, going through the shit we've gone through, and maybe for once we're going to get it right.

Do I still resent her for some of the decisions she made? Of course I do. Do I still resent me for some of them? Damn straight.

But the question I keep asking myself is, if they went home tomorrow, would it be a relief that they're gone? Would I revel in the silence and the lack of kid shit all over the house? Would my cold beer on the back patio be more enjoyable without Nickelodeon on in the background somewhere?

Or would I sit in the studio all night because I no longer had something to look forward to afterward? Would I go into Jagger's room and sit on his bed and miss him? Would I walk into the great room and miss the sight of Bristol sitting at the kitchen table, head down just like Jagger's as she helps him with his remote schoolwork?

It's so fucked how you can love your life one way and within a few short weeks, realize it wasn't as fucking perfect as you thought it was.

Another laugh. A screech by Bristol as she's play-tackled again no doubt. A "Momma" expressed through belly giggles.

It's like this is a new normal I want. A new normal I can accept.

It's just like Bristol to blow my world up and then hold my hand as the pieces fall around me . . . only to make the most beautiful fucking mosaic from them.

The jagged edges are cushioned with mortar. The broken is now a masterpiece.

But there are a few pieces of that mosaic still missing. Either that or they're too big, too overwhelming, that I need to chip away at their edges so they fit in the picture I want left.

How do I chip at them? How do I get rid of the ugly edges to fit them in?

That's what I need to figure out.

That's the only way I can move forward.

CHAPTER
forty-five

Bristol

"**M**AKE A WISH AND BLOW OUT YOUR CANDLE," I SAY, CATCHING Jagger's flash of a grin, dramatic squeezing of his eyes, and then his theatrical whoosh of breath on video on my cell.

Since the boat ride the other day, it feels like things have shifted again. With Vince. With us. Things just *feel* different.

There seems to be less ... darkness, less pensiveness, in Vince's expression. He seems more at ease. Lighter. Dare I say, more hopeful?

I'm the queen of reading into things, so I'm trying not to infer too much into what I'm seeing. I'm scared to hope. Scared to wish for the more I see when he looks at me.

But I am.

"What did you wish for?" Vince asks, coming up behind him and tickling him so that he wiggles.

I take mental pictures of the moment. Images I can burn in my memory to never forget.

Click. Vince behind Jagger. Their faces side by side. Their heads with matching party hats on. The grins both lopsided and happy.

"I can't tell you that," Jagger says. "If I did, it wouldn't come true."

Click. Jagger faces Vince. Their profiles identical.

"Then I guess you don't get your presents," Vince teases.

"That's not fair. Wait—"

Click. Jagger's shocked expression and Vince's knowing one.

"—you got me a present?" Jagger asks.

"Yes. Seven of them," Vince says.

"Because I'm seven?" Jagger asks.

Vince nods but also looks at me.

Click.

Bittersweet happiness in his eyes.

Seven presents—one for each year he missed.

"If you're not going to tell me your wish, then what should you do to get them?" Vince asks, the slipped guard he let me see, he let me capture, now firmly back in place, replaced with a grin for Jagger.

"Tackle hugs," Jagger says and launches himself at Vince so that he falls backward. They erupt in a tickle fest.

Click. Vince's arms wrapped around Jagger. His face buried in the curve of his neck. His eyes welled with tears. His smile, one I think I'll remember for the rest of my life.

Cake is followed by opening presents, by then playing with presents (riding his new bike everywhere), and then a quick FaceTime to my mom and dad so Jagger could talk a million miles a minute, telling them all about his presents and that he now knows how to drive a boat.

It killed me not being able to share his birthday in person with them this year, but they both graciously didn't tell me how hard it was for them. They both know how important this time is for me, for Jagger, and for the possibility of our future.

I did catch my dad giving a little look to Vince though, before he ended the session. The kind of look that says *don't fuck this up or you'll have to answer to me.*

The family FaceTime party was then followed by a campfire and s'mores on the back deck. The last thing Jagger needed was more sugar, but his one wish was a campfire under the stars so a campfire he was going to get.

The s'mores were Vince's idea. No doubt he's never had to wipe heated marshmallow off a squirmy kid's face and hands, but he handled it like a pro by making a game of it.

"This has been the best birthday, ever!" Jagger says, the sugar hitting him soundly by the way he can't sit still.

"It has?" Vince and I ask in unison.

Jagger nods emphatically. "Why'd you get me so many presents?" Jagger asks Vince.

"Jagger," I admonish. "The words are thank you, not—"

"It's cool. He can ask," Vince says.

"So why did you? I usually get one or two, but you got me seven. SEVEN."

Vince chuckles. "Because you're seven, buddy, and as your d—" Vince stops himself as my heart skips a beat. He clears his throat and shakes his head, almost as if he can't believe how easy that was to say. "As your *best buddy*, I get the right to spoil you. Seven presents for seven years."

Buddy. The word sounds so strained. The struggle on Vince's face real.

The word he almost spoke, the most real of all.

He looks up at me over Jagger's head and smiles. It's a tentative smile that hides truths I'm desperate to know . . . but at least he's showing them to me.

More baby steps.

Each day that passes, every moment that's spent, our relationships are building. Vince and Jagger's. Vince and mine. The three of us together.

This feels right, Shug.

It sure as hell does.

"I'm gonna go put this stuff up in my room," Jagger says, interrupting our connection.

"Your bike can stay down here," I say to which I get a very teenager-ish roll of his eyes. I'm definitely not ready for that yet. "Do you need help?"

"Nope. I got it." He loads his arms up with a Lego set, a new game to play, and some guitar picks among other things. He hits the house and turns back. "Hey, Momma?"

"Yeah, bud?"

"I hope we never leave here," he says before walking into the house and shutting the door.

Me too. This bubble away from the outside world is magical. Me-freaking-too.

I stare at the shut door because it's so much easier to look there than to meet the weight of Vince's stare.

"Thank you," I whisper. "For making his birthday special." For this time. For . . . the forgiveness I hope you'll grace me with.

"No need to thank me." In my periphery, I can see him shift in his seat. It moves him a bit closer to me so he can grab another piece of wood to toss on the fire.

"Yes, there is. You didn't have to buy him presents."

"I have seven years to make up for."

His words are there but they don't feel as cutting as I'd expect. They feel resigned and resolved, if there even is such a thing. "I know, but you didn't have to make up for anything. The last thing I want is for you to think that I—"

"Stop talking." His lips are on mine and his hands cradle my face in that way that I love. The way that has always made me feel like I'm his whole world.

I should be surprised by the action, but I'm not. It feels so real, so natural, so perfect, so *us*.

I don't let my heart begin to hope, but rather I simply let myself enjoy the moment. Enjoy him and the simplicity of being in front of a fire and under the stars with a man I've always loved, regardless of the shitty circumstances life has thrown at us.

His kiss is soft and tender. A touch of tongues. A few brushes of lips. Short and brief . . . but the meaning behind it is so much more poignant than I have ever felt before.

When the kiss ends, I reach my hand up to his cheek and meet his eyes. He speaks before I can overthink everything.

"We're figuring this out, Shug. At our own pace. In our own way. We'll figure this out."

The quick inhale of breath has the two of us jumping back and looking to meet Jagger's wide-eyed stare.

"Jagg?" Shit. What do I say? What do I do?

"I knew it," he says and laughs with a carelessness that I've rarely heard from him.

"Knew what?" I ask as Vince chuckles under his breath.

"That you wanted to be boyfriend and girlfriend."

I sputter for a response. A responsible response that won't get his hopes up for something that might not happen—especially with our history.

"Vince looks at you like the way people do on Nana's shows." He makes a blech sound. "The ones where sometimes she has to cover my eyes so I don't see things I'm not old enough to see yet."

"Jesus," I mutter under my breath. Vince just laughs until he doubles over to hide it. "You're not helping." I jab him with my elbow.

"Sorry. Your face though. That expression is priceless," he says and then tries to have a stern expression before he turns to Jagger. "You okay with that?"

"Vince, you just can't—"

"Yeah. I'm cool with it," Jagger says and then fist-bumps Vince like he's sixteen years old.

"See?" Vince says. He stands and grins, proud of himself for handling the situation. "You ready for me to show you how to pop a wheely on your bike?"

"But it's dark out," Jagger says, grabbing Vince's hand like it's so natural. Like we didn't just have the conversation we had, and he didn't just see us kissing.

"Don't ever let the dark spoil your fun. That's what lights are for."

I stare after them, a huge grin on my lips, and feel settled for the first time in weeks.

This just might work out.

CHAPTER
forty-six

Vince

"THINGS COULDN'T LOOK BETTER," GRETA, MY CONTACT AT SONY Music, says. "The single is killing it. Rising up the charts. Getting more airtime each day."

"Just as we anticipated," Xavier chimes in on the conference call. "When can we expect you back? You need to be visible right now and escaping off to the wilderness isn't helping that."

Neither does you firing Bristol. But circling back to that hasn't happened yet, you dick. It will. It will or I might just be heading back to CMG.

"I'm busy writing the rest of the songs for the album. I'm sure Greta won't complain about that."

"Not in the least," she says.

"I'm planning to write a solid fifteen that we can pick from. I also have some others from Steven," I say, mentioning a well-known songwriter, "if we need something more that I don't have."

She whistles. "You've been a busy man."

"I've gotten my muse back," I say and look out the studio window to the empty yard below. I rise and stick my head out to see if I can see Bristol and Jagg, but they're nowhere to be found.

Is it normal to feel that punch to the gut of worry? To wonder if they're okay even when you know they are because your property is a freaking fortress of security?

"Right, Vince?"

"I'm sorry. What was that?" I ask, forcing myself back to the conversation and out of my own irrational head.

"I said, music to my ears," Greta says through a laugh. "Quite literally. But Xavier *is* right. We do need some face time with you. I'll be out in Los Angeles next week. Can you arrange to meet up? Even if for a bit?"

"I'll see what I can do," I say.

"I need more than that," Xavier says. "I need to know you're going to be here so I can plan some additional meetings for you. Press junket. Whatnot."

"Yeah. Sure. Fine." I force myself to pause and remember that Greta had nothing to do with Xavier firing Bristol.

"I know there has been some . . . upheaval in your life as of late," Greta says, "but the time is appreciated since we want to hit this hard while your visibility is trending."

"Work comes first," I say, but for the first time in my life, when I hang up the phone, it doesn't feel that way.

Normally after a call like that, I'd be buckling down to clean up lyrics and perfect some of the melodies. I'd forget the hours, hell, even forget what day it is, and not surface until what needs to be done is done.

So why am I tossing my cell on the desk in front of me and walking out of my studio to see what Bristol and Jagger are up to?

Why does something feel more important than the music for the first time in my life?

Talk about something different to wrap my head around.

They're not in the game room. Not in Jagger's room. Not in the front yard. I'm just about to call their names when I walk into the great room and find them.

Bristol is lying on the couch with Jagger spooned in front of her. A book that I assume they were reading is on the floor in front of them.

My whole world.

The thought comes into my mind and settles there like there's always been a place for it. Like it's completely meant to be.

But how can I think that? How can I make that one-eighty? I knew the high school version of Bristol inside and out. Her favorite foods. Her pet peeves. Her annoying habits. I loved her till it hurt. I loved her so much I walked away from her.

But I don't really know the version of her that's asleep with our son in her arms. Does she still have the pet peeves and annoying habits she did back when she was seventeen? Is she still afraid of heights but doesn't mind going on amusement park rides that go upside down? Does she love tomato sauce but hate tomatoes?

It's the little things I don't know, that I haven't thought much about. The bigger picture has overshadowed everything.

But do those little things really fucking matter, Vin?

We've loved each other for close to fifteen years. She's still fighting for me. She still loves me despite every fucking shortcoming—*and there are a lot.*

It's natural to question the whys and the hows, but how about I just accept that it is? That we can be. *That we are.* And move the fuck forward.

Funny thing is, I think I already have. These days and nights here have been some of the best of my life outside of my professional highlights. I'm not just getting to know Jagger, but I'm getting to know Bristol too. That doesn't say shit about the things I'm learning about myself.

I'm not just growing to love my son, but I'm also falling head over heels in love with Bristol when I already thought I was.

I'm finding out, I was nowhere close before.

The love I have for them is so intense that I wake up some nights from the tightness in my chest and move from room to room, simply to watch them sleep.

Just to make sure they're not a dream.

Just to make sure they're still there.

Just to make sure I haven't fucked up this time.

CHAPTER
forty-seven

Bristol

"**I**S THIS WHAT IT'S LIKE TO HAVE A DADDY?"

Jagger's words stay in my head long after sleep catches him, but eludes me.

Maybe it is.

Such a lame response for a mom who was completely caught off guard. For a mom who felt the guilt lance through her for robbing him of it. For not being able to tell him the truth when a similar reasoning is what got her in this situation.

"Can't sleep?"

I look over my shoulder to where Vince stands on the opposite side of the room. He's wearing a pair of gray sweatpants, an intense look in his eyes, and nothing else.

"Not tonight, no. Done working?" I ask. Normally he spends the days with Jagger and me and then works all night while everyone sleeps. A part of me thinks the routine helps him avoid having to talk about the hard stuff with me. The other part of me has stood at that closed studio door, fist raised to knock, needing Vince in more ways than one.

It's hard to be content with a few kisses here and there when your body knows what his can do to yours.

"No work tonight."

"Really? Why not?"

He walks across the room to where I'm sitting and was staring out the window. "There are other things that are way more important. Things I've been neglecting. Matches I was figuring out how to stay lit long after they are supposed to burn out."

"Vince. I . . ."

"This feels right. You. Me. Jagger. More right than any part of me feels I deserve to have. But . . . I'm working on it. On me. On realizing that my past doesn't have to be my future."

"You're right. It doesn't."

"I've spent my whole life loving the idea of you but have never allowed myself the reality of it. Of there being an us." He looks down for a beat, and it looks like the weight of the world that has been heavy on his shoulders these past few weeks has lessened. "You're right, you know."

"Be careful," I tease. "Those four words might come back to bite you in the butt at some point."

He offers me a bittersweet smile and nods. "I had every intention of sleeping with you while I was here and then going back to my regularly scheduled life when I left. But what was easy in concept was fucking brutal to actually do. I don't know if it's because of the time that's passed or that we've both gotten older, matured, but fuck, letting you go that night—on your porch—was the hardest goddamn thing I've ever done. It broke me in a way that I'm more than certain I've broken you in the past. It was like I was in a tank of oxygen and yet I couldn't fucking breathe."

I nod, understanding exactly how he felt.

"But I had to walk away. Because that's what you wanted. Because that's the chickenshit I was. Because that's who my dad tried to persuade me I was . . . so much so that I believed it."

"Then Jagger happened," I whisper, and he nods.

"Then Jagger happened." He glances toward the stairs where our son sleeps and gives a subtle head shake. "I struggled with the enormity of the situation. And as much as I hate the fucking press for scaring the two of you,

I'm so goddamn grateful they did because it gave us this time here. It forced me to be here when history dictates I might have run the other way."

He says the words, makes the confession, but in my heart of hearts, and after seeing him now with Jagger—in hindsight—I know he never would have. How much I would have given to know this before though.

"I know you want promises and assurances, and you deserve every single one of them . . . but I can't give them yet. That doesn't mean they aren't there, though. They are. They're beside how I feel about you and how I feel about Jagger. They're just harder for me to put words to because of *me*. Because of the shit I need to sort through when it comes to myself. But the fact that I'm working on them when I've never cared to before . . . I'm hoping that will tide you over until I can say them."

He meets my eyes. The raw honesty in both his words and his guileless expression is like a salve to the wounds I've been waiting to heal over the past few weeks. Maybe even the past few years.

He's working on his demons so he can be a better man for us. A better father. A better lover. A better partner. A better friend.

They may not have been the words I thought I needed to hear, but they are most definitely the right ones for this moment in time.

I rise to my feet and reach my hand out in the space between us. Asking. Inviting. Wanting. He draws in a shaky breath but takes it without hesitation.

I lead the way to the stairs.

There's been enough hesitating.

We walk up them one at a time.

Enough questioning.

We move down the hallway.

Enough wondering.

We enter his bedroom.

Now it's time to show him how he makes me feel. For me to love him with words I can't express but desperately want to show.

For me to love him.

Our lips meet. It's the simplest of intimate actions. The soft sighs. The tender touches. The cupping of my face and angling of my head to give him more access.

Every part of me burns for him. My heart with hope. My skin for his touch. The very sweet ache between the delta of my thighs. My soul with the possibility of a future.

We move in the darkness of the room. No words needed. There is no show of getting undressed this time. No time needed to pause and admire the other. Our bodies are already known to each other. Our hearts already beating as one.

I scoot back on the bed, our kisses still intense but softer now. Each one reminding us of our past. Of the present. And of our possible future.

Vince crawls over me as I spread my legs for him. I reach out to touch him, to help him put the condom on. With one elbow pressed beside me and both of our hands encircling his cock, we both guide him into me.

There's an effortlessness to us tonight. A sweet resignation of acceptance when for so long there has only been uncertainty. But our bodies don't know that. Only our heads and hearts do.

And so we let our bodies take over. We let them guide us with his slow push and his muted groan as he pulls out. With him guiding my hand down between my thighs so he can watch me pleasure one part of myself while he takes care of the other.

The ache turns to pleasure. The burn builds into bliss.

We're reduced to moans of rapture and long slides of skin. To hitched breaths and murmured praise. To his fingers gripping and my fingernails scoring.

We make love without words, cementing emotions we've felt for what seems like forever. Emotions we've been scared of, we admit. Now that they're in the light, we'll never be able to hide them in the dark again.

Just like the dust particles dancing around us.

We love each other. With each push in. With every pull out. With our fingers laced on both sides of my head. With the slow grind of his hips. With the scrape of his teeth over my shoulder and the soft kisses to my neck.

It's a slow dance of skin and sensations and emotions. Of met eyes and soft smiles and lips parted in pleasure. Of lifted hips and arched backs and squeezed hands.

We work together to reach our highs. My climax a slow build of pressure that detonates with a warning of its presence but not of its intensity.

I fall under its haze of pleasure. The white-hot heat rolls through my body like a live wire snapping before slamming back into my core. My back arches and hips buck and fingers grip his.

Only Vince can do this to me. Can evoke this from me. Only ever Vince.

"You're so gorgeous when you come," Vince murmurs before meeting my lips with a bruising kiss. The heat of his tongue. The grind of his hips. The feel of his body against mine.

Every damn thing overwhelms my senses so I do the only thing I can. I hold on to Vince. With arms and hands and legs. My own orgasm pulling him with me. He buries his face in the underside of my neck as he begins to piston his hips faster, harder. My body tenses around him as its not finished yet, and all I can do is hold on for the ride.

His breath is warm against my skin. His stubble a tickle as he moves. My moans are soft compared to the harsh pants of his breath. The slap of his hips against mine is the underlying beat.

He pushes my legs farther apart and begins to thrust harder, faster, relentlessly—my body his to use. Then his guttural groan rumbles through the room as he presses his forehead against my shoulder and claims his own orgasm.

Our panted breaths fill the room as our bodies shudder from the rush of adrenaline slowly ebbing from our bodies.

We lie here like this—with his body on mine, his face in the curve of my neck, and my hand idly running up and down his spine.

We lie here like this—soaking up the moment and wondering with hope if this could be a reality we can make work.

If the closeness we feel right now is a hint of what our everyday future could be.

CHAPTER
forty-eight

Bristol

M Y WORDS SOUND PANICKED. ALMOST THE SAME KIND OF PANICKED my heart felt when Vince walked downstairs a while ago with a packed suitcase in his hand.

But I'm trying to rein it in. I'm trying to avoid Jagger seeing my fear.

I'm trying to not imagine history repeating itself.

"It's just for a week," he says. "Maybe a few days more."

But you haven't mentioned it to me.

"I'm going to be super busy though. Early meetings upon midday meetings upon late-night evenings. I'm not going to have much time to do anything other than work. I've been here for so long that I have like a month's worth of work to catch up on."

A reason why we can't talk. An excuse why he's creating distance.

"Yes?" His footsteps stop a few feet behind me. "Why aren't you responding?"

"Okay." I speak for the first time as I wipe down the counters with a fervor only rivaled by Mr. Clean.

"McMann. The head of Sony Music. The morning shows. The late shows. I've got to meet with them and . . . there are some other things I need to take care of."

He's leaving—running—when he said he wasn't going to run anymore.

"I'm sorry this time here made you fall so behind."

"Don't be. That wasn't what I implied. I was—"

"Don't worry about us. I'll make arrangements for Jagger and me to head back home. He's missed too much in-person school as it is. I've put out some feeler applications for jobs. I need to get on that. I had one month's rent saved, but—"

"Rent's paid. I sent money for your mom to take care of that a while back. You don't need to worry about money—"

He can't say goodbye so he's going to start with saying it'll only be a week.

"I don't need your money, Vince." I scrub harder. I scrub spots that don't need scrubbing. "I told you, I don't need or expect anything from you."

Then the week will turn into a month.

"Bristol."

And the month will turn into excuses.

"We'll head back home and—and—we just need to get back home. Get our lives back."

Then the excuses will eventually stop.

"If that's what you want." His voice is low, questioning. "I can get my driver to take you to the airport when the jet returns." When I don't respond, can't, he continues. "If I'm honest though, I'm not comfortable with you going back to your place yet. I'd much rather you two stay here where I know you're safe and—"

And away from you.

The thought comes out of nowhere but hits me like a ton of bricks.

I don't want his driver.

I don't want him telling me where to go.

I don't want him telling me what to do.

My hands start trembling, so I squeeze the sponge with ferocity to control it. "I have to return to my life sometime."

Maybe that's what he wants. For him to leave and for me to feel weird here so I go home on my own. Then he can return to an empty house and the strings can be cut with precision since we won't be face-to-face. So he won't have to see my face when he leaves this time.

"*Shug.*"

"I'm fine. This is fine," I murmur, willing myself not to cry. Not to feel. Not to be anything other than the strong girl I was when I let him walk away the first time. Then the even stronger twenty-one-year-old, when I lied to his face and said I only wanted sex and just the one night. And finally, the woman from a few weeks ago who lied on her front porch when she told him she loved him, but it wasn't enough.

Vince closes his arms around me from behind. My body tenses at the feel of him against me, at the comfort I've come to find in it, when he rests his chin on my shoulder. "Talk to me."

This is how we are.

"There's nothing to say."

This is what we do.

"Look at me." He tries to turn me around, but I just grip the counter.

But now there's Jagger who will be heartbroken too.

Don't cry. Don't cry. Don't cry. "Have a good trip." My voice breaks despite the feigned nonchalance in it.

"Dammit, Shug." I can feel his jaw clench on my shoulder. "If this is going to work between us, you don't get to shut down every time you get scared. I'm not allowed to, so neither are you." This time when he tries to turn me, I let him. His eyes search mine with an honesty he's been showing more and more and that I need to get used to accepting. "Talk to me. Why are you so upset?"

"If your trip turns into longer than a week. Say a month. Say however long . . . just know it's okay. I understand. We gave it a good run."

He uses his thumb to brush away the tear that slides down my cheek. "It won't."

"But if it does, just know it's okay. Just know I love you. Just know Jagger will be loved." Every part of me aches in fear that when he walks out the door, he won't come back.

He's done it before.

"I know you have nothing to go off but the past, but I'm not going anywhere." He brushes a kiss to my lips. "You want me to fight for us? Then I expect the same of you."

I nod but the tears keep coming. The fear still burns bright. "Sometimes it's too hard to hope."

"Then don't hope. *Know.* Trust in me. Trust in us."

He presses a searing kiss to my lips before leaning back. "The offer is there. You can go home and go back to your life like nothing has happened. Or you can trust in me and stay here. I'm leaving the ball one hundred percent in your court. If anyone's going to walk away, it's going to be you."

Our eyes hold before he gives me a brusque kiss and then walks outside to say goodbye to Jagger. I hate that once again, I'm looking at his back, watching him walk away. It feels like déjà vu, except this time, there's so much more on the line.

"*You want me to fight for us? Then I expect the same of you. Trust in me. Trust in us.*"

Then he climbs in the waiting car.

How do I trust in us when I'm not sure what us *means?*

Then he is on his way to the airport.

How do I trust in him when he's never fought for us before?

And I'm left wondering if I've just said goodbye to him for good again.

How do I trust when I've barely survived every other goodbye?

CHAPTER
forty-nine

Vince

MEMORIES ASSAULT ME.

One after another just like his fists used to. Just like his words that left layer upon layer of scars *still* do.

Nothing's changed. The house still has the same oppressive feeling that it did when I walked out the door eleven years ago. The same heaviness to it from the man who reveled in controlling his son with fear.

And everything's changed. The couch color. The brown carpet that's now vinyl wood planks. The box television that's now a flatscreen on the wall.

The man lying in the hospital bed in the center of the family room.

He looks like hell. Sunken eyes. Hollow cheeks. A gray pallor. What's left of his hair that was once dark is now white from the stress of the chemo.

But his eyes—neither age nor sickness have dulled the spite in them.

I've spent the last week being the Vince Jennings everyone knows. Surly. Cocky. Talented. Rebellious. I've gone to meeting after meeting. Done interview after interview. I've held my ground professionally and personally.

The personal side has come at a fucking brutal cost. I left the house, I boarded the jet, I arrived in Los Angeles, all while telling myself that Bristol was being ridiculous for worrying about me coming back.

So I challenged myself not to call her. Not to text her. To see if I can live without her this time around. To realize how goddamn miserable I am without them. To validate my reasons for everything I need to do. To keep her as far away from the man this moment with my dad might turn me into.

If she's nowhere near this, then I can't hurt her or Jagger with what comes of it.

The only thing that's made this misery easier is being so goddamn tired every night I collapse into bed. But that doesn't mean I don't miss the fuck out of them. That I don't pick up my phone, go to write a text, and then set it back down as a reminder of what life would be like without them.

Because I'm still not the man they deserve.

Not yet.

But after today, after I stand here in a house that holds only terrible nightmares, I need to be a man I've never been before. The man *I* know I can be. The one I want to be the moment I leave this house, knowing I'll never return again.

"Vincent," my dad murmurs.

We stare at each other for a long span of time but don't speak. I have so much to say, but walking into this house is like stepping back in time. My thoughts and words immediately tangle with the fear of fucking up. Of not making myself invisible enough to avoid what inevitably comes next.

It's incredible how three steps into this room and I'm reminded of how it made me feel. How he fucked with my head. How when I grew calloused to that, he then bruised me with his fists.

Nothing will ever be able to erase that. Not his sickness. Not an apology. Not his death.

His nurse stands abruptly from where she sits in the corner. She eyes me with distrust. It's a valid thing for her to feel considering I'm staring at my father with disgust. She glances around the room as if to make sure there aren't any weapons I can hurt him with. Only after she seems confident there aren't, does she excuse herself from the room.

She neglected to realize bare hands are weapons too. Just ask my father. He was the master of using them.

I stay where I am. Back leaning against the doorjamb, arms crossed over my chest, stare unyielding.

"It's me you have to thank for your success, you know."

Fucking classic Deegan Jennings if ever I've heard him. Narcissistic asshole. It's always about him, even when it isn't.

"If that's what you think."

"It's what I know. I gave you the foundation you needed to be who you are."

Foundation? Jesus. Does he really believe the shit he's spewing?

"I fed you. I clothed you. I put a roof over your head."

I let him talk. I welcome the words. I hear the bullshit in them. I recognize the things I feared for far too long. The things I believed.

"And you beat me to a pulp for simply breathing." My laugh holds anything but amusement as I clap dramatically. "Award for Father of the Year most definitely goes to you."

"You always were an unappreciative fuck, you know that?"

"Appreciative? How about I *appreciate* you showing me everything I never want to be as a human. As a man. As a father."

He angles his head to the side and purses his sallow lips before they turn up in a taunting grin. "How's that boy of yours, anyway?"

"My son is none of your fucking business," I grit out.

"I'm pretty sure he is being family and all."

I clench my jaw so hard it hurts, determined to resist letting him push the buttons he's mastered.

"Did you take pleasure in it, Dad? To get paid to hurt me? To try and fuck me over? To sell your son out one last time so you could feel like you were still in charge?"

His chuckle says it did.

"And for what? Because you've resented me my whole life because Mom left you, and God forbid you had to take care of your son?" I shake my head. So much hurt and fear from the years slowly ebbing so I can see the truths I was too blinded to see before. The bullshit I dealt with was about him. About his shortcomings. About his failures. Not about me.

"I was doing you a favor."

"Bullshit. You're a selfish son of a bitch who was only thinking about getting one last dig in at his son before he died. One last *fuck you* to revive your black heart."

His smile is half-assed. His wince in pain has me holding my breath momentarily and selfishly wanting him not to die so I can finish what I came here to do. "Or maybe I was trying to teach you a lesson."

"A lesson? That's some fucked-up logic coming from a man who doesn't have a leg to stand on."

He pauses and meets my eyes with a smugness I've seen more times than I care to count. "My blood's running through him too, sonny-boy. Don't you forget that."

I'm at his bedside in a flash. My anger rioting. The urge to grab his sweatshirt and yank him to his feet so we can be eye to eye owns me. So he can feel the fear I used to have every time he used to do the same to me.

But I don't. I grip the bed rail till my knuckles turn white as he sits there and gloats. He got what he wanted. A reaction to know he hit the nail on the head.

That he got his final dig in.

Even in death, my dad wants me to know he'll still be there. He'll still be around. That I should still fear if what's in him is in my blood. Is in my son's blood.

I don't want to ruin his perfect.

I refuse to take his bait.

I refuse to let him leave this world thinking that he was successful in planting that thought in my head.

Instead, I take a few seconds to look at a man who used to strike fear in me. Now all I can feel is pity.

He's just a man. Just flesh and bones.

He is not me. I am not him. I'll never be him.

How could I ever think otherwise?

I shake my head and lean down close to his face. "You know what? I came here thinking maybe the fact you're knocking down death's door might have made you want to say things, make amends, right some of your wrongs . . . fuck if I know. But it's clear you don't. It's clear you'd rather die alone with your anger than with a clear conscience."

"Vin—"

I can see the fight in his eyes. The spite, and I cut him off before he can spew it. "I look at you and feel sorry for you. Nothing more. Nothing less. You wasted your life being bitter and brutal, only feeling good about yourself when you were tearing me down. Well, guess what. It didn't work. Not your abuse—look who I became. Not your deception—look what I now get to love. Not the groundwork you laid for me—because I'll never be like you."

His stare is hard. His jaw is set. Even in death the fucker won't bend.

Well, neither will I. Over the years, I've bent enough for him. Bent so much I thought I was fucking broken.

Not anymore.

Never again.

"Goodbye, Dad. I'm sorry it couldn't have been different. I'm sorry you couldn't find it in yourself to love. Just know that when you take your last breath, I made it. I'm everything you said I could never be. I'm everything I ever wanted to be. *And I'll never be like you.*"

I walk to the door without another word.

Tears well in my eyes. Not for the man he was, but for the man he could have been to me. For the man I needed him to be but never had.

I'm not angry at him. The past is the past. A phrase I've been saying a lot lately. But I resent him for the opportunities he robbed me of.

It's his degradation and abuse that had me walking away from Bristol at age nineteen.

It's his lies that possibly stole eleven years of time that we could have been together.

But it's him who pushed us all together. And that's the greatest *fuck you* to him I could ever hope to have.

CHAPTER
fifty

Vince

Hawke's resting his ass against the rental car when I walk out of the house. I told him I didn't need him to come with me. I played it down and told him there was no way he wanted to come to this hellhole town. But did he listen to me?

Of course fucking not.

Instead, he sat next to me on the flight. He listened to words I didn't speak and then held a one-sided conversation with me where he answered all the questions I'd been asking myself.

If you think that you're like your dad, how is it so damn easy for you to love Jagger?

How many times over the past few weeks have you wanted to tell Jagger what a worthless piece of shit he is? How many times have your hands fisted and you felt like throwing a punch at him?

I've never whipped my eyes up so fast in my life as that moment. But I was met with a shit-eating grin and a lift of his eyebrows—my reaction to him an answer in and of itself.

Of course, I haven't felt that way. Not even fucking close. But Hawkin, in his shock value, got the point across.

I'm not my fucking dad.

I never have been. I never will be.

And when I walk out of the house and see Hawkin standing there, I'm glad he didn't listen to me.

"You good?" he asks from where he's no doubt studying me from behind his sunglasses.

"I will be."

He nods in response and then climbs into the driver's seat. I stop for a beat and look around one last time at a neighborhood I will forget and a town I refuse to come back to.

The only lasting thing Fairfield gave me was Bristol.

Other than that, it can burn to the ground.

"I think a drink *or eight* is in order," Hawke says. "Tell me where to go."

I give him directions to a bar near our hotel and try not to read too much into how much this feels like old times. Hawke. Me. A car. A bar. Or maybe it's the fact that he's sitting beside me.

My best friend even when I don't deserve him.

We drive past places I used to take Bristol. A park where we used to make out in my back seat. A movie theater where we'd skip from theater to theater on a single ticket to beat the heat. The burger joint where we'd sit and drink milkshakes way after her curfew because I didn't want to go back home and she sensed the unspoken reasons why.

Bristol.

The need to call her all week has been there, but never more so than it has in this moment. *I did it, Shug. I slayed the dragon. I'm free to be the man you think I can be.*

But I hold tight to the promise I made myself.

I have one more right to wrong before I can talk to her. Before I can hold her. Before I can strike the goddamn match for the final time.

"Wanna talk about it?" Hawkin asks after we take a seat at the bar.

"Not really."

"Did you say what needed to be said?" he asks, being the only person other than Bristol who knows the real Deegan Jennings.

"Yeah."

"Do you feel better for it?"

It's a good question. One I mull over as Hawkin motions the bartender over, talks him down from the shock of who is sitting at his bar, and orders our drinks.

"I said what needed to be said. I said what I would have regretted had I never had the chance to say it. Feeling better is beside the point."

"Fair enough." He nods and then lifts his chin to where the bartender is lining up two rows of five shots each. "The jet's slated for takeoff in two hours."

"And you plan for us to be shitfaced before then?"

"No. I plan for us to be right again before then." He picks up a shot and places it in front of me before grabbing one himself. "We're celebrating."

"Celebrating what?"

"Five things."

"That's very specific," I joke. "Care to tell me what they are?"

"Yep." He nods and taps the first shot against mine. "For letting your dad go." He holds a finger up to correct himself. "I should say for finally letting go of the choke hold your dad has had on you."

I stare at the shot and nod before downing it and then cough over the burn.

"Hurts like a motherfucker," Hawke croaks. "At least we know we're fucking alive."

"Amen to that," I say as he scoots the second shot toward me. "Whoa. What's with the breakneck pace?"

"When it comes to you, the path of least resistance is to get you drunk fast."

I laugh. God, it feels good to have him sitting here beside me. To have him here when I need him because he *just knows*.

He lifts number two. "For finally pulling your head out of your ass when it comes to Bristol." I stare at him. "Down it, Vin."

"Who said anything—"

"You've loved the woman your whole life. I know it. Rocket and Gizmo know it. You even know it. Now down the shot like a good boy and admit she's it for you so you can move on like a mature fucker and make an honest woman of her."

"I'm working on it," I say to which he throws up his hand and cheers.

"You've been working on it for eleven years. Why don't you work a little faster? Cheers, fucker."

The second goes down smoother, with a bout of laughter and a sharp pang in my chest.

I miss her.

Fuck, I missed her the minute I left the house. But I needed this distance to clear my head. To work and to realize how much better it would be to have her to go home to afterward. To have a piece of normal amid my crazy. *To just have her.*

"Number three—"

"You do know the last time we sat down together, you were pissed off at how much I was drinking, right?"

Hawkin slaps a hand on my back and squeezes my shoulder. "That's because you were drinking out of misery. Not from happiness. *This?*" He throws his arms out. "This is all happiness. This is all good." He nods to make sure I'm listening. "Now pick your third up. If I'm getting fucked up celebrating you, you best be doing the same."

I laugh. "Number three."

"To Jagger. Sometimes facing your biggest fear can be your greatest reward. I have a feeling he just might be that." He taps his glass against mine.

The shots go up but fuck if it has to slide over the lump of emotion in my throat as it goes down.

He's right. I stare down at the empty glass and just shake my head. He's fucking right. How can I miss someone I just met this much?

"I can't wait to meet him," Hawkin whispers and pats my back again.

"He's the coolest fucking kid in the world," I say.

"Of course he is. He's yours."

I laugh and eye him when he pushes the next shot in front of me. My head is already swimming with this frat-boy hazing drinking shit.

"What's this one for?" I ask.

"For doing this." He slides his phone across the bar. On the screen is the Billboard Top 100 chart and sitting at number one is *Sweet Regret*.

I stare at it. The irony's not lost on me that the day I let my dad go, figuratively, is the day I reached the one thing he said I could never do. My eyes blur and my throat burns.

I did it.

I hit number one.

Just me.

"Congratulations, brother. I'm proud of you."

I lift the glass. I down the shot.

But the expected happiness barely crests. Pride is there but it hits differently.

It feels hollow.

Empty.

Because I'm missing the one goddamn dot that connects all the good things we're celebrating. Bristol. She's been a part, a reason, a driving factor behind all these things I'm rewarding myself for. For the courage to see that I'm *not* my father. For never stopping loving me. For giving me a son. For giving me this song. *The* song.

I wish she were here to kiss. I wish Jagger were here to high-five. It feels empty here without them beside me. But it's not just them. It's celebrating this huge milestone without my bandmates here. The only people who can sit beside me and marvel about this crazy, fucking life we have.

I'm happy . . . but it also makes me sad.

"You okay?"

"Yep." I swallow it down to dissect later. It's probably just the alcohol. Just the moment. "What's the fifth one for?"

"That depends," he says.

"On?"

"On if we're celebrating you coming back to the band. We're thrilled about your success. We never doubted you could do it. But, Vin, we want you home, with us. You're our family. Our brother. It's not the fucking same without you."

I look at the shot in my hand, I look at Hawke, and then I down it without question.

"Guess that means we're celebrating then," he says before grabbing me and hugging my neck.

For the first time in my life, I'm exactly where I want to be in all things.

All things save for one.

And that one thing is sitting at home waiting for me. Waiting on me. Waiting to make a life with me.

This week has proven I can live without her and Jagger.

But more importantly, this time away has only cemented that I don't ever want to live my life without them.

They are my life.

CHAPTER
fifty-one

Bristol

Wᴏᴏ's Vɪɴᴄᴇ ᴄᴏᴍɪɴɢ ʙᴀᴄᴋ?

Hasn't that been Jagger's question of the day—hell, the past couple of days really—and the one that's been a constant on my mind?

Because while I've had a blast exploring with Jagger and spending one-on-one time with him—more than it feels like I've been able to in forever—there's a hole without Vince here. An indescribable something missing in the norm we've created over the past few weeks.

It's amazing how easy you can fall into something—even a major life change—and never realize it.

And it's currently the question I've fallen silent over because I don't have a response to give.

"So he still hasn't called or texted?" Simone asks.

"No."

"And you haven't called or texted him?"

"Uh-uh."

"Unwanted advice alert here, but you two might just be the most stubborn people on the face of this earth."

I chuckle. She has a point and yet . . . "I've thrown Vince into *you have no choice but to grow up* fire, and I tossed him into it without any warning."

"You didn't throw him into shit. His dad did."

"Semantics."

"Extremely important semantics. I mean, you were willing to go on your merry way and not tell him."

"Exactly, which is a problem in and of itself if you're standing in Vince's shoes." I lift my face to the sun and welcome its warmth, Jagger's random boy noises of space invaders crashing into the top step of the pool a constant in the background.

"And this gives justification for you guys not talking to each other, why?"

When she puts it that way, it sounds silly. "He had to leave to promote the new material. I get that. But it's also the first time since finding out about Jagger, that he's been away from us. That he's had time to think without Jagger front and center in his face."

"I'm not following you."

"Maybe he needs time to digest it all. To make decisions now that he's had time to take a step back and process it."

"I can understand that. But that doesn't explain why you haven't reached out to him, especially if he's telling you how right it feels and all of that."

"I'm trying to respect his time. I'm trying to show him that I believe him when he told me to trust him. That's a hard one for me, but if I'm texting him constantly, doesn't that say the opposite? That I'm afraid and am checking up on him?"

"Are you afraid?" she asks softly.

"I'm trying not to be. Each day that passes doesn't make it any easier, truth be told. I mean, it was reflex to want to call him and congratulate him on hitting number one, but no matter how many times I typed out the text or picked up the phone, I put it back down."

"Maybe you're overthinking this."

"Maybe I'm trying to prepare myself for life without him. For not being able to pick up that phone and for him to not be on the other end."

She snorts. "While you're living in his mansion."

I laugh, her comment making me realize how ridiculous I sound. "I can hold out as long as needed. He needs to be the one who makes the next move."

"Hopefully he's not thinking the same thing about you."

I scrunch up my nose and give a nod she can't see. "Don't make me second-guess myself."

"Isn't that my job?" She chuckles. "And even with all that, I know you still want to ask."

"Am I that obvious?"

"Girl, you've been hiding away in a mansion in the land of lakes, only answering texts, and then all of a sudden you pick up the phone and call me?"

"For what it's worth, I wasn't picking up because you only call late at night and—"

"And you were too busy getting railed by the rock god to pick up. I get it. I understand. I've got you, girl."

I roll my eyes. "I was going to say my phone is usually on do not disturb at night so it won't wake up Jagg, but you paint a much better picture."

"I do, don't I? And you're going to have to forgive me because I might have painted that picture off skew and added me in your place for one fleeting moment when he walked past me the other day. I nearly died from his . . . looks, voice, cologne, broodiness . . . just damn everything."

"You're forgiven." *But . . . how did he look? How was he? Does he seem okay?*

What answer will she provide that gives you any indication that he's missing you?

None. Zip. Zilch.

He's at work. He has the number one song in the country. Of course he's not going to look like anything other than cocky, edgy Vince.

"He looked good, Bristol. I know you want to ask. Like a hundred pounds have been lifted from his shoulders."

"Hmm."

"And, no. Don't go thinking he seems less burdened because he's here, away from you, and is planning on jetting. It was more . . . I don't know . . . he looked *content*. God, I sound like my mother using that word, but that's the best way I can explain it."

"Okay. Content is good." *Here with me is better though.*

"He stopped by your desk, you know."

"My old desk?"

"Nah. It's still yours. McMann hasn't done anything with it. He didn't do the normal have someone pack your shit up in a box and leave it at the front desk thing. Your stuff is all still there, right where you left everything."

"*Oh*. That's news to me."

"Rumor is, Vince went to bat for you and told McMann that if *you go, he goes* type of shit."

"Jesus Christ. The last thing I need—"

"It's the first thing you need. *Your man going to bat for you?* Threatening for you? Girl, eat that shit up. Let him feel like he's taking care of you even though we all know you can take care of yourself."

"I know, but . . ."

"But nothing. Vince hasn't texted you, he hasn't called you, and yet he's still trying to take care of you. Why don't you use that to ease your worry—and don't say he's getting your job back for you because he's planning on leaving you. No, he's doing it because he values how fiercely independent you are and knows there is no way in hell you're going to let him pull the Cinderella shit on you."

"Cinderella shit?" I laugh.

"Yeah, sweep you off your feet, hide you away in a castle, and never let you work again."

The thought does sound appealing—the not having to work for McMann part—but she's right. I'd totally overthink it. I *should* find comfort in the fact that Vince knows me so well he's trying to retain my independence for me.

"For the record, he was standing in your cube, with the framed collage of you and Jagger in his hand, just staring at it with a soft smile on his face. I thought you might want to know that."

Tears well in my eyes as a smile ghosts over my lips. Yeah, I definitely wanted to know that. Needed to.

I clear the emotion from my throat. "Hey, Simone?"

"Yeah?"

"Thank you. I needed to hear all of this. To talk to you. Thank you."

"Girl, I'll talk you off the ledge any day." She sighs. "And don't worry. I'll think of ways that you can repay me."

I throw my head back and laugh. "I'm sure you will."

We hang up, a smile on my face, and my heart lighter than it has been this past week. We've been holed up here without anything but each other, calls to my parents, and nothing but time to let my thoughts run wild.

Simone was what I was missing. What I didn't know I needed.

"Was that him, Momma? Is Vince coming back?"

I shield my eyes, look his way, and smile. "Not yet. Soon. I promise, he's coming home soon." And for the first time, I truly believe it.

CHAPTER
fifty-two

Bristol

"**C**ONGRATULATIONS. I'M SO PROUD OF YOU." TEARS WELL, BUT I BLINK them away as Jagger sits in front of me on the computer and makes funny faces at Vince through the screen.

He finally called—or even better, he FaceTimed so I can see his handsome face. So I can be reassured by the look in his eyes and the smile on his lips. So I can see what Simone saw.

He looks good. *Content.* Like the same Vince who left here but with less of the world weighing on him.

Maybe all this worrying was for nothing.

Maybe I was right to finally trust him. Trust that he's coming back to me.

Maybe—

"*Hey, Shug?*"

"Yes. Sorry." I smile and even through the connection, I know he can see the relief and love in my eyes. "What?"

"*The two weeks hasn't turned into a month.*"

I nod, not trusting my voice. Not wanting to show Jagger the worry I've hidden from him this whole time. "Okay."

"I'm glad you decided to stay at the house. In Washington."

"We did." I couldn't bear to be the one who walked away with so much at stake. "We stayed." I smile through the lone tear that slips over. "I'm still fighting."

"Me too," he whispers. "Don't plan on me ever stopping. Be home in a few days."

Our eyes hold before Jagger demands more attention, pulling laughter from us. And for the first time in thirteen days, I feel like I can finally stop holding my breath.

Home.

Is that what this is? Because right now, home feels like wherever he is . . . and he isn't here.

But he will be soon.

CHAPTER
fifty-three

Vince

OPEN THE FRONT DOOR IN SILENCE, WANTING TO SURPRISE BRISTOL and Jagger. I also want to rush in, wrap my arms around them, and never let go.

Talk about how quickly life changes.

A part of me wants to call out. To announce I'm home. To get the fanfare that comes with it. Something I've never experienced before.

The other part of me wants to walk in quietly and surprise them. To see the looks on their faces when I do. To make it about them and not about me.

I saw the worry in Bristol's eyes the other day. The fear that I was going to run. If she only knew the only place I wanted to run was back to her.

I set my stuff down in the entryway and move quietly into the great room. My feet falter when I see Jagger. He's sitting at the kitchen counter with a partially built Lego set in front of him. His brow is furrowed as he reads the instructions.

My entire body fills with a love like I've never known before.

How could I fear that I'd ever treat a child like my father did me? I don't understand how that's even possible when I look at him. *I love him.* It's an insane concept considering the short amount of time we've known each other, but I do.

"Jagg," I whisper and catch him in the hug he gives when he launches himself at me.

I hold on. I breathe him in. I love on him in a way my father never did to me.

What's with this dad shit and getting emotional?

"You're back." He leans back and looks at me, arms still around my neck.

"I am." He studies me as if he's making sure I look the same. "Where's your momma?"

"Shh." He holds a finger to his lips. "She's on a Zoom with her professor. I'm supposed to be quiet, and if I am, she'll give me a treat when she's done." I take in the smear of chocolate on his lips. He notices that I do and smiles sheepishly. "I might have already snuck one."

"So I noticed." I laugh and lift him up and set him on the counter in front of me so we can be pseudo eye to eye. "But I'm glad she's on the Zoom because I wanted to talk to you about something, man to man."

"You do?" He sits a little straighter. "Even before you see Momma?"

"Even before I see your mom." I rest my hands on the tops of his knees.

"You're not leaving again, are you?"

"No," I say immediately. "I'm here. I'm back. And Jagg, buddy? I'm ready to handle all of your awesomeness."

The words are out before I can stop them, but the minute they are, I wonder how his young mind will compute them. Will he realize I'm his real dad? Or will he understand that I'm just a man making a choice . . . and I choose him?

His eyes widen and his lips purse. "Does that mean we get to live together? Like all the time?"

I chuckle and reach out to ruffle his hair. "Well, that's what I needed to talk to you about. You see, you've been the man of the house for seven years now. I need to ask you if you think it would be okay if I shared those duties with you."

"Really?" His cute nose scrunches up and his chest puffs out.

"Really. I love your mom an awful lot. I have for a long time. And—"

"Do you think you could love me too?" His bottom lip trembles and my heart all but shatters.

"What I was going to say, Jagg, is that I already love you too."

A tentative smile spreads as he blinks back his tears. He whispers, "I already love you too but felt silly saying it."

I pull him against me and just hold on. His little hands press against my back and his warm breath hits my chest. "Don't ever feel silly telling someone you love them." I press a kiss to the top of his head.

Did my dad ever do this to me? Did he ever tell me he loved me?

It doesn't matter, Vin.

This is what matters. *Jagg* is what matters. Doing it right this time is what matters.

"What do you say?"

He looks up at me with eyes identical to mine. "You'd have to marry her, you know."

I throw my head back and laugh. "That's the plan, buddy. That's most definitely the plan."

"Jagger? You okay? I heard . . ."

Bristol stops in the hallway when she sees me standing there. Her hair is piled on top of her head. Her face has the barest hint of makeup. Her skin is golden from the sun.

She's the prettiest thing I've ever seen.

And then she's jogging toward me, jumping in my arms, and wrapping her legs around me. I stagger backward from the force of her momentum, my grunt making Jagger giggle, but welcome every single inch of her clinging to me as if she thought she'd never see me again.

For a man who likes to wander, I've finally found the one thing that makes me want to stay put. *To settle.*

"You're here," she says, her face nuzzled against the curve of my neck, her lips moving against my skin as she speaks. "You came back to us."

My hand is in her hair as I breathe in everything about her. This is the shortest amount of time we've ever been apart and yet it feels like it's been for-fucking-ever.

"I told you I would." She lowers her legs and my hands are on her face, brushing loose strands of hair away. I brush my lips against hers, the sob in her throat making my chest swell.

If Jagger weren't sitting here watching us, I'm pretty sure the kiss would turn into us stripping out of our clothes and frantically fucking on the kitchen counter.

"I know you did, but . . ." She shrugs sheepishly and blinks back tears.

"Momma, you're not supposed to cry when you're happy."

"I know, baby. I know."

"He hasn't even told you the good part yet," Jagger says.

"What good part?" Bristol eyes me.

I laugh and shake my head at Jagger. "You're stealing my thunder here, Jagg."

He shrugs. "*Then tell her.*"

"Vince?" Bristol asks.

"So I did this thing while I was gone, Shug."

"What type of thing?" Her eyes narrow.

"I bought us a house in Los Angeles."

Bristol blinks rapidly as she tries to take in what I just said. "What do you mean, you bought a house?"

"Exactly what it sounds like. Six bedrooms. Four baths. A big yard with an incredible pool and view of the city. A detached granny flat for when either of your parents want to stay over. *A house.* Something for us to start new in."

"That sounds like a palace, not a house." Laughter bubbles up in her throat as Jagger sucks in a breath.

"You told me we always strike the match but then it burns out. I figure, a house is made of wood. Wood is considered kindling. So this time when we strike the match, we have enough to keep it burning for a lifetime."

"You're serious?"

"I'm serious." I run my hands down her sides and link my fingers with hers. She glances over to Jagger, who has his hands clasped over his mouth in excitement.

"Buddy?"

"He's ready for my awesomeness, Momma."

She chokes over another sob and looks at me. "That's the best way I could tell you that this is real," I murmur and brush my lips to hers again, reveling in their softness. In the moment as a whole.

"You sure?" she asks cautiously.

"I've never been surer of anything. I've let you walk away one too many times in my life. You've let me, too, and for damn good reasons. But not this time. Not ever again."

"You're putting roots down," she whispers.

I nod. "The only person I've ever wanted to put them down with is you. Is with Jagger. Are you ready to strike that match with me?"

"I've never wanted anything more."

epilogue

Vince

One Year Later

JAGGER'S NERVOUS LAUGH CARRIES ACROSS THE ROOM.

"It's okay. Try again," Gizmo urges as he steadies the vibrating cymbal that Jagg just hit, which messed up the beat he was learning. "Stiffen your wrist this time."

Jagger draws in a deep breath and tries again. He creates a groove on the drum kit. It's juvenile in nature but pretty damn fucking good for an eight-year-old who's just learning.

"That's fucking perfect," Gizmo says and then scrunches his nose. "Sorry. Your mom will have my ass for that."

Jagg laughs again but then puffs his chest out, trying to be cool. Older. He loves being backstage with us.

"It's okay. I'm used to it. My dad says it all the time."

Dad.

The goddamn word still squeezes my heart like a vise every fucking time he says it—but in the best way.

I catch his eye. He grins and holds up the drumsticks that seem so big in his little hands.

"Looks like you'll have to buy a set of drums next," Hawke says as he looks Jagger's way. "We better watch out or he's going to come after all our jobs."

"No shit," I say and take a pull of my beer.

To say we've had to make an adjustment to our past backstage antics is an understatement.

Is there still drinking and partying? Yes. Are women still brought back for Rocket and Gizmo? Definitely.

Just a little more on the sly these days.

But I'm fine with all that because fuck if I'll ever get used to looking up and seeing my bandmates—my brothers—hanging with my son and treating him like he's one of their own.

You failed, old man. You thought a son would break me. Wrong. He made me more of a man—a better man—than I ever could have imagined.

Hawkin nudges me.

"What?"

He lifts his chin toward the doorway. "Look who made it after all."

I still do a double take every time she walks in the room. It's impossible not to when you spend years telling yourself you can't have someone, then make it so you have a lifetime to spend with them.

And yes, the proposal is coming. She knows it. I know it. But there's no fucking rush because us being together forever? That isn't a question. What is though, is how to propose? How do I make that moment as special as she is?

Have I fucked up over the last year? Slipped a little in worrying about who I am? Yeah. I'm not proud of it, but it takes more than one year to undo a lifetime of abuse.

But Bristol has waited me out each time. She's talked me through it. She's held my hand—or poured me a drink—and not stopped loving me. Often reminding me that my different is my beautiful.

Just like hers is.

She high-fives Jagger where he sits at the drums—he says she can't hug him around the guys—and then looks up and meets my eyes.

That look still packs one hell of a punch.

I rise from my seat and walk over to her.

"Hey, look," Rocket says as he enters the room. "Crystal's here."

Bristol just gives him the side-eye and shakes her head at this running joke and then says, "Real funny, Rock. Real funny."

"Crystal. Crystal," Jagger chirps, having no idea the significance behind the term.

"Hey, you," I say, hooking my fingers in her belt loops and pulling her against me so I can brush my lips against hers.

"Hi." She brushes my hair off my forehead, her smile holding some kind of secret.

"You're dressed up. You look incredible. And you have that look in your eye. What's going on, Shug?"

"We're celebrating."

"Celebrating?" I ask, before brushing another kiss to her lips and then whispering in her ear. "Is this the kind of celebrating that makes Uncle Gizmo watch Jagg while we go 'celebrate' in the dressing room alone?"

She lifts her eyebrows and trails a finger down my chest. "This is the 'Bristol just got accepted to law school' type of celebration."

"No way." All my thoughts fade away as her words hit me.

She nods frantically with a smile that could light up the whole goddamn state. "*Really*. I just found out. I'm stunned. Shocked. I mean . . ."

"You did it." I pick her up, wrap my arms around her, and spin her around. She slides back down and finds her mouth with mine as she does. "You really did it. I'm so proud of you."

All those years on her own. Being a single mom. Working a job and going to school. Sacrificing her sleep and her sanity to give everything to Jagger while still trying to chase her dreams. Finding the courage to tell McMann no thanks when he offered her job back to her.

All of them just realized for her.

"Dreams do come true," I say.

She reaches out and cups my cheek. "*They really do.*"

epilogue

Bristol

Later That Night

"SO WE'RE GOING TO DO SOMETHING A LITTLE DIFFERENT IN THE show tonight," Hawkin says as he moves across the stage, pulling my attention from my phone. *What mischief is he up to tonight?*

I know the performance by heart. Bent's set list. The jokes they tell. The looks they give when one of them fucks up. The banter they repeat like a rehearsed skit.

It's not that I'm bored by it, but let's just say I don't hang on every note like I did the first twenty-something shows of this tour.

So when Hawkin breaks the routine, it most definitely grabs my attention.

I glance toward the doorway Vince's personal assistant took Jagger through to go to the bathroom. If there's something different tonight, I want him to see it.

"You see, two years ago, like any family, we"—Hawkin points to

Vince, Rocket, and Gizmo—"needed a little break from each other." Boos fill the audience. "I know, I know. I felt the same way." He holds his finger up. "But something really good came out of that break. My brother here." He walks over and hooks an arm around Vince's shoulders. "Had a single that went crazy popular, and I want him to sing it for you tonight."

What? This is most definitely a change.

"Really?" Vince asks, playing it up.

"Really." Hawkin walks over to a waiting stagehand and grabs Vince's acoustic guitar. He holds it out to Vince and exchanges his bass with it. "You see, it's a good song. Fucking great actually. I'm kind of jealous I didn't write it myself." He laughs. "So, will you play it for us?"

The crowd goes so wild I have to plug my ears.

"Okay. Okay," Vince says. "I'll play, but I'm going to need some help."

"What, are we not enough?" Rocket asks, propping his elbow on Hawkin's shoulder.

"You're enough, all right," Vince jokes, "but someone I know has been working really hard on learning this song and wants to help me play it tonight."

My head can't process what my heart already knows, seconds before Jagger shuffles onto the stage with his guitar in hand. The one that matches Vince's. I gasp and put a hand to my heart, the tears already forming before they even do anything.

Jagger reaches Vince and looks up at him with a huge grin. "You want to say hi to everyone, Jenzo?"

He lowers the microphone and Jagger waves to the crowd, his high-pitched voice booming out of the speakers when he says, "Hi, everyone."

The crowd says hi back as flashes light up the darkness.

Each one of the guys fist-bumps Jagger and ruffles his hair as he's getting set up beside Vince. My heart pounds in my chest and every mom cell in my body is overwhelmed seeing the two of them together like this.

"So, I wrote this song a little while ago," Vince says as he takes center stage. "It was for the only woman I've ever loved. A woman who has never given up on me or her dreams. A woman whose different is her beautiful." He adjusts the mic and looks out toward the press box where he knows I am. "Jagg and I have added an extra verse to it tonight. I hope you enjoy it." More cheers. "You ready, buddy?"

"Yep. Ready to rock," Jagger says and elicits laughter from the crowd. My heart is in my throat as I watch them.

The familiar chords of *Sweet Regret* fill the arena. The cameras to the big screens zoom in on Jagger. On the furrow of his brow. The bite of his teeth into his bottom lip in concentration. To the way he positions himself on his guitar.

And when the camera zooms out, both of my boys are side by side, almost identical in all things but height. I couldn't be any more in love with them than I already am.

Vince begins to sing. He pulls me under with his sexy voice and the lyrics I know by heart. With the ones that convinced me we had to say goodbye. With the ones that made me love him even more.

And when he finishes the chorus the third time through after the bridge, he looks straight into the camera and sings to me.

> Time lost. Time apart.
> But we found our way, new lives to start.
> Healed hearts. Our souls consoled.
> You and me, baby, let's grow old.
>
> I look at him. I look at you.
> The love we have keeps shining through.
> I did forgive.
> You did forget.
> Losing time with you, my one, true regret.

I stare at the screen, awed by Jagger's talent and the love I feel for the man standing beside him.

I never knew I could be this happy. This content. This fulfilled. This loved.

God, I adore them.

They bow and the crowd roars. Then Vince pulls Jagger into his arms and holds tight. It's a moment I'll hold dear for the rest of my life.

So many choices have brought us to where we are today. A heartbreaking farewell in a bedroom window, a ticket to a concert and a phone number from a bitter man, and a colleague asking me to fill in for her one fateful night.

But perhaps the most significant choice of all was to follow our hearts.

That decision led us back to each other.

To this moment.

To a love I always knew existed but never thought I could have.

the end

Did you fall in love with Vince and Bristol's story? Here are some other K. Bromberg books you might like:

Sweet Ache: You met Hawkin Play in *Sweet Regret*. Now find out more about this bad boy rock star with a good guy heart, who has lived a lifetime of cleaning up after his twin brother's mistakes. Enter Quinlan Westin. She knows Hawke's type and is determined to avoid the rocker at all costs—even if their attraction runs deeper than simple lust. Just as Hawke might finally be winning over the girl, his brother has other plans. When Hunter realizes his twin finally has a weakness, he'll stop at nothing to take advantage . . .. *Sweet Ache* is a rock star romance with a twist. Check out Hawke and Quin's story.

Hard to Handle: Dekker Kincade's job is to woo the only man who has ever broken her heart, hockey phenom Hunter Maddox, over to her agency. If getting him signed can help save her family's business, she'll swallow her pride and do what's asked. But sometimes old feelings are hard to forget, and even harder not to act on . . .

Combust: Firefighter Grady Malone has met his match when songwriter Dylan McCoy rents a room in house. Dylan needs time to come to grips with walking in on her now ex-boyfriend and her replacement. Grady needs time to recover from a tragedy at work that has scarred him. Together, they just might be what the other needs.

ABOUT
the author

New York Times Bestselling author K. Bromberg writes contemporary romance novels that contain a mixture of sweet, emotional, a whole lot of sexy, and a little bit of real. She likes to write strong heroines and damaged heroes, who we love to hate but can't help to love.

A mom of three, she plots her novels in between school runs, sports practices, and figuring out how to navigate parenting teenagers (*send more wine!*). More often than not, she does all of this with her laptop in tow, and her mind daydreaming of the current hero she is writing.

Since publishing her first book on a whim in 2013, Kristy has sold over two million copies of her books across twenty different countries and has landed on the *New York Times*, *USA Today*, and *Wall Street Journal* Bestsellers lists over thirty times. Her Driven trilogy (*Driven, Fueled,* and *Crashed*) has been adapted for film and is available on the streaming platform Passionflix as well as Amazon.

You can find out more about Kristy, her books, or just chat with her on any of her social media accounts. The easiest way to stay up to date on new releases and upcoming novels is to sign up for her newsletter or follow her on Bookbub.

CPSIA information can be obtained
at www.ICGtesting.com
Printed in the USA
JSHW010309030523
41188JS00005B/14